The Boughs Withered
When I Told Them my Dreams

The Boughs Withered
When I Told Them my Dreams

Maura McHugh

NewCon Press
England

First edition, published in the UK August 2019
by NewCon Press

NCP 214 (hardback)
NCP 215 (softback)

10 9 8 7 6 5 4 3 2 1

ISBN: 978-1-912950-39-3 (hardback)
978-1-912950-40-9 (softback)

Cover art by Les Edwards
Cover layout by Ian Whates

Edited by Ian Whates

CONTENTS

For Mom and Dad

Your entwined stories began mine

Introduction

Kim Newman

I once told Maura McHugh to remember only to use her powers for good.

Of course, I knew she would anyway.

These stories prove that. They're good, and they're *for* good… in that they agitate, without preaching or unearned sentiment, for better behaviour… and in that they're made to last, reaching deep into myth-pools for eternal, primal treasures.

You'll find that out by reading the collection.

But what about Maura the Woman?

I first met 'the lovely Maura' (as many many people call her) when our much-missed friend Rob Holdstock couldn't be bothered to write a speech to deliver at an Irish science fiction convention where he was Guest of Honour. Rob nagged the organising committee into inviting me as an extra guest so I could interview him on stage. Maura was on that long-suffering committee, and already a force of nature. I prize the memories of that long, hectic, bizarre weekend of adventures – my first visit to Ireland, packed with legendary encounters and hilarious incident.

The next year, when another guest of honour couldn't be bothered even to turn up at the same convention, Maura asked me to step in for them. She proved even more kind and even-tempered in trying circumstances, including while she was dressed up as Neil Gaiman's Death – the comic book character, not the (we-trust long-off) final moments of the author – for the masquerade. Now, Maura is so formidable that Death would have to dress up as her to impress me.

Since then, Maura has become a devoted, reliable, uncynical regular in the critics' section of the annual London FrightFest, rolling her eyes upwards at some of the excesses on view – I don't think I could have sat through quite so many tied-up-in-a-basement movies without her tutting in the next seat – and enthusing about the wonders occasionally on offer. She also helped Rob and me into the 21st century by web-mistressing our still-active sites, an act of charity to the hopeless that we've never adequately repaid her for.

I've written a comic book (*Witchfinder: The Mysteries of Unland*) with Maura, and found her calm, measured and always enthusiastic in the collaborative process of taking someone else's toys, polishing them up and playing with them, bending figures in interesting new ways while hoping not to break off legs and arms, then putting the whole game back in the box for the next play-team. I've edited her as a playwright, braiding her unsettling story into five others for something called *The Hallowe'en Sessions*, which played in London to tiny packed houses and some acclaim.

I've also told her repeatedly to write more stories.

And write books. Which, at last, she has.

I'm telling her here, publically, to write more.

Which, I trust, she will.

Kim Newman,
Islington,
June 2019.

Vic

Vic's room was small and awkward, just like him.

When Father built the extension above the garage the space was intended as a storage closet for chemicals, equipment, and spare parts, not for toys, books, and a boy. The narrow asymmetrical compartment didn't convert easily to a bedroom. Its best feature was the large double window that spied across the fenced-in overgrown back yard, and offered Vic a slice of the street and the houses beyond. The sash only opened a little, but the wisps of air that slipped in spoke of wet grass and freedom, and masked the workshop stench from next door.

The branches of a close-planted sycamore shattered Vic's view into hundreds of puzzle pieces. On windy nights, after Mom turned off the TV – wedged in at the bottom of his cramped bed – he lay and watched the shadows cast by the trashing tree roil across the ceiling and crash against the walls. He invented stories about the chaotic shapes, which usually involved knights or spacemen who were strong and brave and could quest wherever they wanted. It helped him fall asleep when the aches and pains were troublesome.

Sometimes, when it was stormy, the branches groaned and the twigs scraped the glass, and their jabbering profiles told darker stories where heroes failed and monsters triumphed. Then he would pull the covers up to the bottom of his crooked nose, turn the TV on low, curl his back to the window, and watch the screen sideways.

He could never bear to draw the blinds.

The stitches itched.

Vic sat cross-legged on his bed in the shifting afternoon light and busied his hands with the *Big Book of Butterflies* Father checked out of the library for him.

Twap: the sound of a basketball bouncing off paving echoed through the inch of open window. Vic laid the book down on the pillow carefully and gripped the headboard so he could climb up on the mattress. Unfurling sycamore buds waved in a spring breeze, and Vic had to bend his neck like a snake to get a good view of his neighbour's neat garden, which had a pond where red fish swam. The movement triggered a resentful throb, but he ignored it.

A boy, a little taller than Vic, bounced a basketball in between the fragile Cherry tree and squat statues. His lips moved as if he narrated his circuits around the tidy obstacles. On a couple of previous occasions Vic had seen him slip aside a board in the garden's slatted back fence, squeeze through the gap, and bounce his ball down the street to an unknown destination. The boy always came back but his absences never raised an alarm. Vic knew because on each occasion he waited by the window until the boy returned home safely.

A scattershot of rain pelted the glass in an offbeat tempo. Vic placed his lopsided fingers over his chest and tapped along to his heart's erratic rhythm, the one Mom called Take Five. "You're a little out of step," she said whenever she pressed her ear to his chest. After she lifted her face, and revealed the scars that rucked her cheek, she'd add, "Keep beating, kiddo."

Vic trampled over the bedcovers to gaze at the bus stop across the street. In the mornings the kids stood there and jostled each other as they waited for their ride to school, supervised by vigilant parents. Now, it was deserted.

Vic hesitated, sidestepped to the bottom of the bed, and stretched for a peek at Rain's bedroom window. Vic didn't know her real name, but she reminded him of the changeable nature of rain: how it freshened up a summer's day, hammered leaves into the ground, or softened the world behind a veil of mystery. Today she worked on her homework at a desk by the window. She chewed on a florescent yellow pen and frowned. Vic was sure she was smart, so it had to be a tough question.

The front door slammed. Vic dropped down on his mattress and pulled the book over his lap. The slow, heavy tread on the carpeted stairs confirmed Father's return. Vic watched the tongue of light under the door. A shadow hesitated outside. Anxiety and excitement soured his stomach. The footfalls continued, and keys jangled. Father entered his workroom, and Vic turned back to the book on his lap.

"Egg, larva, chrysalis, imago," he read as he traced the circular chart that mapped the butterfly's life cycle. He flipped the yellowed pages so the musty library-smell drifted upwards.

A memory rose in Vic's mind like an air bubble drawn to the surface of water: a cheerful elderly librarian with steel eyeglasses and blue hair handed him a plastic-coated book. Vic squeezed his eyes shut and tried to capture the details, but they melted under scrutiny. Sometimes strangers' faces haunted him with uneasy familiarity.

Vic opened the front page. Old dates were pressed on the paper higgledy-piggledy. He tried to figure out how often the book had been borrowed and for how long. A rash of loans clustered around the same period every year, probably for a school project.

He imagined Rain's hands on the pages as she researched her paper, bit her pen, and wrote about the *Nymphalidae* species and their spectacular colours. His fingers slid across the glossy image of Blue Morpho, with its iridescent turquoise and aquamarine wings.

Drip.

A black splotch covered the image.

A machine hummed into life next door.

The stitches were barbed wire strangling his throat, but Vic focused on the book. He couldn't let the page stain. Not on Rain's favourite butterfly. His hands shook as he daubed at the paper with a corner of his cotton bed sheet; it turned navy, as if dipped in ink. *Morpho menelaus* recovered intact.

"What are you doing, Victor?" – Mom's voice from the doorway. He spun in surprise. Alarm remapped the scars on her face into livid lines of fear.

Vic rushed to reassure her. "It's all right, I got to it in time."

Her voice spiked. "Your neck!"

His fingers touched the bandages and felt the damp.

She almost screamed, "Father!"

A *thump* from next door, like a hammer dropped on the floor.

Mom lurched towards Vic, and knocked into the corner of the television on her blind side.

Just as her hand brushed his arm the pain became a saw ripping through his neck. He fell backwards into twilight, the book clasped to his chest.

His mattress became a cloud of multi-hued butterflies, and Vic burst through them, falling into darkness, until they swooped and bore him up into a blinding white sky on wings that pounded a five/four beat.

Vic woke to Mom's touch on his forehead and a pressure on his throat. He blinked crust out of his eyes, and opened his mouth to speak, but she shook her head. "No talking for a while." Pain was cottonballed and distant.

His father slouched in the doorway, a silhouette of unease against the light in the hall. Despite the distance, he reeked of Marlboros and sweat. Mom's good eye was red, puffy, but she smiled. "You need to rest." She levered herself from the bed with her cane but held onto his hand. "Tomorrow, when you're feeling better, we'll watch a movie downstairs on the big television. All of us together." Vic clutched her hand to indicate his delight at the treat.

Father shifted and stuck his hands into the pockets of his trousers, "It's not wise, Mary. The boy needs rest."

Mom dropped Vic's hand and swivelled sharply using her cane. "He needs a diversion!" The pitch of her voice skidded upward abruptly, and its intensity startled Vic. "Being pent up like this isn't healthy!"

"It's for his own good," Father said in his coaxing voice.

Mom's hand tightened around the handle of her walking stick. "It's suffocating. Unnatural." The anger slipped from her voice as quickly as it appeared, but a sloped resignation remained in her shoulders. Father opened up his arm to help her shuffle through the narrow space to the doorway.

"I'll check on you soon," she said, and closed the door quietly.

Vic sat up in bed, and touched the bandages that swaddled the length of his neck. New wrappings bound his wrists. He pulled back his sheets. Virgin strips encased his ankles. Under his crumpled teddy-bear pyjama top a new dressing twisted upwards from his bellybutton. He drew the material back, and followed the trail that criss-crossed older wounds. It terminated above his heart, from where all the other marks radiated.

Shadows moved under the door.

He eased out of bed. Dizziness threatened to topple him, but he leaned against a wall until the crashing in his head abated. He walked to the door and laid his ear against the smooth grain.

Father's voice, low and stubborn: "It's not working." Mom's angry response was muffled. Father's response contained frigid resolve. "No. There's no point. I won't do it again."

"You promised!" so loud it shocked Vic back from the door, but he could still hear the sobbed entreaties of his mother, and the shhing noises of his father.

Barely audible: "We could begin over."

Vic stumbled back and sat on the bed hard. Pain shot up his spine and shook his heart. He shouldn't listen to private conversations, he'd been told so before. Just as it was wrong to explore the house. Bad things happened when he disobeyed.

Memories, tightly barred, threatened to tear open. Behind it images strained: *a small limp foot jutted over the edge of a metal table; a scarlet toenail dripped red; and a clear plastic mask descended towards Vic's face.*

Vic's clenched fists lay on his lap: one dark, one pale. His chest constricted, but not from the wound.

Tap tap tap. The tree clattered for Vic's attention. He scooted around and gazed out the window. The late evening light slanted into the neighbour's pond so the fish glowed. The boy wore a hoodie emblazoned with the word 'Mavericks', and dribbled his basketball around imaginary players. He spun, halted, stared at his house, and back at the fence. Vic's breath caught as the boy weighed his options.

A short sprint; the board pushed aside; and an empty garden. The fish circled the pool.

Vic dragged himself upright using the windowsill and shuffled to the end of the bed. Rain and her younger sister, dressed in party clothes, danced in front of a tall mirror and mouthed words to a song he couldn't hear, their bodies graceful with freedom. His world was a coffin-sized room while theirs was limitless.

We could begin over.

He didn't know why his heart struggled to beat when it hurt so much.

The unhindered light under the door offered a chance. He stood and tested the knob. It turned.

Vic put on jeans, t-shirt, and sneakers. He didn't own a jacket, so he pulled on two sweaters. It would be cold. Underneath the dull heartbreak exhilaration and fear warred.

Out. He was going out.

A sob of lonely hurt hitched his chest. He squashed it. Soon he'd be gone. No longer a bother, a source of tears and fights, or secrets behind locked doors. Without him, they could start over.

He opened the door.

It proved surprisingly simple to escape the house. Father clanked about in the workroom as Vic crept down the stairs. The television blared in the den. In the kitchen the key stuck out of the backdoor lock. A *click*, and he was outside, smelling the breeze, brisk and heavy with the scent of damp earth.

He looked up at the darkening sky, stars and crescent moon ghost imprints on the purple-navy expanse, and for a moment the world tipped forwards and back. The noises of the neighbourhood flooded him: cars rolled past, feet slapped the sidewalk as a pair of children dashed past the house, and dogs barked sulky reminders about their evening walk.

He was out.

Vic propelled himself forward on clumsy legs, anxious to flee the shadow of the house in case the panic submerged by the wonder would surface and drown him. He lumbered through the long grass to the wooden fence. Vic had long ago spotted the broken board that the local cats used to stalk through the garden. He kicked it out of place, sucked in his stomach and wiggled through on his side.

He stood up quickly, trembling, and checked to see if anyone noticed his exit. There were few people about. The smell of cooking food wafted from the houses. Families gathered to eat at this time. Vic knew because he'd watched them.

A man in an overcoat strode past. Across the street a young woman with a stroller glanced at him, smiled, and kept going.

He was part of the world. Accepted by it.

Across the street Rain's house loomed. For a stomach-plunging instant Vic considered ringing the doorbell. He dismissed the idea. Vic didn't know what to say, and... Rain might not like him. The plummet in his gut returned. His feet hurried away from the emotion and followed the same course the boy next door had taken.

Orange streetlights flickered on as he passed, and soon he was at the top of the street, at an intersection. New territory. Across the street a playground guarded the entrance to a park. Colourful tubular towers sprouted from the ground, connected by passageways, and accessed by ladders, ropes, and ramps. Slides and swings dotted the spaces in between. In his rush to reach it he ignored the lights. Brakes screeched and a horn blared as a van skidded to avoid him.

The area was deserted. The glow of the nearby lights slicked the smooth surfaces of the playground equipment. Vic climbed a metal ladder, crawled into the top of a round tower, and looked out of the arched window at the passing people. The wind thrummed through the empty spaces. He found a broken lumpy crayon and wrote "Vic" on a wooden strut in the roof. He wondered if he could live there at night and emerge to play with the children during the day.

Twap: the sound of a basketball. He switched to the opposite window and saw his neighbour throw a ball at a hoop.

Vic whooshed down the yellow slide and approached the boy. He stopped on the edge of the dimly lit court, and waited. After a couple of moments the boy dribbled his ball towards Vic.

"Hey," he said.

"Hi," Vic grinned.

"You play?"

Vic shook his head.

The boy raised an eyebrow at that. "What, never?"

Vic noticed the suspicious tone. "I've been sick."

The boy bounced the ball a couple of times and nodded, as if this information made perfect sense. "Wanna learn?"

Vic bobbed his head, afraid to speak in case he messed up an unknown code of conduct.

"I'm Don," the boy added, and bounced the ball at Vic, who huffed when he caught it.

"I'm Vic," he responded, and threw it back at Don.

The boy tucked the ball under his arm, and cocked his hip. "First, I'll explain the basics."

Half an hour later, Vic's breath rasped from effort. His legs throbbed with the malicious promise of a later reckoning, but he couldn't stop smiling. He'd scored his first point. As soon as his hand touched the ball it was as if the memory of the game was hard-wired in his body, despite its slowness. He had to stop for a breather several times, but Don hadn't complained, and used the breaks to describe tactics, or demonstrate a couple of special moves.

Vic wanted to play basketball with him forever.

Don paused, his cheeks glowing, and his breath visible. "You sure you haven't played before?" Vic shook his head. Don jerked his chin at Vic's hands. "Were you burned?" Fear rendered Vic mute; the bandages and his mis-matched hands were clearly visible. "My uncle's a firefighter," a swell of pride, "so I know about skin grafts."

Vic yanked the sleeves of his sweater over his wrists and dipped his head.

"You home-schooled?" Another nod. Don laughed. "You escape for a night?" Vic's eyes widened, and the boy bounced the ball harder. "Know the feeling." He paused and checked a chunky watch on his wrist. "I gotta go soon. Even my mom'll notice I'm missing."

"Vic?"

Don's stance stiffened, and his gaze flicked to behind Vic's shoulder. Vic turned. His mother hobbled from the direction of the shadowed park, bundled up in a long coat, scarf, and hat. Behind her, the darker blot of Father's presence. Her cane tapped like the rattle of twigs against a windowpane. "I was so worried," she gasped.

"I'm fine," he said, and wrapped his happiness tight about him, desperate to keep it. He stepped back from her. "Just shooting hoops with Don." He loved the normalcy of the new words on his tongue.

She paused about ten feet from Vic. "Don?" she said, and her voice glitched in a funny way.

Father took a step forward. "Don't." She half-swivelled, and Vic couldn't see the expression on her face, but Father didn't move or say anything else.

Don fidgeted and glanced over at the playground and the streetlights beyond. "Well, see ya, Vic."

"Wait, Don is it?" her voice smoothed out, and became the sound of a beautiful, caring Mother. Someone you trusted with your life.

Don stopped, and a hungering need rose in pupils wide from the lack of light. "Yes, ma'am."

"Do you like drinking chocolate?" She glided closer to the boy without a trace of a limp.

"I sure do."

"Why don't I fix you some, as thanks for being such good friends with my boy?" Mom held out a hand, and Vic noticed for the first time that her fingernails were long and sharp.

A memory erupted: *Vic approached the sleeping boy on the table, hoping to wake him so they could play together.*

Don took a step towards Mom.

A puddle of blood glued the sheet to the boy's leg.

Don's hand rose dreamily upwards.

The cloth slid a little as Vic touched the boy, and exposed the...

Vic jumped between them and shoved Don so hard the boy almost fell backwards. "Like I want this loser coming to my house!" Vic yelled.

The enchantment broke, and bitter rejection replaced it.

"Screw you Vic," Don bellowed, and he ran with fast angry steps towards the light, and safety.

For a while there was only the sound of traffic and the crack of Mom's knuckles as she clenched and unclenched her fingers. She sighed, a long release of irritation, and hobbled to Vic.

"I do it to make you better, Vic." She touched the curve of his neck. Dampness bloomed against his skin, and the discomfort hidden by activity sharpened.

Her voice caught, broke. "I *can't* lose you."

Vic stared down at his sneakers, scuffed for the first time. "Promise you'll leave Don alone."

Her silence offered no assurances.

Exhaustion settled on Vic with the weight of sorrow. He staggered, but Father caught and lifted Vic.

"He taught me to layup," Vic said, and closed his eyes as the pain returned with the fury of the repressed. Father kissed Vic's forehead, and in surprise Vic opened his eyes and looked directly at his father for the first time he could remember.

"Don't begin over," Vic whispered, too low for Mom to hear.

His father froze, and guilt tightened the smudged circles under his eyes. He bent his head and gripped Vic tight. Vic buried his face in his father's raincoat, inhaled the smell of cigarettes and formaldehyde, and cried.

Father hugged Vic close to his chest as they walked home. Mom held onto the crook of Father's arm. As they left the playground, Rain and her sister bounced by, giggling and chattering, on either side of their mother. A blue enamel butterfly glittered among Rain's curls. She smiled briefly at Vic, and he imagined how she saw them: a father carrying a son tuckered out from activity, his wife by his side; a family.

Later that night the shadows of the sycamore combed the walls and ceiling of Vic's room with urgent movements. He lay under Mom's hand-stitched quilt and groggily watched the shapes become tall lean basketball players who tossed a ball to each other, dodged, dribbled, and dunked. Thousands of shadow hands applauded the game.

The injection Father gave Vic softened the world, and dragged his eyes closed.

Vic remembered Rain dancing, loose-limbed and radiant, and Don's frowned concentration as he leaped with the ball. Their beauty suffused him and his heartbeat lurched.

Mom stroked his forehead and Vic cracked open heavy eyelids. She smelled of soap and tears. The bed creaked when she settled beside him. She placed her hand on his chest, and her fingers echoed the stuttering rhythm. The words of the lullaby she crooned were mixed up and fragmented, jigsaw pieces of songs that didn't fit together.

It was hard to breathe.

Father sat on the bottom of the mattress and placed his hands on Vic's feet. He nodded.

Vic closed his eyes.

Mom kissed his cheek. "You're a little out of step," her voice cracked.

Vic kept beating for as long as he could.

Who Hears Our Cries in Forgotten Tongues?

The wind shrieks across the barren hilltops, scraping moss from our cairns and carrying our wild laments across neighbouring bluffs. Nothing remains of our race except these humps of grey stone that surface like whales cresting waves of foaming grass. Few visit. Wearing crackling material that defies rain, they are deaf to the story of our people. They never linger.

Until today.

She lags behind the group, and our cunning people recognise the patterns of intuition that flare from her mind. Her far-seeing eyes track our movements as we creep close.

Let me see, she imparts. Fearless, she perches upon tumbled rock and *opens* her mind to the images that leap like salmon across the weir of time.

Together we walk upon straw-strewn floor, and nudge the sleeping hounds from the hearth so we can cut slices from the spitted boar. Songs echo in the hall as slaves carry mead to our chief and his warband, who display the heads of our enemies with pride. The hag speaks of our ancestors, who watch from their lofty tombs until prepared to return in the round bellies of our children's children.

The runner arrives, panting. He is revived to warn of invaders who have traversed the ninth wave to set foot upon our noble isle. Men and women grab spears and bronze swords, and speed in eager packs through the thick forests to the beaches and to battle.

The sands sink with the blood of our warriors.

The invaders swarm across the land and slaughter our people. Their hard eyes glitter under iron helmets, and they know no mercy for the aged poet or the mewling child. We cannot withstand their new magic; spells fail upon the lips of our wise folk.

Our passenger in time turns away, but we cannot stem the memories that rush from the severed veins of our grief.

Chilled by biting wind, we make our stand on our most sacred site, and face the army of our foes: pitiless, cruel, unending. None survive to welcome our souls back from the grey hinterland bordering life.

We are doomed to watch the conquerors teem across the hills, carve their names in foreign words upon our monuments, and claim our legacy. We remain in legend as the phantoms of the hills who wove lies and died easily.

Between eyeblinks, more invasions occur. The conquerors become servants. From our high fortresses we witness the death of the forests and their creatures, as buildings multiply in the soft vales and fragrant meadows. Dark snaking paths mark this dominion, and we abide in the unforgiving reaches to avoid the madness of their belching towns.

We are alone, forgotten, and unheard.

Until now.

"I will craft a tale of memory." She leaves, her mind gravid with the souls of our people.

Tonight, we dance under a moonless sky, and howl the delivery of our lives into a new race.

The Boughs Withered When I Told Them My Dreams

The woman rushed Joanna as she opened her car door.

"Excuse me, Mrs Wynne," she gasped.

Startled, it took Joanna a moment to recognise her since the wind spun her fine, dark hair into cobwebs across her face. Memory jolted into action: she was part of the coterie of parents at the school drop off, in the era before Oscar was too embarrassed to be seen in the company of his mother.

Niamh Colman. The name drifted up to rescue Joanna from embarrassment as the woman finished a jerky introduction. The boys had been in a play together… Christopher; never Chris, she recalled. She hadn't seen Niamh since their sons graduated St Joseph's.

They engaged in a stilted exchange of information – Christopher was studying drama, Oscar was doing a business degree. Catching up via exchanging information about other people.

"It's lovely to see you again, Niamh," Joanna began as a preamble to leave and placed her hand upon the car door again. It was getting dark. She wanted the boundaries of home and an escape from unwanted presences. She'd had enough of intrusions.

"I know this is odd Joanna, but…" Niamh looked up – her expression was strained. Joanna felt a spike of fear. Was she being asked for money?

"… have you ever visited the Crone House?"

"Sorry, what's that?"

Had Niamh turned into a New Age boor? The only son had left the nest so she poured herself into another vocation? It wasn't as if Joanna wasn't familiar with the ache. But that's what hobbies or jobs were for. Perhaps a cat.

"It's in the woods by the hospital. It's old, before the housing estate was built. Three women live there. Always three." She started to speed up, having noticed Joanna's recoil. "It's not officially Crone House, that's just the nickname, because of the women. They're elderly you see."

"I've no idea what you're talking about." Joanna heard the sharpness in her voice and wanted it there as a warning.

Niamh sighed. "I know this is weird… I don't want to upset your evening. You look tired. It's just… They can help you."

"What are you talking about?" Anger stirred in her so when Niamh placed her hand on her arm she yanked back from it.

Niamh held on.

"I dreamt about them last night. They said they can help you. With the man."

Joanna froze.

"They helped me once. You know, having Christopher."

"You had IVF."

"Yes, three rounds. Then… *them*. And it *cost* me." Her mouth twisted into a skein of pain. "But I have Christopher now, so it was worth it."

Joanna felt Niamh's fingers dig in through the padding of her jacket.

"I'm obliged to pass the message on. What you do is your business. But if they've offered help you must need it."

Niamh released her hold and patted the spot, apologetically. A gust of wind obscured her face again with a haze of hair.

"But it will cost you."

She dropped her head and turned, walking furtively, her shoulders hunched.

Joanna sat down in her car seat with a thud.

She'd seen his type before: the young, brash fellow, who took up a little too much space and talked a little too loud. His jokes were ribald but not rude enough to annoy anyone important. Just enough to pinpoint how far he could take it the next time. Conor Brophy knew how to flatter and do just enough work at the right moment to appear industrious.

Joanna was part of the old guard in her department: efficient, reliable, and the keeper of legacy information about the company. She maintained a professional distance at work – it paid the bills, but she wasn't there for friendships. She knew some people thought her aloof, but she planned to retire from full-time work in another five years. Oscar would finish uni that summer and already had a job lined up with a financial firm in Dublin. He had mapped out his career since he was fifteen, the year after his Dad died. He'd even started dating an equally poised lad called Ben.

They were serious, but Oscar was serious about everything.

Despite her rule to maintain a calm demeanour at work, Joanna could not ignore Conor. He was always in the kitchen, with his *banter*, or playing *hilarious* squawky videos on his phone to anyone in the room. Joanna no longer liked to be in there. Before she'd always enjoyed sitting on the high stool by the counter, with her back to the room, for a break with her cup of milky Barry's tea and a Hobnob.

He developed a habit of stopping by Monica's cubicle whenever he passed – this meant he hung over her partition, partially in Joanna's space.

She despised his badly ironed shirt, perpetually half pulled out, his silly superhero socks, and skewed nylon tie. Nothing he did was complete or precise, yet he had a way of inveigling others to cover for him.

Joanna recognised the ratcheting resentment she harboured toward him and realised she was showing it through barbed comments about punctuality and neat dress. He always turned her remarks around to depict her as prim or lacking a sense of humour. Worse, she recognised those traits in herself because she disliked them too. They were patterns of behaviour she longed to untie but the knots defied her.

More and more she found her thoughts obsessing over every zinger he launched at work, or his lazy, informal style of writing emails. During the drive home she'd clench the steering wheel and replay conversations they'd had that day but with added damning commentary. She considered it her *l'esprit de l'auto* – she was capable of wit when given a little time.

It came to a head during a meeting about their biggest client. Conor made a significant error when calculating their bill in the coming quarter. When reading through the reports she'd noticed the mistake but waited for the meeting to point it out. The boss was annoyed and praised Joanna for her close attention. She relished the moment, but in the periphery of her vision she spotted the red hatred heating Conor's face and it stirred unease in her.

From that time forward, it was war… Nothing direct, but a constant picking on everything Joanna said or did. No slipup was too small for Conor to correct. No comment was too innocent that it couldn't be transformed into a ridiculous jibe. She raised the matter once with her superior and was informed that Conor had already complained that her 'impossible high standards' were a cover for bullying. She was warned to be more considerate.

Someone hacked her Facebook page and covered it in derogatory gay porn. She felt humiliated and stressed during the days it took to sort it out and Oscar was appalled – Ben had seen it. She began to worry that Conor had installed software on her computer at work that was keeping tabs on everything she did. She could be under surveillance. There were cameras in every screen, and they could be hidden anywhere. She'd seen a TV show about it.

Her personal email address was used to register for hook-up sites. Going through the rigmarole to end the lewd messages drained her. She considered changing her email address except she'd used the same one for twelve years, and she worried that Conor would uncover her new one anyway. Perhaps he had hacked her home laptop. She bought and installed software to detect malware and beef up her firewall. She placed tape over the camera to prevent spying. She had no confidence it would keep him at bay. Determined people always find a way, one expert explained.

Text messages arrived late at night from strange numbers. "I will slit your throat and watch you die choking on your own blood," said one. She reported the incident to the Guards. They took it seriously but added it to their list of things to investigate. Likely just a crank, they stated, but instructed her to keep records of everything. She had to turn off her computer and phone at night to bring peace, but it didn't extend to her mind. She had no refuge, no place of safety. Her sleep suffered.

Every work day she had to meet Conor and paste on a mask of indifference. He avoided being rude to her in front of others but smirked and rolled his eyes at everything she said. Her colleagues began to treat her differently. Where before she was trusted, now she was micro-managed. Twenty years of diligence undermined in six months by a canny idiot.

She drove by the house slowly. It waited at the end of a path secured with an iron gate choked in ivy. The trees drew close on three sides, like conspiratorial friends. It was a grey two-story house. Neglected but ordinary. Yet as she crawled past she felt like she was being sized up. She didn't have the nerve to orchestrate another drive-by. Someone might notice. It was a populated spot that was cunningly hedged away from neighbours.

As she turned the car wheel to leave, waves of rooks erupted from the woods in a raucous flood. It looked like the trees were bleeding black blood into the air.

Her breath seized in her throat. Her foot hit the accelerator.

Behind her the clamour of rooks smudged her view.

That night Joanna dreamed about the crones.

The strangled gate opened with a stifled protest. Above, a smoking chimney tilted on the bowed roof. The tall windows were veiled by jaundiced lace curtains, and the front door had a brass knocker in the shape of a snarling wolf's head.

It growled low when she approached through the thickening twilight, but the door swung open. A long dim hallway past a darkened staircase led to the kitchen. She passed a living room, where aged furniture mouldered and motes of black dust hung suspended in the air. Standing by the cold fireplace were three children wearing white shifts. The tallest with a fox's head, the middle one with its crow's head cocked to one side, and the littlest with a hare's head, unblinking big eyes, and long ears.

The fox's yellow eyes gleamed and it licked its sharp teeth.

"Mother." It said, garbled.

"Monster," the crow cawed.

"Myth," the hare whispered.

The dream granted it logic. Joanna nodded at the child beasts and moved on.

The women waited in the kitchen. The oldest, a hoary hag with long silver hair and bright bird-like eyes, perched on top of a high stool, her knees by her ears. A stout woman with a plaited rope of grey hair curled around her head rolled out dough on a sturdy oak table. A pie dish lay beside her piled with glistening meat. Nearby, the gutted carcass of a rabbit, and a flensing knife. Gore splattered her apron.

By the antique range the last woman, tall with short white hair standing upright on her head, stirred a huge cauldron with a pitted white stick. She was all lean muscle and angles. The heat from the range permeated the room, but there was little light. Candles dotted the shelves and nooks, and the long wide window over the sink looked out onto a wild garden, barely visible in the advancing night. A massive, gnarled tree dominated the view.

"So you came," said the piemaker, busy with her work.

"You knew she would," replied her sister, stirring madly.

"Will you help me?" Joanna asked. She knew these ladies would have no truck with preamble. Their lives were measured by a shorter scale.

"You have it in you," the woman at the table noted. She lifted her skin of dough carefully and laid it upon her pie dish. "It depends on what you want."

Squatting on her tall perch, the oldest cackled and shook her head.

"Hush, Mother," said the one by the range.

At that, Mother leaped across the room, as agile as a monkey, and landed on the back of the woman to yank at tufts of her hair.

Joanna expected bedlam, but instead the tallest reached around, and with an impossible movement, lifted the Mother off her back and circled her to her front so she was cradled like a baby. She lifted her shirt and offered her small depleted breast to the crone – who latched on and suckled with gusto. She rocked and crooned the bundle of old bone and hair.

Joanna pretended she did not want to gag.

"Tell the tree," the piemaker said, and nodded to the window. "And then we'll see."

"And you'll pay," the tall woman added, and all three howled.

Joanna walked to the door. The women became motionless with intent.

The round handle turned smoothly in her palm, allowing her access to the garden.

Outside the air was bruised purple-black, but the sky was cloudless, so the marvel of the stars was visible. But it was a strange array of lights. Joanna was no expert but their arrangements appeared replicated as if many skies lay upon each other but slightly out of synch.

The thick roots of the huge tree boiled out of the grass, a tangle of serpentine damp knots. She could not ascertain the girth of the trunk and it towered so high it was impossible to determine where its branches ended and the sky began.

She clambered over the coils, slipping, aware of the women's gaze upon her from the kitchen window. The tree's bark was craggy like primordial rock and yet there was a faint warmth when she laid her hand upon it. Its vast expanse was covered in whorls and cracks, but she noticed a section which evoked the memory of the angle of her mother's jaw when she tilted her head to listen to one of Joanna's questions. She sidled to it and lay her cheek against the rough surface.

A fierce longing erupted in her chest, for the surety of childhood, when she had believed that someone watched over her, taking care of all the bad things in the world… but it was temporary; an illusion. Her mother couldn't protect her from betrayal and loss. Sometimes she'd caused it.

Tell me your dreams, daughter.

And she poured out the rot inside her: the fury that curdled within her constantly and her elaborate fantasies for revenge.

The tree seemed to sigh, settle, and a creaking began above her that escalated into a squealing wail. Joanna looked up: the boughs were withering.

They darkened, twisted, and shrivelled until they became blighted vestigial nubs.

She glanced at the window. The three crones watched with rapt delight.

Joanna picked her way through the swirl of roots, unsure of her path but aware she had power.

She returned to the kitchen and the old women carved her a slice of their pie.

It tasted delicious.

Joanna rose from her bed, imperious.

She stood in the middle of her bedroom, with its bland walls and unassuming decorations, and did not recognise any part as representing her whole.

This was the illusion. A cocoon she had spun from digested fear and shame.

She picked up the framed picture on her bedside table of her late husband Dermot with Oscar, taken at an all-Ireland hurling match when Oscar was six. Oscar had hated the crowds, the noise, and the game itself but his father had insisted he come, trying to duplicate a beloved memory from his childhood, determined that Oscar feel the way he had felt a generation earlier.

And Joanna had traipsed along with them, organising sandwiches and soft drinks, keeping the peace between the disappointed man and the sulky boy, and coaxing a false, cheery photo from the disaster of expectations.

Joanna noticed the unhappy strain around her son's eyes and the angry loop her husband's arm made around Oscar's shoulders. Why would she want to look at this image every day? There were better pictures of Dermot, and Oscar's Instagram account was full of photos of him and Ben together, laughing, sure of each other.

She smashed her fist into the middle of the picture frame and the glass shattered, cutting her knuckles. She threw the mess into her bin.

Blood dripped on her snowy white carpet. She glanced at the pattern and twisted her arm so the drops created a jagged circle with a man in its centre.

She slashed a line across its thin throat.

She smiled and dressed for trouble.

Joanna strode into the office with a new haircut, and boxes of artisanal donuts. She listened as her co-workers ate their sweet treats and drank coffee, and she even cracked a few jokes. She told them to call her Jo. When Conor appeared she made sure to stand too close to him and look him directly in the eyes when he spoke. She could smell his confusion. She went out to lunch instead of hiding in her cubicle.

Once she cracked open her guard allies materialised. Conor had pestered a lot of people.

Getting access to Conor's phone and PC was easy: he was careless and predictable – his password was hidden under his keyboard. After that, evidence emerged. She wasn't the only target of his harassment – he was digitally stalking his ex-girlfriend and one of his co-workers at his old job.

Luckily for Joanna he had used the work machine to maintain his vendettas, and after that it was a matter of tipping off the IT department that something might be awry with Conor's digital practices.

He was marched out of the office by a security guard, and Joanna was called into a meeting with HR where they sensitively explained what they had discovered on Conor's computer. Joanna realised they were angling to cover their liability. She was gracious, but negotiated a raise, extra holidays and an assistant. They disclosed their discovery to the Guards, and Joanna heard though the office rumour mill that he was being prosecuted by his ex.

It wasn't enough.

Joanna knew, with a clear certainty that he would feign penitence and present a defence as the socially awkward bumbler, get the lenient judge who disbelieved harpy women, and Conor would return to destroying people's lives because that's the only way he could feel powerful.

In her bedroom the symbol in the carpet had dried into rusty flakes.

She lit a candle and sat before it with the darkness upon her back.

She remembered how the boughs withered.

And she sang of her corrosive dreams and they seeped out of her and into the carpet. They sought out the jagged circle and poured into it. Inside, the man writhed as the line looped around his neck.

Three pairs of bony hands supported her shoulders. Three mouths joined in with her song. Their music stirred her hair.

And the man's legs danced as he hanged.

Joanna laughed and the crones behind her jabbered.

And you'll pay, she heard.

"Gladly," she replied.

Joanna walked to the house on a thin winter's day with a bag in her hand.

Six figures in black shuffled down the narrow path with a coffin on their shoulders. The hearse waited, but no one else.

The two crones lingered inside the doorway, safe in the shadows of the house. At the window, the beast children had flipped up the yellowed lace to watch their mother depart. They raised a din of farewell.

Joanna felt a twang for Oscar, but she'd given him the best of herself.

Now she would savour her worst.

Joanna waited for the hearse to depart before opening the green-coated gate.

The Light at the Centre

Sheila leaned slightly over the steering wheel, driving slowly, squinting as she studied the narrow country road picked out by the headlights of the car. On either side from the darkness the crooked limbs of hawthorns and hedges reached into the road, trying to snag us as we passed. Beside her, Mike's face was lit from below as he examined the route on his smartphone.

"Not far now. It'll be on the right," he said.

"How did I let you talk me into this?" was her reply.

Behind them, I snorted. Sheila was the one who had reacted with unusual enthusiasm when I'd received Diz's invite earlier.

"What was that message again, Claire?" she asked, stress tweaking her voice.

I sighed, and pulled out my phone.

Adopting Diz's laconic accent I read out: "Hear ye! Pop-up Party House at the Kilroy Ghost Estate tonight @ 10pm. Halloween Blitz. BYOB. Tunez spun by DJ Diz. Bring your scary faces, bitchez!"

"Bitches!" she muttered, "I'll bitch him if this isn't the best party ever –"

She braked, and I slid into the back of her seat.

"What the hell is that?"

Mike started laughing. "Class."

At the entrance to the derelict housing estate a blow-up doll dressed in a tattered black witchy dress with a pointy hat waited for us. It writhed in the breeze, fighting the binds that tied it to the stake. One of its arms pointed into the rows of empty, grey houses. "BOO!" said the sign around its neck.

I glanced up at the wide, scarlet mouth. "It looks like it's screaming."

"Yeah, she's probably seen the state of the party and was horrified," Mike said.

Shelia turned the wheel and the car into the housing estate. A faded billboard depicted the estate as it had been imagined: rings of white houses, and green circles for children and dogs to play on. 'Kilroy Hollow' the sign blazed in comforting letters. 'Your New Home'. Some wag had crossed out 'Home' and replaced it with 'Hell'.

"How did they ever think houses would sell out here?" Sheila asked. "The bloody hubris of it!"

As the car bumped along the unfinished road of the first circle of houses, the headlights splashed across grim, ashen buildings, their doors and windows boarded up with pale wood bruised with mould. Skeletal outlines of garden walls fronted them. The street lamps looked like gibbets.

"Cool," I whispered. Then louder, "Diz is a genius. This location is perfect." Already, I was considering its potential for a film I was working on.

"If we can find it," Sheila said. "These estates always seem to be planned like an Escher painting."

Mike shot her a surprised look, which she noticed. "What? I can know art."

He shrugged, "I didn't realise it was a requirement for nursing."

I noticed Sheila's eyes narrow and leaned back into my seat.

"Art is a requirement for *life*. If you want to do something other than just exist." She let out a breath. "I see enough pain and death every day to know we all need beauty in our lives."

Mike held up his hands, "Okay, sorry. I wasn't trying to imply anything."

She didn't reply but her fuming was almost audible.

We bumped along in silence for a few moments. The houses gaped at us.

"Sorry," she said finally. "It's why I wanted to get out tonight. Rather than another night watching a DVD or you two killing aliens on some stupid game. And I wanted to dance, and feel my heart pound, and forget about that jackass Chris."

"We could all do with a night out," I said, even though I really wanted to drink rum and cokes at home and re-watch the classic Universal monster movies.

"We could all do with a shag," Mike said.

"That too," I agreed.

"I've been in a bit of a dry spell," he added, with a wistful tone.

I laughed. "What, a week?"

"If you must know it's been ten days. Liam said he was coming tonight." I could hear his filthy grin. "I'm certainly planning on it."

Sheila slowed down the car. "What was that?"

Mike looked about. "What? I didn't see anything."

"Something moved there, dark and low to the ground. Fast."

"Probably a cat, or a fox," I offered.

"Or the ghost of the Kilroys," Mike said in a voice that wove up and down like a theremin. He took our silence to be ignorance, and added. "You know, this used to be the estate of the Kilroy family. They were notorious hereabouts. Landlords. One of them was supposed to be a brutal old bastard who had a dungeon where he locked up people to torture, slowly."

Our breathing seemed loud in the car. Outside, the clouds covered up the moon's face in horror.

"Apparently the tenants burned the big house down, and salted the earth after Ireland got independence. They say that one of the daughters was caught in the fire, and her ghost haunts the place, along with all the anguished souls who died there over the years."

"Jesus," I said, quietly. But in my mind I could see the vengeful expressions of the faces illuminated by the flickering flames of the torches, the great conflagration erupting in the mansion, and then the screams, and how cinematic it would be.

Neon lights spun and glinted ahead. We passed a trio of cyclists dressed in Lyrca with lime green and lurid pink highlights. Rainbow coloured fluorescent lights sparked all over their bikes.

"We're going the right way at least." Sheila sounded relieved.

My cynicism kicked in, late. "Was any of that story true, Mike?"

"Fuck if I know." He laughed. "It's something I heard. I'm not a native. I'm only here for our glorious employer."

Mike and I worked at a mobile games company for our day jobs. I coded, he did tech support. Both of us believed we had the harder graft.

A scarecrow dressed as a business man loomed suddenly in the dark, his pumpkin face carved into a hideous grimace. 'WE OWE YOU!' written in heavy black marker on the cardboard that flapped around his neck. The 'e' in owe had been struck out and an 'n' added so it read 'own'.

"Nice use of props," I conceded. My hopes rose for the party.

As we crawled along the pockmarked path we passed more people, some dressed up as zombies, superheroes, and of course, slutty schoolgirls.

"She must be freezing," I said as I watched a young one with a skirt as wide as a belt, totter down the uneven pavement. "It's Baltic out."

"No doubt warmed by vodka and drugs," Sheila said, grimly. "I'm sure my colleagues in A&E will be dealing with the spillover from this party later."

Mike and I groaned at the same time. We'd heard many of Sheila's war stories. "Not tonight, Sheels," Mike pleaded.

She slapped the steering wheel. "You're right. Sorry. And… we're here!"

Cars lined the street on either side, with some of them parked in the empty driveways. One large mansion at the end, clearly meant to be the deluxe version of the standard three- and four-bedroom residences, was festooned with blinking lights. A ghost with a streaming tail swept back and forth from an upstairs window like a metronome. The boards on the downstairs windows had been removed and their empty sockets were edged in white skull lights. Music with a thumping beat blared out.

It was a bright beacon in a dead zone. Promising pleasure amid the darkness.

"That's what I'm talking about," Mike exclaimed.

I pulled on my gloves, zipped up my parka, and picked up my six pack of beer. In each of my pockets I had a naggin of whiskey. "Good to go," I said, and pushed open the door.

Just before we joined the party-goers, Sheila stopped us. "Synchronise watches."

Mike and I dutifully extended our wrists out of our coat sleeves and consulted our watches. "It's ten thirty-five pm. We meet here again, at two am. Unless this ends up being a total bust, which doesn't seem likely right now. Are your phones fully charged?"

We grinned and held up our phones, touching them to light them up, displaying their strong battery life. "Yes, Mammy," I said.

She waved her hands at us both "Off you go, my children!"

Mike and I joined hands and skipped towards the bright lights and music, giggling.

ꕤ

After a couple of hours I had a decent buzz going, enough to quash the pervading dank that radiated from the floor and walls. Everything was raw concrete. It was the bare minimum for a house, lacking everything that made it a home. It had one flushing loo downstairs, which quickly became unusable. There were two rooms for music: the massive open plan kitchen/dining room, which seemed designed for giants, was the dance-your-face-off zone, and the chill-out room was located upstairs in the enormous master bedroom and assorted alcoves (intended for closets and en suite), which had plastic cartons for seats.

I'd danced for a while with Sheila, both of us executing ridiculous dance moves without caring who was watching. We'd separated when I went to get a beer – my six had disappeared, so I helped myself to a can from someone else's stash. After that I'd nipped away at my whiskey, danced for a bit, and nodded at some people I knew from work.

Mike had come along later and offered me half a pill. "Who gave it to you?" I shouted.

He leaned in and I saw his pupils were already dilated. "Jeff." His breath smelled of jellybeans – he'd been drinking some ghastly alcopop.

I gestured 'no thanks'. He pantomimed an L-sign over his forehead.

I shrugged in acceptance. I'd learned my limits, and the locations where I'm willing to really cut loose. This wasn't one of them.

He boogied towards Liam who was giving him come-hither fingers.

I wandered through the house, a little floaty and disconnected from all the happy people. It was a familiar feeling. Like being an observer of my own life. Directing the *Film of Me*, while also being separate from it.

A familiar melancholy rose up but I dodged it temporarily by finishing one of my naggins.

I swung by the chill-out room. In the corner, perched on a crate, Sheila was having an intense conversation with another woman I didn't recognise. Diz was on the deck, washing the atmosphere with a groovy neo-soul vibe. When he spotted me he waved. I gave him the thumbs-up to acknowledge him. He tapped a woman with a mane of pink hair curling from under her woolly hat, and handed her his headphones. She nodded and glided forward into his position, her fingers already changing the dials and knobs.

He picked his way through the bodies and we hugged. His soft leather jacket squeaked, and he smelled of expensive cologne.

"Fancy a smoke?" He rolled a joint between his fingers. "Good stuff. Pure weed. No hash. The way you like it."

I arched an eyebrow at him. "You know how to get on a girl's good side, Diz."

"Let's go outside."

"No one's going to complain if you light up here." I passed my hand through the fog in the room.

He shook his head, and the row of rings in his ear jangled. "Naw, I want to get an overview." He spread his hands, "You know, enjoy the magic of it all." His beatific smile was charming.

"Sure," I said, and we wandered downstairs, threaded our way through the manic bodies hopping up and down, and out the back of the house.

We stood on what was meant to be a grand patio. The darkness in front of us was absolute, yet from behind waves of light and beats from the party surged over us.

I took a deep hit from his proffered spliff, letting the warmth spread from my lungs into my limbs.

I blew out a long stream of smoke, thinking that I could be a dragon. "Nice." I handed the joint back. "It's a good gig, Diz. You've come a long way."

He nodded and directed his smoke up at the sky. A sheen of silver gleamed here and there through the muddy clouds, hinting at the moon trying to break free.

"I want to show you something," he said.

"It better not be your cock."

He exploded with laughter and that turned into a small coughing fit. I patted him on his back while he gasped and shook.

There had always been something between us, but I was never convinced it was sexual. It was more like an understanding; a recognition between one soul and another that are travelling in similar directions but on very different paths.

In college – when he'd attended – we'd liked the same films and books and had admired each other's choices: his purist approach to drop out completely and live his passion for music and performance art, and mine to stick with the nine-to-five job while also making films on the weekend and during my holidays. He'd scored the soundtrack to my first short film.

He smiled and offered his hand. I took it. It was square and warm, and my hand felt comfortable in its loose grip.

We moved away from the house of light and delved into the hushed night.

"Careful with your footing," he warned, and we ascended a damp grassy hill.

I puffed a bit at the end, acutely aware of all the time I sat at a computer for work, or in front of a screen editing. Never mind the gaming.

After we struggled to the top, he gently took my shoulders and turned me around.

Despite the gloom I could just make out the entire housing estate laid out. At its centre was the glow of Diz's party house.

As if on command, the clouds scudded back and the moon spotlight turned on.

The design was obvious now.

The pulse of the house was a heart, pumping life into withered veins.

He pulled out a plastic bin bag and spread it on the ground, and we sat down on it companionably, our bodies pressed together on one side.

"You see, don't you?"

"Yes," I breathed.

"I'm glad you came. I wasn't sure if you would. And who would I share this with then?"

We looked at each other and smiled, filled with the joy of connection beyond words.

I broke away from it to marvel at the project again. For an instant I had considered kissing him, but with a flash of clarity I knew where that would take us, and it would not be to some happy-ever-after ending.

Intimacy does not always have to involve sex. A lesson learned from past mixed-up creative endeavours that devolved into bruising relationships.

"I got funding for this, you know," he said after a few minutes, during which he lit the last of his joint.

"No way!" I exclaimed.

"I shit you not," smoke curled out of his lips like a magician. "EU money. One of those "Revitalising the Community" art grants. It's part of a project I'm developing."

"If you ever need any video elements, you know who to call."

He raised his fist, and I bumped my knuckles against his.

In the filtered moonlight his expression was that of someone who had pondered a problem for a long time. "What makes a house a home?"

I knew he was being rhetorical, so I offered no suggestions.

"People," he answered, and stared down at the circles of grey radiating from the luminous centre. "We build houses to become homes for families. Without us, they're thwarted shells, rooted in our landscape. Beacons of discontent."

Spread below me the deserted estate now seemed the loneliest place I had ever seen before. The malaise I often experienced drifted up inside my heart to meet the *absence* that flooded me from that vista. I inhaled a shaky breath, and dug my fingers into the wet grass to anchor myself.

Diz put his arm around my shoulder. "You've always had that sensitivity, Claire. The kind that feels the aches in the world and wants to fix them."

He squeezed me a little. "It's a tough edge to live on."

I shrugged, not trusting my voice to remain steady.

He pointed at the estate with the fading ember of his joint. "We made a pact in stone. If we don't honour it then old grudges, buried in the land, will compound new failures. The whole mess will transform into something deadlier."

I frowned. "You think this one event will ease that… obligation?"

A breeze picked up and I shivered. The clouds moved, obscuring the moon again.

He shook his head slowly, sadly. "No. This is triage."

Below us the light and music snuffed out. A shared moan of surprise drifted up on the breeze. Bobbing dots of light appeared as people turned on mobile phones.

Diz's grip on my shoulders tightened, and his voice hardened. "We promised, Claire."

The first scream shocked me. I flinched, but he held me in place – determined to keep an audience for his drama.

"What have you done?" My mind was moving too slowly, dulled by weed and an inability to process Diz's insane theory.

He whispered close to my ear. "Sacrifices must be made."

The cries and shrieks gathered momentum, and one by one pinpricks of light began to vanish. Even in the gloom the house at the estate's epicentre grew darker, *denser*.

My stomach spasmed and a retch threatened. Blindly, I snapped my elbow up into his face, and heard a satisfying *crack*.

Diz tipped backwards like a felled tree.

I staggered upright, weeping because the cacophony was too awful to bear. I plugged my hands over my ears thinking of Sheila and Mike and the hordes of people who had congregated in that place to celebrate, forget, or experience bliss for a time.

I broke into a sprint, barging through nettles and bushes, desperate to save my friends.

Until it felt like gravity changed, and I stumbled to a halt, my shoulders sagging under an oppressive weight. The slumbering need, sated, wasn't content.

It demanded what had been guaranteed.

In my mind I heard the question, and I forced myself upright.

"No," I replied.

It gathered the full force of its bitter, horded resentment.

I clenched my fists and remembered Sheila's maternal spirit, and Mike's generosity. This I possessed, clear in my heart. The bright light at my centre.

And then the wave broke upon me.

A Rebellious House

The doctor's office is odd-angled, with stark walls and a black and white zigzag carpet. His desk is positioned before the frame of a huge bay window, so he is an imperious shape stamped upon panels of grey – here in Holstenwall the view is either dull skies behind serrated trees or an enveloping mist which obscures the world.

You see him as a flat, pancake-faced villain who unfurls from his leather chair to approach your seat. His tread is light, cat-like, but you imagine a flip-flap sound of paper soles slapping against the peculiar floor.

He's been speaking to Conrad, your husband, about your condition. You are used to people talking about you as if you are not truly present. They mistake your lack of engagement with absence, or idiocy.

The doctor gently touches your right arm, pushes it upwards, and bends it at the elbow so it appears as if you are hailing him. He steps back and your arm remains in the position he has determined. You stare ahead and focus on the opalescent sheen of his waistcoat buttons. They are water wells in his chest. In each you can throw a coin and make a wish. Not that wishes comes true.

"This is classic waxy flexibility, one of the effects of Penelope's depressive catatonia," the doctor says.

You cannot see Conrad's face, but you picture his expression of helpless fear. He has heard these descriptions before – there have been many consultations since you became *afflicted* – and each medical term provokes an emotional flinch. He does not want a wife with a mental illness. This has always been his greatest horror: the withdrawal of the mind into an alien landscape that allows no trespass.

Conrad's whole life has been an exertion of rationality and scheduling as a defence against disorder. His joy emanates from numbers and equations that can be wrestled into submission. You bent yourself into the square box that he wanted because you hoped his calm, fixed certainty would solve your erratic interior life. And for a time it provided a barricade. You followed his regimes and agreed with his opinions, and for that you were rewarded. You seized upon every validation he offered for your correct behaviour as a stone in the bailiwick against the furies in your head. Your interests – hobbies, Conrad termed them – atrophied. Your existence revolved around the needs of others. Your martyrdom of self became a sick satisfaction.

You woke up one grey crepuscular morning to a hallow pain in your breast. The dusty artefact that beat within was merely a decoy to fool others. Yet life, with its barrage of tedious demands, kept happening. Ending it turned out to be difficult. But you could decide not to accept its torture.

Exerting the continuous minute control to shut down every reaction to the great monster of life becomes your distraction against the blizzard of torments in your mind. The vigilance required to be impassive against its constant assault keeps you occupied. You perch within your meat cage, acutely observing everything but denying it your reaction, and reimaging the world as you will.

"You won't reconsider electroconvulsive therapy?" The doctor asks Conrad. You imagine him wearing a top hat, cape, and twirling a cane in a pantomime display of power.

Conrad will never agree. His late great-Aunt Jane had ECT when she was a young woman in this very institution, back in the bad old days of experimental psychiatry. He once described her to you as 'more wraith than real.' The stories she told him gave him nightmares as a child. As supremely logical as Conrad is, he is not immune to his personal boogyeman, which in this case is the image of a woman in a long white gown, strapped to a chair with a gag in her mouth, spasming uncontrollably. He understands that ECT is not administered in this fashion any more, but when the subject is brought up he re-hears his aunt's ghostly voice whispering the horrors of her torturous confinement and logic is repelled.

"No," Conrad says, firmly. "If Penny is to return to me I want it to be because of kindness."

An echo of a throb registers, but you stifle any response. Conrad was never cruel, and often loving. You remember the way he stroked your cheek after your first kiss – a wondering exploration. You constructed a flattering façade he never demanded; that he never peered around its cardboard edges to discover what propped it up was either due to his lazy credulity or a tribute to your talent at devising cut-outs.

The doctor presses on your arm and you allow it to follow his guidance until your hand rests again in your lap. "We'll take good care of her," he assures Conrad.

You hear Conrad stand and fuss with his coat. He feels guilty. In sickness and in health, after all. You understand his dilemma and hate him for giving up at the same time. Anger has been gnawing inside you since you began your boycott. Or perhaps it was always present, but you were too busy covering up. Now, you use it as fuel to be precise in your negation.

You listen to the men exchanging goodbyes. Conrad says he will visit every week.

You wait, fearful, and yet... there is a thread of excitement at your surrender to the unknown.

The doctor returns and hunkers before you so that you and he are at eye level. His direct, powerful gaze magnified by his black-framed glasses is disconcerting.

"I know you're in there, Penelope," he says, softly. "You think you're safe, and beyond reach." He places his hand upon your limp forearm. "No one is beyond my influence."

His thick brows lower and his stare becomes a projection of will. "Stand," he orders.

You harness your resolution to prevent your muscles from even twitching. Your desire to do as he commands almost overwhelms your control. Instead, you fiercely do nothing.

His mouth smiles, but there is a lurking fury in his dark eyes at your resistance. "You're a challenge," he murmurs.

He stands up brusquely and strides to the door, summoning a nurse to fetch you. You note his confident authority, his framed credentials, his ordered desk, his lack of personal photographs. You wonder are these his defences or a reflection of his singular vision. You begin a catalogue of observations. You plan to learn everything you can about him while giving him nothing in return. There are victories that are won through action, and those that come from stubborn patience. You aim to win the war.

You discover that the doctor has a particular interest in patients with catatonia. Every morning you are all wheeled into the sun room – a large conservatory that faces onto a featureless lawn, hedged on all sides by the perpetual conifers. There is rarely sun, just dreary light. Among the mumblers and pacers you still women are pools of peace. There is Alice, Lisa, Gertrude, Margot, and Deirdre. The staff refer to your group as the six statues; that it also sounds like sick statues amuses them. The nurses like you because you are compliant, easy to steer, and never troublesome.

One of them, a young woman called Natasha, is fond of plaiting your hair. She hums as she brushes your long locks, and her kind touch and deft movements are a pleasure. She tries a variety of styles on you, and always shows you her handiwork in a mirror afterwards.

"Is nice, yes?" She will say, but you do not respond.

There are streaks of silver in your hair now that you no longer colour it. You notice a strange youthfulness to your slack features. Not smiling or frowning has a benefit, and you have been liberated from concern about your appearance. That has been a surprising relief. You put down a burden you were not aware you carried.

Natasha sighs, pats your shoulder, and moves on to the next patient. Rosie is a big, broad woman, prone to quoting scripture, and one of the more agitated inmates. She always insists on the same hairstyle as you. She watches you with a hot, intent focus while Natasha fixes your hair. You see the danger in her gait and her habit of accidently knocking into your chair or dropping something on you. Once it was a hardback book that cut your temple. You sat, with blood slipping down your cheek, as she wailed her sorries to Nurse Sara.

Somehow, she knows you are capable but stubbornly refuse. You can't figure out if she is envious of your fortitude or furious at your falsehood. There is no reason for her fixation on you, but none of you reside in the house of logic.

There is piped music in the sun room which is meant to soothe jangled nerves, but its earnest blandness irritates you more than most things. It often works on Rosie if she's responding well to her meds, so you appreciate it for that side-effect.

A craft table sits in one corner of the room, with puppets, books, stuffed animals, and simple toys. A patient called Elena, an older woman with white hair but a child's mentality, often acts out stories that she invents. They are a strange mish-mash of ordinary situations with fairy tale details. A plush pig rescues a ragamuffin doll from having to go to the dentist. They celebrate by eating as many sweets as they like until their teeth fall out. The dentist creates sets of dentures for them from acorns. Then they dance and sing in a circle in the forest. But a crafty squad of squirrels steal their teeth, and when the evil swans fly down to peck out their eyes no one can understand their screams. But the firemen arrive and give them ice cream to cheer them up, so they all end up happy.

Elena tells her bizarre tales in an upbeat sing-song tone, which makes the eerie elements even more unsettling.

Sometimes your dreams continue the stories. You are always one of the toys, usually the patchwork princess with the yellow yarn hair – a fact that makes your question your deep-seated desires. A giant Elena looms above you and the other playthings in these visions, manipulating you to fit her stories. She dictates the plot and you must do as she describes. Even if that is to disembowel the bunny. It does not bleed stuffing, but ropes of sticky intestines.

Elena screeches at the sight of them and points her enormous finger at you. "You're a bad Penny," she bellows. "You're a bad Penny."

You do not sleep the rest of the night after waking up from that nightmare. You lie and count the time in between the nurse's inspections, or when they are called to a room by a more disturbed patient. No night passes without some interruption.

You imagine the liberation of walking on bare feet in your hushed, dark room... but you are worried they have planted a hidden camera or a microphone. It would be a shame to be caught by such a simple stratagem. So you remain immobile and practice minute control of your muscles.

Every other afternoon there is physiotherapy with Annie, which keeps your body from wasting. You eat the soft meals they put in front of you with slow, automatic movements. You are instructed to start and you stop when you don't wish to eat any more. You take the meds they give you and make a show of swallowing. You can be directed to the toilet and you comply without hesitation. The more you make life easier for the nurses the more complacent they become around you. After a time you learn the easiest ways to spit out pills or throw them up again in the privacy of the bathroom.

Twice a week the statues are brought into a therapy room where the doctor waits for you. It is another off-kilter chamber with too many walls and a black floor. He takes your pulse and checks your reflexes one by one. Two of you – Margot and Deirdre – have sluggish reactions. You wonder if their medications prevent them from recovering. Deirdre has a gleam in her eye. A woman who wants to get better.

There is a raised platform at the rear of the room with a short ramp for ease of access. The doctor herds you up there and encourages you to stand. He places you in various groupings or in a wide circle as if figuring out some obscure configuration of bodies that will unlock mysteries. He moves your arms or legs into poses, leaves you in those positions, and takes photos from in front of the stage. He regularly consults an ancient, battered leather-bound journal during these sessions. You hawkishly watch every time he picks it up to spy on it. You only snatch a couple of faraway glances: the thick white pages are covered in a black scribbled script, sometimes with diagrams, and formulae. You do not recognise the language.

He uses a stopwatch and takes notes with a voice recorder, remarking on rigidity of limbs, or if any of the poses shift. You begin to realise that he wants guaranteed stillness, until he commands motion. He works particularly with Lisa, Gertrude, and Alice, instructing them to make simple movements. They do as he says every time. He teaches them a small set of coordinated steps, almost like a dance. He adds simple music, and there is a hypnotic quality to their dipping movements and waving arms, which they execute perfectly to his commands.

Over a period of weeks you notice that outside of the therapy room none of you are improving. You have learned enough about your condition to know that long-term, acute catatonia is unusual. Many people recover quickly under the right treatment. You six are stunted in your release from paralysis. You consider demonstrating some sign of change, but you are curious. You want to know what the doctor is planning.

He continually works with you during your therapy sessions, making eye contact, and ordering you to stand, or sit, or move your head. You refuse, despite the immense effort this takes to resist. You notice a difference in the colour of the pills the nurses give you, and do your best to avoid eating them completely. Sometimes this is impossible and your thoughts become elastic, pliable. Your body wishes to move as the doctor commands, but you have habituated it to only recognise your cues, so it resists even when your faculties are affected.

He is frustrated by this, but Margot and Deirdre are similarly recalcitrant. He adjusts his plans, and begins to situate the three of you in cross-legged poses on the dais with arms raised straight up. Your three companions are directed to circle in between your fixed points, while executing their choreography.

One day he brings in another doctor to observe you. She is young, petite, with a razor sharp cropped hairstyle, and a jewelled septum nose piercing. They consult quietly together first, and you overhear him call her Deborah. The doctor sets you, Margot, and Deirdre on the platform in your usual spots, and sets the others dancing. Deborah taps the screen on her phone and the speakers in the room play a strange tune. It sounds old, somehow. As if recorded in a Minoan temple. You don't know why that thought comes to you, but it seems apt.

The dancers' movements suit the rhythm exactly. They are more graceful with the accompanying tune, as if they are inspired by the music to refine their steps. Their clothes flair out slightly and brush against your skin as they pass. A breeze begins, and you sense something else stirring and uncurling in the room. As if another sleepwalker is being stirred into unconscious dance.

Deborah taps her screen and the music ends. The three women continue their silent dance, until the doctor calls a halt.

"Good," Deborah says. "It's almost there."

"Who will speak?"

She regards your group, and shakes her head to indicate her lack of knowledge. "Whoever is chosen." She pauses, "Maybe all of them."

The doctor seems taken aback by this. "Surely not. His notes indicate there will be one oracle."

"Your grandfather only dared work with one subject. And often in uncontrolled environments."

He bridles at her criticism, and shoots her a haughty look. "With ambition comes risk."

She bends her head as one does to a superior. Her words are those of an acolyte repeating a well-worn response. "The way to know is to do."

Since that last session with the two doctors there is a subtle change in the institute. It's like a new scent is in the air and everyone can smell it, the patients most of all. It reminds you of the nature documentaries they play on TV endlessly: the group of zebras with heads raised, tails swishing, muscles trembling with the need to spring away from danger. But you patients have nowhere to dash from the watering hole.

You are bunched together, restless, vulnerable.

Two days later a dense mist sweeps down from the mountains and over the tree tops. It swaddles the glass of the sun room on all sides, sealing you in grey. Natasha doesn't braid anyone's hair, and Rosie shoots you angry glances from where she is slumped in the couch as if she blames you for this omission. An edgy lassitude possesses you all. You worry that if one person is set off the whole room might erupt into berserk energy.

Elena dumps out all the dolls and bricks in the middle of the floor for one of her storytelling sessions. She creates three strongholds of multi-coloured blocks, and plunks the princess in the centre. She picks up the ragamuffin doll, the swan, and the bunny in both hands and begins to dance them around the ramparts. She hums a tune. It's off-key but it's similar to the one Deborah played in the therapy room. As best you can you glance around at the other statues. You think they are paying attention despite their frozen postures.

Rosie stands up and begins to clap to the tune. Elena beams up at her and sings louder. The toys caper faster. Two more patients rise to their feet and clap. Nurse Sara drifts to the doorway and watches, but doesn't intervene.

Rosie begins to chant, "Dance, dance, dance, dance..."

Lisa, Gertrude, and Alice quietly stand up. Sara issues a startled gasp, but now she is the one frozen in place.

All the patients clap, and Elena's singing becomes manically loud. The three statues converge in the centre of the room and commence their dance around the blocks. At once, the atmosphere shifts in the room and Elena's voice seems to resonate and double as if others are singing harmonies with her.

Sara is released from indecision, and enters the room, her hands already raised in a calming gesture. One of the patients is on her in an instant, her arm locked around Sara's throat, keeping her immobile. Sara claws for release but is stretched back with little purchase.

Rosie's head turns and singles you out in the room. You see the malice slip forward from its hiding place. Still clapping, she skips over to your chair and lowers her face to look you squarely in the face.

She raises her fist and slowly uncurls her fingers to reveal a secreted pencil. "Daughter of man," she whispers to you, "you dwell in the midst of a rebellious house, who have eyes to see, and see not; they have ears to hear, and hear not: for they are a rebellious house."

Rosie grips the pencil like a weapon. "You are a bad Penny, among the righteous. Without you, I can step upon the path again. And see the glory anew."

She strikes at your eye but your hand whips up to catch her wrist in a surprisingly firm grip. Rosie's eyes widen first in surprise, then with satisfied glee.

You head-butt her.

She roars in pain and staggers back. Your skull reverberates from the contact and your vision is spangled with stars of agony. Amidst the dazzle and the noise a figure stands up in the centre of the room: a woman in a straight white gown, and long dark hair. Her face is a cluster of stars in an empty void.

Your head rings and feels twice as heavy as normal. The figure begins to move towards you, but in strangely displaced movements, as if she is warping from one spot to another, to avoid contact with the other patients.

Suddenly she is in front of you. You see the sparkling white of her shift, but you will not raise your head to look into that face, even though it feels as if a thousand hands are upon your skull, pushing it up.

You are a rebellious house, Penelope, says a voice in your head.

"DESIST!" The voice booms from the doorway. The doctor is a blot overlaid on blossoms of pain. Elena drops into a foetal ball on the floor, the statues refreeze. Rosie retreats to her couch, blubbering, with her hand over her forehead. Nurses swarm into the room bristling with injections.

Soon you are tucked up in bed, in a haze.

But the imprint of the woman remains on your drugged vision. She is the strip of shadow underneath the door, the spear of light through the window, a presence which slips between the empty spaces looking for a way out.

You are glad for the drug that keeps you fuzzy, because your instinctive reaction to Rosie's attack has woken something in you. Now, in the background, hums a desire to move again of your own volition.

You resist the urge. Not until you observe the doctor's special rite.

The waiting wears on you. The usual routines recommence, except for the sessions in the therapy room. The doctor pays special attention to

Lisa, Gertrude, and Alice and has extra treatments with them alone.

He enters the examination room when you are being scrutinised by the resident physician, Dr Allen. You have an angry bump on your forehead, but it's not as bad as Rosie's black eye. The cameras in the sun room did not catch your interaction, although they captured Rosie's staggered retreat through the bodies back to her couch. You discover she is insisting that you attacked her. Given both your records, Rosie's account is the least credible.

Allen checks your pupil reflexes, and you relax as much as possible at the invasion of light. You sense the unseen woman standing behind you in this moment. You can feel the icy regard of those dead stars upon your neck.

"Any signs of concussion?" the doctor asks. He is observing you very carefully.

"Apart from this impressive goose egg on her temple, she checks out fine. Well," Dr Allen raises your wrist and lets it go so it remains in place, hanging, "as fine as she can be in this condition."

He frowns and studies your chart. "Perhaps we need to change up her medication. She should have improved by now."

"I've consulted with Dr Olsen about this case. She outlined a therapy we've been investigating. I have hopes it will be successful."

Dr Allen stands, and pulls off his gloves now that the examination is over. The doctor moves before you to bend and stare directly at your face. Your flat gaze locks with his piercing regard. "If that doesn't work then Deborah believes she can convince Penelope's husband to try ECT."

It's hard to suppress any flinch of surprise.

Dr Allen nods as he jots notes on your chart, "It can be effective in these cases."

Behind you the phantom presence presses against your spine.

The doctor smiles at you. "I've no doubt Penelope will respond to the right course."

The desire to spit in his face causes a muscle to twitch in your thigh.

The therapy sessions recommence. There is a new tension in the doctor, and he monitors every part of your ritual exactly. Deborah returns to watch another run-through. She stands behind you so you cannot see her reaction, and her conversations with the doctor are too low to overhear.

Outside the sessions Rosie and you are kept apart, and Elena is no longer allowed to play with the toys. She sits, defensively curled, her expression blank. You wonder if she will retreat further into herself, and become a statue. And you wonder how she knew that tune, and what is her history of treatment?

You cannot be a sleuth because of the path you have chosen. Answers come to those who hunt. They do not drop into dormant hands. Frustration agitates your mind, and threatens your control.

Previously you were convinced your inaction was the best revenge, now you waver. You remember this kind of intractable attitude was never one you admired. Before.

The released spirit lurks close by. You consider there may be other ragged remnants teeming all around this place. Inescapable observers.

You are a rebellious house. You keep hearing that phrase.

You wonder if you should open the door and free what you have shut away.

It happens unexpectedly. Late one night, Deborah enters your room and urges you up and into a wheelchair. The corridors you are wheeled through are empty except for bouncing light. You are dozy, and strain not to squint against the glare.

The room is lit with large white candles in three tall candelabras. A huge backdrop hangs behind the platform. On it is drawn a jagged path in black pointing to the top of a cliff, upon which perches a lighthouse signalling a diamond flash of light. The flickering shadows from the candlelight dart across the faces of your fellow statues, and you can feel the wraith skipping in and out of the moments in between.

Deborah eases you into your position on the stage, facing front, and you hear whispering. The doctor moves into view and there are other people with him. It's hard to discern them in the darkness as they all wear black clothing. Their shiny faces exude a simmering excitement.

The doctor wears a vaudevillian outfit with exaggerated makeup. He is stepping into a part, and taking the power of that mantle upon him. "Ladies and Gentlemen, you are witnessing a rare re-enactment, and those of you who have questions will be answered. All secrets will be penetrated, if you remember our instructions and keep to them exactly."

The audience nod their heads, and stare at you with open fascination.

Deborah starts the music. It's a more complex version, with strings, drums, rattles, and odd hissing. Lisa, Gertrude, and Alice begin their sinuous weaving between the three seated positions, and to your mind's eyes you are wrenched somewhere else: a black plane on which stand three white towers, while three priestesses carrying snakes wheel around a white-flamed fire.

The great presence permeates: it is the heat, the bricks, the tongues of the serpents, and the breath of the women. You are both the tower and the motion, and your stillness in the distant room is imperative to experience the ecstasy of the whole.

A penitent resolves from beyond, and you observe him dispassionately.

A question hovers in his mind, a stupid one about investments. You can answer it easily enough as it is simple to pick it out from the threads of man's predictable patterns, but it is odiously dull, and will not grant you egress.

What you want, what you always crave, is to slip out of this flat realm and into the curves and curls of human interactions. To embroil yourself in the passion and pull of fleshy existence. Where you can cascade change in delicious combinations.

Here, on your territory, they are easy to influence. Mistakes are made when they are pulled out of their world and made to walk in your unusual spaces. Only those who are practised at stepping outside the familiar can resist your sway.

You perceive his thought processes clearly. The question, in this weird unspace, seems foolish, corpulent. How can he pass on this rare chance to force insight of one of the great mysteries?

The question flashes into his mind, "When will I die?"

You are out, and in his world.

Shudderingly, you are wrenched back into the room, along with the vast presence. All the statues are compelled to stand, even you.

The doctor, he who thought he had planned so carefully, grabs the seeker and attempts to push him to the door.

Deborah stops the music but that will not prevent this prophesy.

Your voices speak together, and you pronounce his death: "Now."

He clutches his chest, his face contorted in shock at the pain and his finality, Gasping, he drops to the floor. Deborah attempts to help him but the body is winding down and his spirit is already unspooling.

The doctor steps forward, and he has one of the old devices that even you must respect. He has prepared. But so have you.

He speaks the words that disrupt your connection, and you are scattered back.

You fall upon the dais hearing the panic and the crush as people bolt away from death.

A cool breeze from the bright, clean hallways rushes into the stuffy playhouse.

Three of the statues have returned to their inert position.

You sit up slowly, careful with muscles unused to activity. Near you, Margot and Deirdre stir.

Deborah kneels by the dead man, her hand on his chest, but her face is turned to you. She is riveted.

The doctor raises a hand to stall you, to explain. "This was theatrical therapy," he says, but his voice cracks. "To break the construct you have created. By playing a part you are forced to confront the role you have subsumed yourself into."

He has no idea. You witnessed the unreal world. All the old obsessions, the paranoia, the fears that proliferated in your mind are cut-out replicas of this world's illusions. They have been knocked over and blown away by the whirlwind you experienced.

You delight in your solid skeleton; the feel of your ligaments bending; the scrapes on your skin; how your lips moisten when you lick them; the clash of teeth.

You help Margot and Deirdre stand, and there is a fleet, faint tingle of connection between you. You move to the doorway.

The doctor dithers, but decides to step in front of you, determined to re-assert his control. But he still wears the greasepaint and the costume.

You notice a flake of white sticking up from his cheek. You reach forward, pick at it, and *peel.*

You strip back the mask in one long rind, exposing the emptiness. He shrieks as you roll him up into a tight coil.

Under your scrutiny the persona collapses flat. You crush it in one hand and toss it into the air where it disintegrates.

When you glance at Deborah she presses her forehead to the floor.

You walk across the threshold.

It is time the rebellious left the house.

BEAUTIFUL CALAMITY

"I never finish anything, because it never ends well," she said the first night we met, at *Les Neuf Soeurs* club, in the noisy, cramped Helicon Bar, literary hub of the East Village. It was known among the art house crowd as Hell because of its crimson walls and hissing cast-iron radiators. I realised then that most of them didn't get out much.

"I dunno," I said, and rattled the ice cubes in my slick of bourbon like dice. "How can you start something new if you don't finish anything?"

She laughed, her smile an epiphany. "I'm Mel." She stuck out her hand, and I cinched it in a firm grip. She didn't give me the feeble back-off-buddy handshake I was expecting. Her hand was supple and confident.

"James," I responded. It was one of my cover names. I imagined James as a welder, with a mongrel terrier, and a mouthy fiancée. I tried to exude a love of steel.

Her fingers slid across my palm as we disengaged, and the heat and pressure of her hip against my thigh came to my attention. We were crushed together in the only booth in the bar, sitting on cracked vinyl between curvy Betsy the burlesque diva and Torquil the pencil-thin master puppeteer.

Mel sipped red wine from a glass she cradled in her palm, her fingers scissored around the stem. She flashed me a sidelong, appraising glance. "Are you a writer, a director?"

I sucked back the last drabs of Jack, and crunched ice. "I don't create." I kept a watch on Clarence Hastings across the room, my target for the night, and thought, *I only tear things apart.*

She leaned into me so I could see the sweep of her bronzed neck and the curve of her small breasts, tight to her white silk blouse. She smelled of sandcastles and salt. "I don't believe you," she whispered.

She raised her gaze to meet mine. Her eyes reminded me of sunlight filtered through seawater. The world ebbed away for a moment; a commotion from the stage startled me back to the heat and din of the bar.

The MC, a petite blonde called Lia, shaded her eyes from the spotlight's glare, and squinted at the audience. "Mel, Mel," she pleaded from the tiny platform, her voice distorted by the cheap microphone, "you next. Please. Clarence plans on boring us into a coma with his latest epic." Clarence pressed the hand-written verses to his waistcoat, blushed, and sat down hard on his stool. "Only kidding, Clarence," Lia grinned, and snapped one of the braces holding up her pinstriped trousers as penance. "You know we adore your work as much as *The New Yorker* does. Come on, Mel."

Mel shook her inky curls, her face downcast. A babble of encouragement rose. I elbowed her softly in the ribs. "They won't let up until they've had blood." She turned her face towards me before she stood, and her resignation stabbed me with a sudden regret. In that instant I wanted to circle her wrist with my fingers, ease her back down on the seat, and spend the rest of the night yapping about stupid inconsequential things.

"Let me out," she said.

Torquil and I jumped up, and she swayed among the tables of writers and performers who sat hunched knee to elbow, and shoulder to shoulder. Lia handed Mel the microphone after a kiss on the cheek and darted into the gloom to squeeze between the patrons lined up at bar.

In the unforgiving light Mel's thin nose and high cheekbones cut hard shadows into her face. "This is a work-in-progress," she said, and it roused a laugh from the crowd.

"Is there any other kind?" some smart aleck quipped. I eyed the press of bodies between the bar and me and wondered if I could wade through without too much fuss. I guessed I was going to need another drink.

Mel bowed her head for a moment, and under the toss of hair her lips moved as if in prayer. Before I could make my excuses she spoke: "Andrea left, as she always promised to leave, on an unkind day in Spring, after the reign of snowdrops but before the promise of daffodils."

Mel lifted her head to silence. "Shirley ghosted through the following two weeks: she haunted her job, drifted through the deli and bought groceries, and even attended a birthday party for her older sister. No one noticed her insubstantial state. Instead they asked after Andrea, which ground glass further into Shirley's heart."

"On the third week Shirley cut off her small toe. She divined the bleeding as a good sign. Alive after all. But then she paused, the severed digit in her fingers, her foot up on the bathtub rim, the shoelace tourniquet soaked black, and wondered: do phantoms bleed? How could she be sure she hadn't expired the day Andrea left. She could not remember when she last drew breath."

"That night she hobbled out to the worn patch of dirt and grass behind her apartment building, and scratched a small grave for her toe, which lay in a navy jewellery box coffin that once contained an enamelled broach, bought by Andrea at an antiques fair. Its lightness surprised her. She buried it with the distant cry of a police siren as eulogy."

"Shirley held onto the banister as she climbed back up the worn steps, and wondered when she would feel real again."

Mel paused, and suddenly her voice rose in song. It carried the heartbreak of Piaf combined with the earthiness of Holiday, and although the lyrics were in a language I didn't understand they sounded old. A dirge that untied knots congested in my heart, and loosed unwanted memories: the smell of baking cookies and cigarette smoke; and a fiery blaze sucking air from my lungs.

The last note hung high and long and Mel finished to a hush. She bowed, and the audience started as one, as if broken from a trance, and clapped its enthusiasm. She left the circle of light.

Lia sashayed onto the stage. "Who could follow that?" She arced a hand at Clarence, "My dear, you'll have to wait. We require fortification." A murmur indicated a collective agreement. "After a stiff drink I demand bawdiness and ill-advised humour!" Lia waved at a volunteer at the back, and the house lights flashed on.

Betsy and Torquil abandoned the booth and jostled towards the bar. I glared at my empty glass and decided against the urge to strangle conjured memories by booze or my departure. I had a job to do.

Clarence skipped through the press of bodies to dodge in front of Mel. He waved pages at her face. She paused and dipped her head to examine his prose, and he sidled in cosy. His hand touched her shoulder, and she didn't shake it off. Until that moment I thought Janice's suspicions about Clarence were part of her usual drama queen fantasies. I only took the investigation to stop her constant phone calls, and because when we were kids she was the only one of my cousins who ever stood up to my dad.

I turned towards Mel and Clarence and clicked the top of the pen in my jacket pocket to activate the camera. I couldn't hope for high quality in this light and across that distance, but it would capture their proximity, and give me an image of Mel's face.

I wanted to know who she was.

A week later a bitter November draught chased me up the crooked staircase towards the rumble of voices in the Helicon Bar. Lia stood near the doorway and gossiped with Torquil until she noticed me pause on the threshold, momentarily stunned by the heat and colour.

She narrowed her eyes in vague recollection. "Back again?" She moved towards me with a clipboard of scrawled names. "Will you read tonight and forgive me sweetie but I can't recall your name. An awful lapse on my part." She laid a chagrin hand upon my forearm.

"James Monaghan," I said, "and I don't write."

She punched my chest playfully. "Don't be shy, if we didn't hear new work," she raised her voice and caught the attention of a tall woman with ropes of greying dreadlocks, "we'd be forced to listen to the same authors over, and over..." The woman frowned at Lia and turned away. Lia dropped her voice, conspiratorial, "That's Sophix, yes *that* Sophix," I nodded as if it that meant something. "Her novel was slammed in the *New York Book Review* last week despite its obvious genius. She's gutted. Now, what did *you* bring tonight?"

"I'm a philistine."

She favoured me with an unimpressed stare. "Darling, philistines don't admit to it."

I scanned the crowd. "Is Mel here tonight?"

Lia nodded at the corner. "She's in the booth." I spotted Mel, and beside her, Clarence. Pages were fanned out on the table in front of them. Two other people crowded the space and ogled the work. "Clarence is smitten." Lia shrugged. "It's always the serious ones."

"Does Mel perform often?" I asked. In between my other cases I'd shifted through the surveillance reports on Clarence. He'd been attending rehearsals for a play, but there was no evidence he met Mel during that time.

"On occasion. Her voice... well, it makes your heart stagger."

"Who is she?" I noticed Clarence place his hand over Mel's. She slipped her hand away to point at a line on a page.

Lia's silence warned me. When I looked back at her she appraised me in a frank fashion. "Have you a crush on Mel?" She stepped in close before I could protest and slipped her arm in the nook of my elbow. "Forget it. You're not gloomy enough. And besides, you don't write." She laughed, and stepped back, her attention on the door as more people entered. "People say she's a Eurotrash heiress trawling to marry a brilliant writer to piss off Daddy. The truth is more banal I'm sure. She's probably an accountant." She waved at somebody. "You should ask her. Must dash." And Lia danced through the bodies and brandished her list at another target.

I nodded to a couple of people I recognised from the last meeting, and ordered a beer from Jacek, the hard-eyed Polish bartender, who I later heard was a celebrated poet in Russia. "That's a big fuckin' market," Torquil said in his rapid-fire patter. We sat at a rickety table. His bulbous eyes looked like they were being squeezed out by invisible pressure to his forehead. "Huge territory, twice the size of Canada, and a place that appreciates the artistry of puppetry. Obraztsov. Ever hear of him?" I shook my head and watched Mel banter with Clarence. "Brilliant. No fuckin' Henson, thank Christ. Technical master of the form."

I interrupted him, "What do you know about Mel?"

The puppeteer glanced over at the booth. "Great voice. Been with Clarence for a couple of months."

"They're dating?"

"They're chummy. And Clarence's play opens soon. Makes him popular with the ladies." Torquil slurred the word ladies and made it sound obscene. "Wonder if his wife knows."

I'll tell her as soon as I find out. A splatter of applause heralded Lia's appearance on the stage.

Torquil nudged me hard in the side. "Mel favours the artistic types. She was the best of friends with Sophix a year ago." His leer had the exaggeration of a cartoon character. I hoped an anvil would drop on his head.

The lights dimmed, and my back slumped as the first poet took the stage. I wished I could see Mel's face so I could search it for the famegrubber of Torquil's story. It didn't match the woman I'd met the previous week, and years of watching and reporting on people had honed my instincts. Still... an attractive woman was a distraction.

The performers didn't suck, but I couldn't concentrate. In my mind I saw Clarence slip his pudgy fingers over Mel's hand, over her shoulder, and over her...

"When Nanci walked home at night from the diner…" I jerked my head up. Mel stood on stage, and gripped the microphone with both hands. "She watched the shadows reach towards her and then stretch behind as she walked from street light to street light. Thin dark bodies that mocked Nanci's curves and thick ankles. She longed to reverse their situations, until she possessed their lean legs and graceful arms. At her front door the shades thinned, snapped back to the bottom of the lamp posts, and watched her struggle up the steps and into the house of second-hand insults, where her kids interacted with video games, and her husband slapped her ass and suggested the latest diet he'd seen advertised on TV."

"One night, after another long shift on her swollen feet, Nanci paused between two posts and observed the daisy chain of elongated bodies. She closed her eyes and with the force of suppressed anger and cancerous resentment willed herself away."

"The shadows seeped into the soles of her sneakers and filled her up and Nanci fled into the current, where she could flit from lamp to lamp and reflect the journey of the middle-aged woman slouched in a cardigan but bid her goodbye at the door."

Mel sighed, closed her eyes, and lifted her face to the spotlight and the foreign song that poured from her throat transported me back to my mother's kitchen, to the aroma of baking chocolate-chip cookies. It was the only time Mom felt safe to sneak quick drags from a cigarette as she leaned out of the tiny kitchen window. Dad had a bloodhound's sense of smell, and if she smoked on the landing or on the apartment stoop word got round to Dad and then she'd have a reckoning. I flapped a dishcloth as she puffed out a nervous haze and she joked we were sending smoke signals to heaven.

The burst of applause wrenched me from the past, and I slammed my palms together to drive away the sickness in my stomach. Mel stepped into the darkness, and a poet took her place. I couldn't concentrate during the following recitals. The beer wouldn't wash the taste of melted chocolate from my mouth. Instead it reminded me of kneeling by my bed with my hands clamped together, urging God to answer our desperate messages. For an angel to intercept Dad's hand, or for God to transform him – like Paul was changed on the road to Damascus. If God did it for Paul, why not for Dad?

The house lights flooded the room, and I stood, stinking with old fear and rejection, and elbowed to the bar where I signalled Jacek for another beer. I moved to the niche where nobody stood because of the steaming ancient radiator. I welcomed the painful heat and swallowed the beer fast. My focus returned as I finished it, and I searched the crowd for a sign of Clarence. If he was fucking around I was going to nail him.

I pulled out my notebook to jot a couple of notes. I always kept it handy, and it wouldn't stand out in this crowd. I clicked my camera pen, and wrote:

She sings of beautiful calamity.
Bees from her mouth,
Which sting with honeyed words.

"James?"

I looked up at Mel, and the pen stalled in my hand.

She pointed to the page. "I thought you didn't create."

I snapped the notebook closed. "Grocery list."

Her smile was wistful. "Liar."

I couldn't speak.

She lifted her hand and brushed my cheek; her touch blazed. I felt a *clunk*, like a key grinding in a corroded lock. "The boy, his prayers, and the fire are the shattered centre. All your stories splinter outwards from it."

I stepped back, and the radiator burned my calves. My tongue was too thick and heavy to vocalise the pain.

She moved towards me, and I couldn't retreat. "Tell your story." Her eyes were the breathless plunge into the ecstatic void.

"This is very snug," Lia's words hauled me from the dream. I skittered from the radiator and banged into a short ponytailed man who spilled half his drink. As I mumbled apologies Lia put her arm around Mel's waist, and looked up at her. "You can't have *all* the shiny ones Melpomene."

Mel blinked, and her forehead creased. "Lia," she murmured, and her gaze cleared. She glanced at me and her cheeks flushed ruby. "I have to go." She turned and fled through the crowd.

Lia sighed. "That girl needs to relax." She eyed me. "You all right?"

I nodded, but I noticed Clarence's furious gaze upon me, and how he shoved through the group to follow Mel.

Lia studied my face and shook her head. "I'm jealous." She disappeared into the throng.

Two weeks later my surveillance guy caught Clarence coming out of a hotel with the actress who played the lead role of the agoraphobic amputee in his play. When I showed the photographs to Janice in my office she wrote a cheque, thanked me calmly, and left. The next day, a week before the opening night, Janice shot Clarence dead. "I couldn't let him have it all," she said as she was led away in handcuffs. It generated huge publicity for the play. After the premiere's standing ovation, and in between hiccupped sobs, the actress dedicated her performance to Clarence's memory.

During my subsequent two-day drinking binge I tried to slaughter as many brain cells as possible.

In one of the photographs that appeared in the dailies afterwards I spotted Mel in the background – an oval smudge with dark fathomless eyes. I blew up the image, cut out Mel's shape, and pinned it to the corkboard where I tracked all my live cases.

I continued going to the *Les Neuf Soeurs*. Mel didn't turn up, and I couldn't generate any leads. When questioned closely no one knew her, not even her last name, and the grubby images I'd taken on my camera didn't match anyone in the databases I searched. The one time I cornered Sophix in the Helicon bar she refused to speak about Mel. "Forget her if you can," Sophix said, her intense eyes bright in her gaunt face.

Lia showed up a couple of times, but when I tried to approach her someone would sidetrack me or interrupt. I attempted to tail her after those meetings, but always lost her. It was like following a ghost.

The only clue I had was the full name of Melpomene – the Greek muse of tragedy – and the fact that Mel might have been an heiress from Europe. I called in a lot of favours and spent too much money chasing that rumour. It only uncovered old gossip and twice-told nonsense. Like how Vincent Van Gogh referred to Melpomene in his letters to his brother, and Virginia Woolf described the muse in her diary like a lover. Franz Kafka even wrote testimonies dedicated to her. No facts, no solid information. Just myths and apparitions.

I dreamed of Mel. She stood on the shore of a radiant sea, and seaweed and froth manacled her ankles. The salt breeze carried her song to where I stood sinking in the wet sand, unable to move toward her or escape.

When I woke I had to *write*. I scribbled memories, poems, snippets of scenes, short stories, and dialogue between characters that looped in my mind until I recorded it on paper. I tried to stop writing once, but after three days I was so distracted I almost crashed my car while trailing a woman suspected of insurance fraud.

I got to know the regulars at *Les Neuf Soeurs*. I went to one of Betsy's shows – just to offer my support – and her sexy witty performance surprised me. Torquil was a son of a bitch sometimes, but he curated an exhibition on puppetry at the New York Public Library with ferocious professionalism. I came to enjoy the debates about who were the best writers at the meetings, and what books were overrated. The gang bought me drinks when I told them I'd broken up with my fiancée because she declared my writing worthless. At least I still had Twain, my faithful pooch.

I never planned to show my writing to anyone, but Betsy pestered me, and Torquil joined in too.

A year after I attended the club for the first time, I hunched in my overcoat against the winter breeze that whistled down the narrow streets. I could only think about the pages zipped up in my leather briefcase. I rounded the corner for the Helicon bar. Sophix stood outside. Beside her, Mel, her scarlet raincoat a slash of colour on the grey streets. I backed away and knelt on the filthy icy pavement by the building's corner and fussed with my shoelaces.

Sophix's voice snapped like a high-tension wire. "Why did you leave?"

Mel's soft response wasn't audible.

"Don't tell me what's best for me!"

A new voice spoke: "Sophix, go home and take your meds."

I gave up pretence, stood, and turned the corner. Lia wore a white wool coat. She stood at the bar's entrance, her hands on her hips, and smiled up at Sophix. Frustration corded the tendons in Sophix's neck.

I strolled towards the trio, and called out, "Do you need any help?" I kept my voice neutral.

Lia threw up her hands when she saw me. "Oh great."

When Sophix turned her expression of hatred stopped me. "Fuck off!" she screeched.

Mel touched Sophix's shoulder, and Sophix whipped around and swung her fist. I broke into a run, but I knew I couldn't intercept the blow.

The punch never landed. From behind I saw Sophix's angular

shoulders suddenly relax, and her arm drop to her side as if a string attached to her arm was cut. Mel hugged her and spoke into her ear. The tall woman nodded and crossed the street with long strides. Sophix disappeared down a side street before I reached Mel.

I sweated from the burst of activity, and my cheeks burned from foolishness and the shock of seeing Mel again.

"Our saviour," Lia warbled, and wrung her hands. Mel stared down at the pavement. A yellow cab whisked by and a plastic bag ballooned into the air and drifted past us like an air-borne squid.

Lia pointed at my briefcase. "You better read tonight hero." She was poised to enter the doorway but glanced back at Mel. "You okay, sis?"

"Go on, Thalia," Mel said. Lia left.

The lights above us flickered, and our shadows lunged towards each other for a second.

"I dreamed about you," I blurted, and immediately regretted the words.

"You've been writing," she said matter-of-factly.

I lifted the briefcase and held it in front of me like an offering. "Yes."

"I wish you hadn't."

A sliver of pain pierced me. "It's probably not very good," I said.

She lifted her face, "If it's honest it will have power." The path of a tear limed the curve of her cheek. She squeezed her eyes closed for a moment as if she wanted to block out my image, or a bad memory. "It always ends badly," she whispered.

I longed to crush her to me, to imprint her on my body as flesh and bone, and not an illusion, or a dream. I raised my hand to bridge the gap between us.

"Don't," she said, and her eyes flashed open.

I froze.

The reflected streetlights were diamonds circling her pupils. "I will break your heart."

An artic breeze raised hairs on the back of my neck. I shivered.

She entered the dark doorway.

I waited until the echo of her footsteps faded before I followed, unable to keep away.

I couldn't see through the barrier of light. There was only the microphone, and the page in front of me. Above the tinny whine of the amplifier a murmur of voices hinted at the existence of the crowd. And among them, Mel.

I cleared my throat to dislodge the terror. "My name is..." *Fuck.* My voice gave out.

I shut my eyelids against the glare for a second. A dissatisfied rumble rose among the people beyond my sight. I opened my eyes again and sucked in a lungful of frigid air. The heating in the Helicon was broken, and the scatter of electric heaters the management provided did nothing to warm the old space.

"Danny Considine. That's my real name." It felt like the temperature dropped another couple of degrees. My breath was smoke and I tasted ashes. "This is a work in progress," I said. A woman tittered. Someone coughed. The paper rattled when I raised it. I opened my mouth to recite the story I'd written, but other words arced across my mind, desperate for release.

I crumpled the sheet in my hand and surrendered to the current. "Sammy began his war against God on Easter Friday, when Jesus was in the tomb and he figured even the all-knowing but indifferent deity had other things on His mind."

"It'd been a snap to find an empty whiskey bottle in his home, but stealing gasoline was tricky. The super of the apartment building, Mr. Cook, watched a soap on TV every day at three thirty and always left the door to the basement unlocked at that time."

"Sammy sneaked down the creaking wooden steps into the darkness, afraid to turn on the light and draw attention to his theft. With a torch held behind his teeth for illumination he poured the gas into the bottle. His eyes teared from the fumes. He screwed the bottle's cap back on and returned the sticky red canister to the shelf beside the tin can bristling with nails and screws."

"The bottle sloshed in his hands. For a moment the rage that fuelled his plans dimmed, and Sammy questioned the wisdom of taking on the Almighty. Then he remembered the constant smoke signals to heaven and the thousands of ignored prayers, the awful *crunch* his mother's nose made as it broke and the fine mist of blood that sprayed across his Dad's white shirt and enraged him further."

"Sammy heard a sound in the darkness of the basement, like an animal stretching awake, and shaking its hide."

"'No quarter Sammy,' it rasped."

"Sammy nodded, and stuck the bottle inside his denim jacket. It grated against his ribs. He stank like an inferno. It would be easy to scrape through the chain link fence at the back of the basketball court to gain access to the boarded-up Church of Merciful Christ."

"Sammy would raise a sign to heaven that even God couldn't miss."

Silence. I stumbled off the stage. Applause followed me, and someone slapped my back, but the drumbeat in my head drowned it out.

I walked to the door without pause, and descended the staircase, stiff like a marionette. The next performer's voice echoed after me. I dragged my right hand against the rough surface of the wall to steady myself.

A cold gust flapped my coat against my legs when I exited the building. I stopped, inhaled deep, and looked left and right.

Mel stood under a streetlight. The sodium glare bleached her black hair. She drifted from me. Her red raincoat winked in and out of pools of light and dark.

I followed her, eager.

Home

On a moonless night in 1678 Lord Alexander Fitzhugh laid my foundations.

With the aid of his architect, Francesco Alberti, he slaughtered a fawn, a fox, a badger, and a raven. The blood washed my heartstone, pooled in the alchemical sigils carved into its surface, and ignited my animating spirit. Afterwards, their bones were sunk deep in the wet Irish soil, under the seal of my stone.

Beneath my slow pulse worms laced between animal teeth, while above, humans busied themselves with my construction.

This is what I gleaned during my assembly:

For his Grand Tour, Alexander had travelled Europe extensively, buoyed by the funds of his ailing, indulgent father. He had scoured libraries and universities, and employed rare book collectors in Paris, Cologne, and Madrid to gather texts on the arcane sciences, ancient architecture, and sacred geometry. His agents acquired a copy of Agrippa's *Fifth Book of Occult Philosophy*, which many sages insisted did not exist in any form in this world. His research was supported by his extensive study of mathematics, alchemy and astrology; Newton had tutored him at Cambridge.

With money and the right letters of introduction Alexander procured initiation with the Fraternity of the Rosy Cross, which admitted him to the association of students of the Invisible College. Via the brotherhood he unearthed Francesco from a mouldering athenaeum in Rome. An ignored but clever apprentice of a famous architect, Francesco required little enticement to purloin secrets, abandon his master, and take service with the ambitious Englishman.

Alexander's father, the Viscount Fitzhugh, had never travelled to the sodden and savage lands of Ireland – not with his gout – but his agents gathered coin from the peasants he'd inherited with his title. Alexander decided that such a place, with its wild and romantic landscape, would be the perfect location to raise a citadel of civilisation, a bulwark against barbarian ignorance, and whose very design would furnish him with the key to the secrets of creation.

Thus, Alexander selected my birthplace.

The Golden Ratio guided my design, and the Tree of Life dictated the number of my rooms and the flow of paths between them. The red bricks that composed my walls were fired in Dublin, and smooth Portland stone, ferried from Dorset, covered my exterior façade. Expert stonemasons followed Francesco's designs with precision, but bemoaned Alexander's strict supervision and the exactitude of his demands.

A phalanx of carpenters carved and fitted hardwoods from the Americas to fashion my sweeping central staircase. My floorboards were local oak, except in the echoing first floor rooms with their arched Serlian windows where Penteli marble – the building blocks of the Acropolis – was selected. Italian artists lay on scaffolds and painted frescos on the vaulted ceilings. French designers haggled over gilt furniture for my interiors and complained about the food and weather. Silks from China and carpets from Morocco adorned my rooms. Troops of gardeners shaped a symmetrical garden designed upon the principles of harmonious proportion.

I flourished under their care and attention.

Alexander poured a goodly portion of his fortune into my construction, and despite the simmering resentment of a conquered people, the natives welcomed the influx of industry. Discussion about Alexander's tastes and particular requests were all the rage at social engagements in Dublin. My location outside the Pale was hardly convenient, yet every gentleman and lady of good breeding desired an invitation to view "Alexander's folly".

In the rusticated ground floor, beneath the ornate rooms and high ceilings of my *piano nobile*, Alexander built his laboratory, centred at the very heart of my structure.

Within, he began a serious foray into arcane secrets forbidden to all sane men.

She arrived after their wedding.

Tiny, delicate, and dressed in a silk dress edged in fur and studded with gems, Lady Claire Fitzhugh alighted from the carriage as Alexander held her hand. She climbed my exterior steps and gazed at my columned portico with wide eyes and a pretty smile. I welcomed her with warm fires to guard against the slanting rain. The row of maids, footmen, butlers, and cooks curtseyed and bowed at her entrance. Her little speech coaxed smiles from them all, even the dour Francesco. Alexander drew her into the bedroom. I watched their coupling with interest and recalled my birth of blood.

At first there were weeks of dances and entertainments, which continued with evenings of cribbage, and harpsichord recitals by candlelight in the drawing rooms. Guests visited often, but when company or family were away Alexander retired to his hidden room, which was bound by charms and spells. Even I could not peer within, as it was fashioned to block prying spirits and contain whatever he summoned. It was a blind spot in my bright and cheerful household.

During Alexander's absences Claire went horse riding across the craggy landscape. When not needed by Alexander, Francesco accompanied her on those jaunts to guard her against local brutes. When inclement weather kept her indoors, which was often, she embroidered, or walked listlessly through the house, her hand upon her belly. On occasion she read books from the huge library that Alexander had assembled (except for the texts locked behind iron).

She screamed all night and I could do nothing.

Her bedroom reeked of fear and blood. The midwives discussed the birth in their native tongue, and despite my foreign design I had roots deep within the land and their thoughts and speech were transparent to me.

They feared mother and child would die. I focused upon Claire's heartbeat, and willed it to strengthen. I sensed the small life's quest for delivery, but it was weakened from the strain of the protracted labour.

Alexander withdrew to his sanctuary. My foundations shuddered, the skulls under my heartstone shrieked, and even I heard his urgent petition for help shoot into the ether.

A terrible darkness invaded me, and I flinched from it, shocked and frightened by its touch. Deep inside I sensed claws, teeth, and an awful hungering need that wished only to corrupt and deceive. A pact was offered, accepted, and I could do nothing to prevent it.

When Alexander emerged from his laboratory his black-stained fingers trembled, and he could speak to none.

Their son, Robert, surged out in a torrent of blood. Pale and weak, Claire could not suckle. Alexander arranged for a local wet-nurse, but she handed back the child after a couple of days and claimed her breasts had dried up. I heard fearful whispers among the locals. Out of earshot of the priests who taught them in the hedgerows they repeated ancient charms to their Saint-Goddess Bríd.

Claire paced the bedroom, rocking her screaming babe, as Alexander whipped his carriage to Dublin.

He returned with Helen Montgomery, chestnut-haired and wide-hipped. A recent widow, her family was respectable, humble, and Protestant. Her brown-eyed boy, James, crawled through my rooms and distracted Claire with his good-natured smiles. She loved him as if he were her own.

Sickly Robert Fitzhugh accepted Helen's milk, and Claire and Alexander were content for a while.

The changing weather and the bloom and decay of the gardens marked the seasons, as well as regular tasks such as the beating of rugs, the polishing of the chandeliers, and the turning of mattresses.

Claire never carried another child to term, although three blood-wrapped bundles were carried from her bedchamber. Despite the tears and heartbreak, Alexander did not enter another treaty with the forces he had invoked to save Robert.

The tiny sparks that failed to flourish within flesh floated free and were caught in the web of my magical structure. I welcomed two girls and a boy into me.

I grieved with Claire when she lay abed for weeks. I missed her laughter in the parlour and her light step upon my stairs. Alexander locked himself away in his laboratory with increasing regularity, and the darkness he invited into me was a constant sore, a damp, dank spot that I tried to disregard.

Instead I focused upon the bustle of the servants, the chatter of the children, and the ebb and flow of human life. Claire recovered, but her deprivations leeched her spirit of its previous vitality. Robert and James grew up like brothers: one red-haired and intense, the other dark and cheerful. Helen remained as companion and nurse to Claire. They confided in one another on all matters.

When Robert was ten years old he stole the key to his father's hidden room, and opened the door. I watched, unable to prevent his entrance to the shadowed realm. Fearful of a beating, James reminded outside as lookout. The door clanged behind Robert, James could not open it, and I could not see within. After a long and anxious wait, Robert emerged, but I saw the mote that floated in his heart; the taint. James started at his friend's appearance, aware of a subtle change, but Robert sneered at him and called him craven.

In that moment the unschooled Robert allowed the darkness out of the room.

It took root and began its slow and insidious assault upon me.

Everything changed after the argument.

Lightning speared from roiling black clouds. The wind ripped tiles from the stables and exposed the bucking horses to fierce hail.

Claire screamed accusations at Alexander, to which he responded with aloof disdain. Earlier that day Helen had left, stiff-faced and red-eyed, with her luggage and a quiet James in tow. Robert had waved goodbye from the bottom step but refused to shed a tear.

My family was riven. The corrosion took advantage of my grief to eat deeper into my structure. Doors rattled in their frames, the servants cried out as shadows flitted after them in my dim hallways, and all heard the wan wail of forsaken children.

Alexander retreated to his laboratory, where he often spent days at a stretch refining his formulas and incantations. Claire, distraught, maddened by solitude and the lonesome cry of long-dead babes, took up a lamp and went down to her husband's detested sanctum with the intention of burning him from it if he refused her entry. There, the contamination was strongest, and my love for Claire twisted into resentment at her treason.

She drew back the lamp when Alexander ignored her hammering, and for the first time I reached out and *touched* her mind. I betrayed the evil festering inside me, her children's ensnared souls, and how they had bloomed like diseased lilies fed upon infected waters.

She froze, her eyes wide and devoid of reason.

Francesco stepped out of the shadows and removed the lamp from her unresponsive arm. He guided her back to her bedchamber and sat her upon the brocade coverlet. Quietly, he warned her against ever attempting such an action. He kissed her. She did not respond or reject his advances.

The blight spread.

The storm passed and I recovered, but I did not forget the memory of that night. The ability to touch the living lay within easy reach, and the voices that dwelled within me urged me to impose my will upon my residents. The power tempted me daily, and as the years passed I lapsed more often.

Visitors complained of a sensation of cobwebs trailed upon bare skin as they traversed my corridors, or the sob of a child from a darkened closet whose door opened without assistance. Indistinct forms flickered behind reflections in mirrors. As dread secrets grew within me they bled into the entire house until the atmosphere dulled and deepened. Occasionally a cadre of men visited Alexander from Dublin and gathered in his laboratory. On those nights my walls vibrated with summoned energies, and the rot quickened.

I watched over Claire, repentant for my cruelty, but she declined after that night. She lost all appetite, ignored her wardrobe and appearance. A doctor asserted it was a profound case of melancholia, and prescribed purgatives and cold baths. Alexander engaged a local woman to watch over her. Nora was kind to Claire, recognising the touch of a greater force upon the lady's mind. Yet, she pocketed the coin Francesco gave her to look the other way on the nights he slipped into Claire's chamber.

Most locals refused to stay a night within my walls, and guests arrived less often. In a moment of lucidity, Claire sent Robert away to England for schooling. Alexander reduced the staff. He embedded himself in his laboratory, and every day the taint strengthened while he conducted his nefarious experiments.

Eventually I savoured contact from the threshold of time and space, where shunned leviathans rested in a stupor and ignored the siphoning of dribs and drabs of their necrotising fluids. Soon I hungered for its taste. All who died under my roof were caught in my structural web, and they supped upon the stale nectar of insane Gods and perverted angels.

Claire's father, a Vicar, had a seizure upon seeing his dead granddaughter, still caught in bloody swaddling, crawl from the empty fireplace in his bedroom and leave a trail of ashes in her wake. I latched upon the man's departing soul, and soon he hummed hymns to his grandchildren in tongues that had not been used in aeons.

I bound my family tight with love.

Alexander, with the iron control that had kept him sane and

prosperous during his years of experimentation, noted the change in my entire structure. As a test, he attempted a ritual outside his laboratory.

During a lunar eclipse he summoned a door in my atrium and stepped through into the Akashic library itself. He plundered its mystical records for knowledge barred to men for centuries.

Claire shambled through my empty hallways and whispered stories to her ghost children. She tossed slips of bloodied hair in her path like confetti. Sometimes she spoke to me during her rambles as a valued friend. Even Francesco avoided her company.

I loved her more than ever.

During the summer Robert returned, and with him came James, radiant and pure. Upon their arrival the boys were told Claire was visiting with her sister in Malahide. In reality she was confined with only Nora for company. From a high secluded window, hallow-eyed and gaunt, Claire watched the young men climb the outer steps much as she had when she arrived for the first time.

Robert and James had met at Cambridge. Their old friendship had rekindled despite the drift of time and circumstances. James was an anchor to a younger, simpler life for which Robert yearned, even as he succumbed to jaded excess, and Robert exerted a fascination upon James like a charged lodestone.

My family was whole again.

On a moonless night Alexander – his temples touched with grey – ordered all the staff from the house. A carriage filled with purposeful men arrived. They eschewed the laboratory since Alexander's influence extended to my entire structure. I was riddled with gateways into unnameable regions.

Robed and hooded, Robert and James were led into the saloon and the circle of adepts. Braziers of charcoal and incense released soporific smoke. My chorus of souls sang grotesque chants in discordant melodies. Hellish shapes capered across my walls. Alexander initiated his son first. As he drew the last symbol in blood upon Robert's forehead, James backed away. Francesco seized his arms, and refused him escape.

Since my attention was focused on the ritual, and I held the summoned power in check, I had not noticed when Nora's chin dipped to her chest or remembered the whiskey in her cup.

Claire, a bald skeleton in a tattered grey dress, glided into the saloon carrying a lamp and brought silence with her. Robert froze, and Alexander grabbed his son by the arm to calm, or restrain, him. Francesco released James and approached Claire with steady hands and a careful voice.

She tossed the oil lamp at Francesco. He erupted into flame, shrieking, and whirled around the room seeking relief. He brushed heavy silk curtains and ran with outstretched arms to Alexander, who leaped back, knocking a brazier.

Flames chased up Robert's robe. Alexander helped his son remove the burning cloth as the fire blackened my wallpaper and reached the ceiling that artists had spent months painting. The stench of roasting flesh and the rising conflagration drove away the adepts who scattered like dark leaves in a whirlwind. In the frenzy, James escaped.

Claire raised a knife, bright with reflected flames, above Alexander's back.

I could not permit it. I reached out and punched her mind. She slumped to the floor.

Choking black smoke billowed from the fire. Alexander pushed his son from the room and returned for Claire.

I saw and felt both of them burn.

My windows exploded – a scream of pain – and the souls trapped inside me hammered for release.

Robert, scorched and weeping, stumbled down the steps into the garden as the inferno blazed through me.

The horrific pain of the fire possessed every room, nook, and closet. The laboratory collapsed with an exhalation of noxious spirits and a searing heat.

It purged me. My heartstone cracked, my magical net frayed, snapped, and faded. The souls that had abided with me for so many years swept upwards with the embers and soot towards the bright heavens.

I burned for days.

No one attempted to rescue me. The locals spat on the ground in front of my charred smoking doorway and thanked their God for my destruction.

Only a shell remained, and I was much diminished.

The fire rid me of the corrupting madness that had seized me. My pulse remained, a slow painful thud, under my chipped heartstone.

I slept.

I woke on occasion to notice the new height of the tree that grew in the stables, or to listen to the cattle call to one another as they grazed on the nettles that populated the old ballroom. A parliament of rooks took up residence in the remnants of the servants' quarters.

Occasionally the local children dared each other to visit my ruins, and their conversation and bright presence recalled happier days. It was a painful pleasure to feel their curious hands touch my stained walls and scratch their names into my crumbling stone. Sometimes, I wished them to remain forever.

Other times I wished I could strike them dead.

One day I woke from a dream of fire and blood to the sound of engines and shovels digging earth. The tree crowned the stables with a whispering green roof. Men in hard yellow helmets conversed by metal digging machines that issued black smoke.

I did not understand much, but I recognised the blue tracery of architectural drawings on large white scrolls.

I yearned for a fresh start free from memories.

Boots stamped the earth around me. Men and women in strange garb sat on tumbled walls, drank tea, ate sandwiches and watched a man with a polished trowel repair my heartstone.

The rooks circled down for scraps.

This time I would be good. I would protect all who lived within my walls. No taint would turn my actions against those I loved.

An exclamation. Drops of blood fell upon soil-clogged charms etched in my stone, and the man with the trowel stood up and brushed earth from his knees.

The bones beneath my heartstone shifted and remembered their purpose.

A slip of air breathed between animal teeth.

My pulse thumped faster.

I would guard a new family, and we would be happy, forever.

This time I would make sure of it.

Moments on the Cliff

The train skirted the graveyard and rattled past flashes of wet marble and old-fashioned granite crosses. I stared through my reflection in the carriage window at the flat, grey winter sky, and wished the rhythm of the train's relentless forward motion would inspire my stalled heart.

Outside, a spotlight of colour shone in the empty cemetery. Wreaths and flowers heaped upon a fresh grave. Laid on top: "Best Grandad Ever", picked out in red roses on a rectangle of wilting white blooms. The music playing on my headphones rose in a plaintive wail, and the train hitched, as if making a polite cough to catch my attention.

I turned from the window and noticed an elderly man sitting opposite, his liver-spotted hands folded on the table between us. The seat, like most of the carriage, had been empty moments before.

He reminded me of a faded blanket that has been scrubbed too many times. He wore a charcoal waistcoat and jacket, and a black shirt that buttoned all the way tight to his Adam's apple. I wondered how he could breathe. He nodded at me, and wisps of thin silver hair slipped across watery eyes lost in folds of loose skin.

"*Good morning,*" he said, without moving his lips. The frail words cut through the din piped through my headphones.

A bubble of panic drifted up from my chest, but my throat cinched shut on it. I dipped my head in acknowledgement, and lowered my gaze to the table where the large paper cup rested that had contained a latte I bought at Heuston Station.

A caffeine-fuelled hallucination then. Heartbreak and coffee just don't mix.

"*There was a good turn-out,*" he said, with a tremor of pride. "*Better than Gráinne's funeral, but she kept herself to herself.*" I raised my head again to make sure he was still there. "*My wife,*" he added, and made an expansive gesture with his limpid hands.

I checked the rest of the carriage. The only other occupant was a sleeping man whose shirt buttons strained to contain his impressive beer belly. No other ghosts. I turned up the volume of my music.

The old man retained the same level tone. "*My son cried,*" he said. I switched off the player, hoping that was the problem – maybe it was possessed – but his words whispered through my headphones anyway. "*The last time I saw him bawl he was ten and had fallen off his bike and scraped both knees pretty bad. Gráinne put plasters on the cuts while I gave out to him and told him not to be such a crybaby.*" He sighed and shook his head with the slow beat of a metronome. It seemed the memory no longer made any sense to him.

I squeezed my eyes closed, and ground knuckles into them. When I blinked my eyelids open he continued to watch me, patient and serene.

"*Where are you headed?*" he asked.

The normalcy of the question loosed a response. "Galway." My voice seemed too loud in my head, and I jerked the headphones off.

"*Me too,*" he said. "*I saw the train go by, and I remembered Salthill beach, where Gráinne and I used to bring the children during the summer. The two of us would eat ice-cream on our blanket and watch them splash in the water. We always got sunburned, but Gráinne never forgot to put lotion on Mike and Yvonne.*"

The train lurched and slowed. The man turned to regard the station as we pulled in. Only a couple of people waited, their heads bowed under the miserable deluge. A tiny woman in a dripping raincoat clattered into our carriage and rolled her bag ahead of her. She sniffed, frowned, and whisked past us into the next compartment.

"*Are you visiting someone?*" he asked, polite.

A sudden rush of emotion swept away my voice. I shook my head.

"*You live there?*"

I nodded.

"*The city's too big for me now, but Yvonne and her brood are settled there. Your people come from Galway?*"

My voice returned. "No. Dublin."

He leaned forward, his washed-out eyes intent and bright. "*No one can disappoint you quite like your own, but never let the relatives you love drift away.*" He settled back again, as if the outburst cost him in some fashion.

"My grandfather died when I was seven," I said, surprised at the words. "He used to sit me on his knee to tell me stories, and his breath smelled like pipe smoke mixed with mint."

This revelation brought a smile to the man's lips. "*Grandfathers love their granddaughters. The little minxes rob our hearts.*"

My eyes burned with tears, but a flare of anger licked up at this echo of a man who wouldn't let me rest.

"Go away," I choked. I hadn't thought of my Grandfather in years, and I couldn't bear to remember him when I was raw from fresher wounds.

"*What's his name?*" the ghost asked. "*This man that's upset you so much.*"

My voice came out louder than I expected. "I loved my granddad. He never upset me." I checked to see if I had woken the nearby sleeping man, but his pudgy fingers twitched from dreams, and he let out a low snore.

The old man waved his hand in dismissal. "*No, the young follah that has you twisted in knots.*"

I shrugged and simmered with sulky resentment. I turned away, and for a long time I stared out the window at the trees trashing in the gale, and the cows and sheep clustered together for warmth in the foul weather.

When I glanced back at him he held the same expression of inquiry. It did not seem possible to annoy or evade him. "Liam," I said. "He moved out this weekend."

The ghost waited. I struggled against the constriction in my throat, and I rifled through my bag on the seat beside me until I uncovered a clean tissue amid the used, crushed balls. "I went home, because I couldn't bear to watch him pack up and leave. And, of course my Dad and my sisters spent two days reminding me they'd warned me about him."

I twisted the tissue in my fingers until it ripped. Tears slid down my cheeks. I daubed at them with frayed paper edges and resisted the sudden furious impulse to slam my head against the window until I could no longer recall the useless fights and the slow dissolution of respect.

"*Gráinne wasn't my first love,*" the man said. "*That was Therese. God, I loved that woman something fierce. After we broke up I went on a trip to the Cliffs of Moher. It was a day like this. Stormy. I watched the waves crashing on the rocks far below, and listened to the wail of the gulls, and it felt like the wind was dragging me to the edge, like it was eager for me to jump into the hungry ocean.*"

"Why didn't you?"

For the first time the man hesitated. "*I don't know.*"

Even to my ears my laugh sounded bitter. "No wisdom from the other side?"

"*Just experience.*" He smiled, gentle. "*I endured. I met Gráinne. We had children. We made a life together.*"

The intercom crackled and a voice announced our imminent arrival at Galway station. I gathered my tissues, magazine, MP3 player, and shoved them into the bag. The large man awoke with a start and grabbed his luggage with noisy haste.

I stood. The ghost remained seated.

He said, "*We all have moments on the cliff, Máiréad.*" For a moment I wasn't talking to another girl's dead grandfather. I could almost taste pipe tobacco and spearmint. "*Keep going forward to the life that awaits you.*"

The train stopped suddenly, and I staggered. The ghost had vanished.

Shaking, I hoisted the knapsack on my back, and dug out my gloves from the pocket of my jacket. Rain sleeted from low clouds and disguised any tears on my face. Everyone's head was bent down, but I raised mine to the indifferent sky.

I imagined the apartment without the big TV Liam brought with him, or the CDs and DVDs we had divided up the previous week during an exhausting negotiation. I envisioned the half-empty closet, the gaping drawers, and the silence of abandonment.

I walked to the bus stop and bought a ticket for Salthill.

The beach was awash with merciless waves and angry foam, so I trudged along the prom and leaned into the squall. The splashes of colour from the flashing lights of the empty amusement arcades seemed a beacon of despair rather than relief. A determined man bundled up in a waterproof coat walked a terrier that trotted close to his master's flapping trousers.

My phone vibrated in my pocket. The message read: "Keys on the table with money for bills. Liam."

Our life together ended with a mundane text. My face was numb from the rain and wind. My heart was frozen. I wasn't sure I had a pulse.

I drifted towards the pier, where the ocean smashed into the unyielding stone and raised a spray of protest.

A couple walked towards me through the haze of rain like flickering images from a silent film. They were dressed for a summer many years ago and were unaffected by the weather. The man had his arm around her waist, and they both licked ice cream in cones. Their transparent faces had a pink tinge of sunburn. They laughed.

I stood before them and waited for some communication. Instead they walked into me, and for a second I inhaled their happiness, and sensed their hidden hurts. Their lives were interwoven threads of joy and anguish.

They moved through me, and I spun, to see them continue on that long-ago walk until they were obscured by drizzle and the gathering dusk.

I shivered. My thin coat had not shielded me from the storm and lay glued to my clothes and skin underneath. My hair felt like a long slick of water plastered to my skull and neck.

A taxi light shone among the slow-moving traffic. I jogged towards it with my hand upraised. It was time to return home and face the empty spaces.

I opened the car door and a gust ripped at it, almost yanking it from my slippery grip, and pushing me a step away from the car.

The gulls shrieked. The surf pounded a hungry beat. Rain dashed into my eyes. I tasted the salt of the devouring ocean, and for a moment I dearly wished to sate its appetite.

Instead, I slid into the car and slammed the door against its entreaties.

The Gift of the Sea

The village squatted on top of a hill overlooking a long sandy beach and the bracing swells of the Atlantic Ocean. It possessed few of the charms of popular seaside hamlets: its buildings were robust, resolute, and grey, with their gardens tucked away at the rear behind protective hedges. During the Irish economic upswing the village had experienced a minor surge in surf tourism, but that vanished after the recession, and the subsequent recovery had not yet reached its doors. The lone exception to this drab façade was the small, stone church at its centre which was built in the 1300s, and miraculously survived Cromwellian excesses, and attempts in the 19th and 20th century to modernise it.

Among the rarefied Irish Art scene the church was famous for its extraordinary stained glass window which dominated the chancel and overlooked the grey slab of pitted limestone that served as an altar. This was the church's only new feature, dating from the 1920s. It was donated to the town by Felicity Goss, a local woman who had escaped its shores, trained as an artist abroad, and achieved fame when she branched into stained glass design. This window was the only example of her craft in Ireland, as her work was considered too *avant garde* at that time for Irish tastes. The parish priest had not invented a polite way to refuse her tribute to her home town, despite attempts.

The piece's formal title was 'The Gift of the Sea', and it was composed of three sections set into the arched window. Dominating it was a large image of Our Lady of the Sea in less than virginal garb: her periwinkle blue mantle clung to her body, and due to Felicity's immense talent the folds of cloth were rendered almost transparent, so Mary's form was easily discerned underneath. She stood with arms and palms pointed down at the rolling crimson waves below her, while her face titled upwards. Many argued over her expression; some deemed it beseeching, while others claimed it was strangely pleased.

Dotted among the foaming red crests, in which Mary's feet bathed, roiled the bodies of men and women, with piteous expressions on their upturned faces. Above Mary the clouds had parted and sunlight streamed down – the Grace of Heaven, it was supposed.

Behind Mary on the right, a man rode a horse made of waves and held a flaming sword upright. To her left, another maiden with an oddly green cast, robed in seaweed and carrying a harpoon, perched upon the prow of a traditional fishing ship and stared out at the viewer in an unsettling manner. Up close, little details were visible, such as fish leaping among the thrashing limbs, and a constellation of unusual stars in the indigo sky at the edges of the frame. The whorls of colour shifted and hinted at other stories depending on whether warm sunlight or silver moonlight shone through its glass.

For many children, and adults, the window provided a subject to meditate upon during the sermons of a succession of unimaginative, elderly priests, sent to the community to finish up their careers. When the savage Atlantic storms burst upon the church's walls and rattled the glass, Mary's defiant pose often comforted those who sought refuge.

Growing up in this staid environment there were only two options: to synch with the rhythms set by the restless ocean, and raise the next generation, or flee to more prosperous and exciting locations. While many youngsters spoke of dreams of exotic adventure, few strayed further than the nearest town after a stint at college, or a few months of travel to faraway climes.

The sound of the sea, they claimed, was never the same anywhere else.

It had been the drumbeat of their lives, and without it they did not know how to place their feet.

But one resident, Gill Desmond, aged seventeen, had *plans*. Ever since she completed a school project about Felicity Goss three years previously, the deceased woman had become her idol.

Not only had Felicity set up camp in Paris and hobnobbed with the gliteratti of the age, but she had never allowed anyone to circumscribe her dreams. She'd painted, sculpted, designed clothes and furniture, mastered the arcane art of stained glass, and upon discovering the new medium of filmmaking had embarked on a final career as a film director and *auteur*. She never married, had numerous affairs with men and women (a fact that her teacher Mr. Devlin said was 'outside the scope of her topic' when Gill gave her presentation), and had lived, with faculties intact and creating art until her death – at age 93.

It had not been a charmed life that had squeezed out success, Gill determined as she leafed through books ordered from the inter-library loan the town over, or swiped through the web pages that documented her life, it had been Felicity's diamond-hard determination, and an unyielding desire to explore new vistas.

If this amazing talent could explode from her home town, then Gill saw no reason why she could not follow suit.

Gill was at her drawing desk, painstakingly recreating one of Felicity's sublime pen and ink illustrations for an Arthur Machen short story, when her mobile phone buzzed. Outside the worst storm of the winter buffeted the house, and sang dirges down the chimneys. She had a supply of candles, matches, torches and batteries near to hand, and extra blankets for the bed. She figured the message for a text update from her parents, who had gone to the city to visit her uncle, and had decided to stay the night after the red alert was issued. People who live by the sea take its tempers seriously.

But it was a message from Rich Clancy, her boss from the café in town.

It read: "Need you to come in. Will pay double."

The house shuddered in the wind, and she shook her head. "I'm not chancing my life."

"One hour. €50. Get here by 7pm."

She stared, incredulous, at the screen. Rich didn't have an extravagant bone in his stingy body, and was a tough manager. One of the reasons they put up with each other was that she needed the money for her art and college fund, and her proximity to the café meant she was always on hand in emergencies.

Five minutes in the shrieking winds, one hour of work, and then a happy period browsing new brushes and paint online.

"See you at 7pm", she texted.

Gill was nearly blown into the street once, when she rounded the corner and the wind sheered into her. Her thick waterproof jacket whipped around her body, jerking her off balance. She flailed out her arm and caught a lamp post. Her glasses were coated in water and the salt stung her lips.

Fifty euros! she yelled into the teeth of the wind, reminding herself of her prize. The storm didn't care for her insolence and attempted to knock her down again.

She jutted her jaw, and walked carefully by the sheltering wall of the row of attached houses before she arrived at Clancey's Café.

The big window was dark, and she banged on the glass door, which had the 'We're closed' sign facing out.

The kitchen door opened at the back, revealing the light, and Rich bustled out, his face pale in the gloom.

"You made it," he said as he struggled to close the door behind her. The bell above them jangled a demented jig.

"Payment up front," she gasped, adjusting to the stillness inside, and peeling her drenched coat off her body. Rich was usually a straight arrow when it came to wages, but she didn't want him to reconsider his generosity later.

He nodded, "Fair enough," and dug into his baggy trousers for notes.

She raised an eyebrow. "Why the urgency?"

He held the two twenties and the tenner in front of her and locked her gaze. "I've important customers coming in. This is the only time that suits them." He placed the money in her hand, and grasped it and her palm tightly. "This isn't just for the service, I want your word you'll say nothing to no one about this. Even your mam and dad."

Gill recoiled slightly. She'd been warned about situations like this.

He must have read her expression, even in the dark. He let loose a whooshing noise and removed his hand. "Ah get away," he exclaimed. "Nothing like that. I don't want people knowing my business." He made a disgusted noise. "I went to your Christening for feck's sake!"

Gill held up her raincoat at arm's length so it wouldn't drip on her. "You can't be too careful these days, Rich."

"I don't know about this world sometimes..."

He headed back to the kitchen and she followed him.

A strange feast was assembled on the table. Fresh fish, lightly grilled, with lemon slices lay in neat rows on a platter. A large pot of chowder simmered on the gas burner. Thick slices of brown bread and a heap of baby potatoes lay in bowls. Curls of butter were piled on a little dish. An apple tart with a golden crust, and a jug of thick cream. Pots for tea and coffee waited. China plates, cups and saucers, glass goblets, and silverware were laid out.

"Here, put this on," he said, handing her a long white linen apron.

She was glad she'd made the effort to change into her black shirt and trousers, her usual apparel for work.

She tied on the apron, and noticed he kept checking his watch, and darting glances at the front door.

"Lay the table in the back room," he handed her a crisp table cloth.

"It's all very fancy, why –" and she stopped when she saw the expression on his face. "Right, none of my beeswax."

She brought the dishes, glasses, and cutlery on a tray into the back room. It was a nice, intimate space, with a proper fireplace. Rich had set a fire with turf. The fire capered madly to the wind's tune, and the fragrance of turf permeated the room. Nine fat white candles burned in groups of three. She laid the table for four, based on what had been left out for her.

She made an effort to be neat and tidy, even spending time on the napkins – fashioning them into swans, a trick that Rich taught her one quite morning.

The dreadful clang of the bell alerted her that Rich's visitors had arrived.

She peered around the door.

A blast of wind shot through the room as the man entered. He was a bit short, but burly, wearing an old-fashioned fisherman's oil slicker. A nest of wet white curls covered his head. He held a net full of mussels in one hand. Water poured off him onto the floor.

"Blessings upon your house," the man said, and he laughed, deep and hearty, and his teeth flashed. "What a night! Makes me feel young again." He held up the net of mussels. "A gift," he added.

Gill thought Rich paled. He held his hands up to demur.

"With no strings," the man said, dipping his head as if he was answering a question. "Except for those in the net of course!"

And he laughed again as if this was the most original of jests.

"Gillian," Rich raised his voice a little, "could you bring those into the kitchen and I'll attend to them later."

"Oh," said the man, and his attention on Gill felt like walking into a patch of sunlight. "Who's this?"

Rich rushed in front of the man and grabbed the net out of his grip. "Just the girl from around the corner. She'll be serving us this evening."

The man's huge grin was infectious, Gill could feel a corresponding smile forming.

"Well, *a cailín*," he said, "I look forward to your service."

She *bobbed* and grinned, seized the mussels from Rich, and shot back into the kitchen.

Behind her she heard Rich guide the man into the dining room.

Inside the kitchen she inhaled a deep breath. She felt *giddy*. Like that time she and her best friend Shona drank a bottle of wine behind the couch during her cousin's wedding party last year.

The bell cried again, and she moved to the door to observe. This time the person was tall, wearing a dark hooded cloak that billowed out around as she entered. Gill was unsure why she determined so clearly that it was a woman, as she could see nothing of the person's form. Rich bustled around the person, head ducked and shoulders bowed as if in deference.

The darkness at the centre of the hood seemed to regard Gill for a long moment, and Gill was rooted to the floor.

Then the person swept by into the room, and she heard the man's voice raised in greeting. "My lady," he said, and then rattled off some words in a language Gill didn't understand. It sounded vaguely like Irish, if it had taken a ramble through India.

Rich almost barged into her as she lingered by the door.

He was sweating, but there was an excitement underneath the sheen of anxiety.

"Get the tea on, none of them want coffee. Loose leaf, brew it thick. They like it strong." He took a short breath, and steadied himself.

"Then bring in the soup, bread and butter. We'll have the fish and potatoes after that. Later, desert."

"Aren't you waiting on a fourth to join you?"

"They're all here."

She blinked, "But that's impossible, the bell didn't ring."

"Get cracking, girl!" And he spun on his heel and left the room.

When Gill entered the room she was concentrating so keenly on keeping the bowls of soup steady that she didn't take a full account of the occupants until she had set down all the dishes. The woman had cast off her cloak, so Gill could see the shimmer of the blue silk dress lying lightly on her broad shoulders and muscled arms. She was deeply tanned, as if she spent all her time outside, and masses of wavy black hair streamed down her back. She radiated authority even though she said little.

And there was a fourth person in the room – a young woman, slight but fierce-looking, dressed in boots, trousers, a waistcoat, and a shirt, who *lounged* in her seat in a provocative way. Like a cat amused by dogs.

Gill departed quickly, and returned with the bread and butter. Nobody had touched any food and they all looked up at her when she entered. She paused and blushed, wondering if she'd inadvertently upset someone.

"We'll bless the food now," the lady said. Her mellow voice had a steel centre.

Gill started to leave, and the man raised his hand.

"No, lassie, everyone under the roof must be present."

Gill thought Rich was unhappy with this, but said nothing. She bowed her head a little and clasped her hands in front of her as a show of respect. Her parents were aware that she had abandoned religious faith several years ago, but it was never discussed. It might be 21st century Ireland, but some changes waxed slowly, especially in a small town.

"The Sea and Earth, ever-bounteous, we thank you for your gifts. Bless this food and our company. As we share food we share ourselves. May we be generous and truthful with each other."

The man raised his glass, now filled with a rich red wine, "*Sláinte!*"

Everyone raised their glasses. Gill attempted to slip out and was stopped again.

"No, no, no, this won't do. The girl must drink with us. What was your name again...? Gillian, correct?"

"Yes, sir."

"Fetch a glass and share a wee drop with us."

She spotted the filthy glare that Rich directed at her.

"Um, I'm underage, I can't drink alcohol."

The man burst out laughing, his whole form shaking with mirth. Gill was unsure how to take this outburst.

He put his hand upon her arm in a friendly way. "Pardon me, Gillian. I'm not mocking you. I took you to be at least eighteen, but among my people it is common for those of twelve to have their first drink."

The lady regarded him in a superior way, "Which is why so little work gets done in the morning."

"Now, my lady," he replied, raising a finger in cheerful warning, "no need to be snippy. We love our feasts but we always finish our tasks." Then he inclined his head, "Of course, if they are accomplished in the afternoon, who cares as long as they are done?"

The younger woman appraised Gill wearing a sardonic smile. "I doubt you've never touched a drop before, but get a glass of milk if you're so prudent, and return for the toast."

Gill checked on Rich, but he stared steadfastly into the wine in his glass.

She went to the kitchen, opened a can of Coke, and poured half of it into a glass tumbler.

When she returned they all swivelled to look at her. She raised her glass, feeling odd being the centre of attention.

"*Sláinte*," she said, and they joined in the toast. The candle flames flickered, and they all drank deeply.

As the man put his glass down, he said, "Gillian, as we know your name then you should know ours, since our host failed with introductions."

Rich spluttered to redeem himself, but he was waved silent.

"I'm Oirbse, this is the lady Medb, and our trio is complete with Gráinne."

She nodded, "Pleased to meet you."

And they laughed, as if she had said something funny.

Gill left the room, but in the quiet kitchen the buzz of conversation indicated the group had plenty to discuss. She did not know what to make of Rich's visitors – they were clearly not local and yet there was something familiar about all of them. She sneaked a slice of Rich's bread slathered with butter, and sighed. It was his Granny's recipe, and no doubt it was handed down from many generations. While Rich churned out basic items for his regular crowd, when he had a special occasion he proved himself a talented chef. He rarely displayed the full extent of his skills but tonight his simple, well-cooked fare was delicious. She slid the crust of bread around the bottom of the pot of chowder and ate it with enthusiasm.

Rich didn't have to call her, as her waitress instinct kicked in based on the change in the hum of conversation. She quietly entered the room and removed the plates, and they remained politely silent. She returned shortly, with platters of food and laid them out.

"Fish!" Gráinne grumbled, disappointment lining her face. "What I wouldn't do for a bit of beef, or even mutton. It's always fish."

"It's traditional," Oirbse replied, before Rich could explain. "He's only following the rules."

Gráinne poked at the fish with her fork. "It demonstrates a lack of imagination. He's petitioning you, after all."

Gill spoke out of the instinct of always making the customer happy. "There's some beef curry in the fridge, I could –"

"I doubt she wants the curry I serve to the plain folk in this town!" Rich sounded furious, and Gill was going to apologise, but Gráinne spoke first, her voice low. She twirled her knife in her hand for emphasis.

"No one *ever* speaks for me."

After a short pause she raised her gaze to Gill and the girl knew she never wanted to cross this woman. "Bring me some of the curry."

Gill nodded, and exited as quickly as possible. Inside the kitchen she sped around, locating the plastic container, pouring the curry into a large bowl, and microwaving it thoroughly. The lack of noise indicated they were waiting. She was so nervous she nearly burned her hands taking the bowl out of the microwave.

She entered the room, heavy with an unhappy hush. Fish sat on every plate except Gráinne's, but no one had eaten. As she laid the bowl in the centre of the table and aimed the ladle's handle towards Gráinne, she said, "There should be enough for everyone, in case you all want a taste."

Gráinne doled out the curry on her plate and sniffed it. "So it's a kind of stew. It smells... unusual."

"You've had curry before, surely..." Gill wished she could take back the words as soon as they tripped out of her mouth.

The woman didn't appear insulted. She chewed her mouthful with a thoughtful expression, and when she was done, she said. "Not in my lifetime," and Oirbse and Mebd chuckled. "I like this curry," she added.

Medb speared her fish delicately. "Potatoes and tea are hardly native either, but it's hard to imagine there existed a time without them."

Oirbse knifed knobs of butter on his potatoes. "Spuds: the fish of the earth as far as I'm concerned."

"If we could direct our conversation back to the matter at hand," Rich held his cutlery rather tightly in his hands.

"Excuse me," Gill said, and removed herself from the room.

"You know, *lad*," Oirbse began as Gill closed the door, "it's usual to feed your guests first, and once their bellies are full and their glasses empty, ease into negotiations."

Gill sat on a chair in the kitchen and checked her watch. She'd been here for over an hour, but she didn't care. She wanted to know why Rich was entertaining these people. Were they potential business partners? Rich was always bemoaning the lack of tourists in the town. He sat on all the development committees in the area, but never made traction on any of his plans. An impassive inertia immobilised the village; a fixed dislike to see beyond what had always gone before.

Gill understood it well. At times it felt to her that if she lived another day in the town she might choke on saying the same things to the same people.

How she *burned* to leave.

An angry shout from the room interrupted her reverie, and she started upright. For a moment she froze, unsure what to do.

She got up, rapped lightly on the door, and opened it, hoping to break any tension.

"Are you ready for dessert?" she asked, brightly.

Rich's face flamed scarlet. The three guests stared at him with impassive expressions.

"*Nothing?*" he yelled, too loud in the confined space. He threw his napkin across the room. It sailed past Gill's face, and she ducked reflexively.

"After all this! After the years of research and learning the correct ways. You refuse me now!"

Mebd laid a cautioning hand on both Oirbse and Gráinne who seemed ready to launch from their seats.

"You can ask, but we can refuse. What you request is base coin. We don't trade in that currency. If we wish for riches we can obtain them easily. You have nothing to offer us because you're mean with your talents and liberal only when you perceive a reward."

She leaned forward slightly, and locked gazes with Rich. "Once, you might have tempted us, when you had joy in your heart. Now, you only see money as the way to escape the trap of your own making."

Malice twisted Rich's features. "What patronising *shite*, from those who abandoned us to hardship, conquest, and misery."

"You chose your path long ago. Do not blame us when you discover it is hard and difficult to navigate."

He roared at them: "*Get out you heathen liars!*"

Oirbse stood, and the house *shuddered* from a blast of wind from the tempest outside. "The hospitality of your race is much diminished," he said quietly.

Gráinne eyed up Rich from her chair, and glanced back at Oirbse and Medb. "I have killed men for less. But, I will abide with your decision."

A gasp escaped Gill's lips, and they turned. She stood with her hands clenched together in front of her chest, fear fixing her to the spot.

Oirbse and Medb shared a look, and they relaxed somewhat.

Oirbse spoke again. "Every day from this day forward, be grateful this young woman served as your witness."

Gill frowned. "Witness?"

Oirbse noticed the flash of guilt on Rich's face. He leaned his fists on the table. "You refer to us as liars when you inveigle a child to attend when she is unaware of the position she is taking?"

Mebd stood, and she was taller now than Gill remembered. The candlelight dimmed, and the storm outside abated. The darkened room seemed to shrink around her. "Nothing you will put your hand to will ever thrive. People will turn from you, even in dire need. You will live a long and bitter life, Richard Clancy, and in the end you will realise how you brought this ruin upon yourself."

"No!" Gill cried, and the light rushed back into the room, and the noise of the storm returned. The three turned to her. "Don't do that. He's not a bad man. No one deserves such a fate!"

Gráinne stepped forward, and there was a friendliness to her that Gill had not glimpsed before. "Are you aware that as witness you were bound to whatever terms he negotiated? That if he failed to uphold his terms you would also be responsible?" She moved closer and clasped Gill's hand. "This man did not care about your dreams, only his own selfish needs. Do you object to Medb's curse now?"

A sickening taste rose in Gill's mouth, it was of rotting fish and awful disappointment. Rich had collapsed in his chair, his shoulders bent, unable to look at her.

"No one deserves that fate," she whispered.

Medb regarded Gill for a long moment.

"So be it," she said simply.

In a sweeping motion the cloak and hood covered her again. Gráinne opened the door, and Medb glided out, followed by Gráinne.

Oirbse glared down at Rich, who finally raised his head to look him in the face. "Stay away from the sea, Richard Clancy."

At that he spun sharply, nodded to Gill as he passed her, and the final jangle of the bell announced their departure.

For several eerie minutes there was only the sound of the whistling of the wind outside. Gill stared at Rich, contempt and hurt in her expression. She did not allow him to escape it.

Eventually, he dropped his gaze, and offered, "I'm sorry, Gill, truly…"

"Rich," he stopped and looked up again. "I quit. I expect my wages for the rest of the month."

She ran into the kitchen, shaking, and grabbed her coat.

Outside, the storm raged, and she was glad because she could cry as hard as she liked and no one would ever know.

At the door to her house the key fumbled in her icy fingers as she tried to unlock it while the wind jarred her body.

She swore loudly, knowing the neighbours wouldn't hear her over the gale.

The door swung open, revealing Gráinne.

Gill stuttered, "What the..."

Gráinne bowed a little, her motion accompanied by a mocking smile, and indicated Gill should enter.

Anger quickly replaced her shock. "I should call the Gards! How dare you come in here without permission!"

Gráinne closed the door. "Oirbse and Medb would like a word."

"Why?"

"They're in the kitchen."

Gill dripped down the hallway, removing her coat, and entered her parent's open plan kitchen. All the lights were on, and the familiar room radiated warmth and security.

Oirbse stood with a mug of tea in his hands leaning against the kitchen island, while Medb perched on one of the tall stools. Her tea steamed in a cup resting on the black granite countertop.

She came at them, hot. "What *right* do you have to break into my home?"

Oirbse raised an eyebrow and spoke to Medb. "Speaks her mind plainly. I like that."

"*I'm in the room!*" she yelled at him.

He winced, and touched his ear as if she had pierced it. "I noticed."

"We have spared Rich, based on your request," Medb began. "Now we will negotiate terms."

A sliver of icy fear pierced the heat of her anger. "What terms, what is this about?"

"You must have some idea of who we are now." Medb stated. "If you're unsure, you may ask."

Gill held her tongue for a moment. Her instinct screamed at her that she must proceed with caution, and she did not want to voice her suspicions out loud.

She spoke slowly, "Rich clearly felt you could grant him some... power. And your names... Medb... I like mythology."

She refused to admit any more.

Gráinne entered the kitchen and loitered by the back door. "The storm is abating," she said.

"Who are you telling?" Oirbse asked, "It is my breath and soul."

The roaring wind outside dwindled suddenly, and the rain rattled down to a desultory patter on the pane.

He smiled. "It's a bit easier to talk now."

"What do you want?" Gill asked.

"No," Medb corrected her, "What do *you* want."

They stood, Medb and Oirse, close together, and Gráinne was a step behind them.

"We were puzzled that Rich could summon us here, despite knowing the right words and sacrifices. But we were curious, and it had been a long time since someone from this town brought us forward out of our place."

They stepped closer to her, and there was a heat rising from them. It seeped into Gill's body, erasing all memory of the cold, and the wind, and the sting of betrayal.

"*You*, the witness, who is also the petitioner."

Gill smelled a warm sea breeze wafting over fragrant grasses, and gulls crying with the joy of boundless skies.

"What is your soul's desire?"

She was somewhere else, on a grassy hill overlooking the endless sea. The soft surf pounded a familiar beat. The sun relaxed her shoulders. The three stood beside her, although Oirbse and Medb seemed more like figures of light. Gráinne was resolutely herself.

"To *go*," she whispered, and the words rose from the core of her, which she had protected fiercely for so long. "To seize life, embrace love, defy fear, and make a difference in the world."

She looked at them directly. "Above all, to reject limits."

Medh and Oirse each placed a hand on her shoulders. "So we have an accord."

She staggered a little, but their touch steadied her.

They would always steady her.

She blinked and she was back in the kitchen.

Medb and Oirbse sipped tea. Gráinne clapped her on the back. "Welcome, sister."

"What happened?" she asked, her thoughts tangled between here and there. Everything that been communicated now seemed foolish in the stark artificial light.

Medb smiled gently, "You will get all you have asked for, and after... you will be in service to us."

Gill glanced at Gráinne, and a realisation dawned. "The Pirate Queen. Grace O'Malley." Her voice hushed.

Gráinne inclined her head. "I got the wild adventures I wanted, and since then... I have seen more."

"Who else?"

There was a knock upon the back door, and Gráinne opened it.

Gill recognised her from the grainy black and white photos she had pasted upon her project board. In Gill's kitchen she was petite, blond, and *vital.*

"Felicity!"

"Welcome, sister," she said to Gill. Then she grinned at Gráinne and they embraced and thumped each other's back.

Gill turned to Medb and Oirbse. "How long will I be in service?"

They raised their cups to salute her.

"Until the rocks crumble and the sea dries up. Then, we will reassess your contract."

Medb winked at her. "Take your passions and make your mark upon the world. For you will wish to look upon it often, afterwards."

Gill placed her hands upon the cool stone counter, and within her elation bubbled up.

She would *soar.*

SUSPENSION

That summer the heat was a creepy perv, Jamie decided. She explained it to her friend Huxley on the phone extension in her bedroom.

"You wake up and it's standing by your bed, you go outside and it presses up against you, and at night, it's lurking in the shadows ready to suffocate you in your sleep."

Hux barked a laugh down the crackly line. "It's the Long Island stalker, and no cop can stop it."

Jamie grinned. She could depend on Hux to spitball an idea. "No firefighter can extinguish its blaze –"

"– 'Cause they're all been canned," he interjected.

"It exists in a dimension between broiling and inferno. This is a journey into a wondrous land of perspiration."

Together they chorused their favourite catchphrase of the summer, speaking like Rod Serling on *The Twilight Zone*: "Welcome to Fear City!"

From the living room her Pop yelled. "Jamie! Get off the phone! I'm not a Rockefeller!"

She groaned. "Dad's freaking out. Probably wants me off the line in case Mom calls. Like that's gonna happen."

"The summer will end. And then you'll be in College."

"I cannot wait."

Her father shouted again. "*Jamie!*"

She shoved the mouthpiece into her mattress, and hollered back, *"Chill out Dad!"*

She lifted it back up, and whispered, "The tightwad's going to lose his shit if I don't get off. Sorry."

"Don't worry Patty, we'll build another sand castle."

She smiled, and recalled when they'd gone to *Snoopy Come Home* at the movie theatre. They were fifteen, too old to see it really, so they'd hung out at the back with their heads down and feet up on the seats, and snuck out early so no one could see them. Hux's dog had died that year, and they ended up hiding behind the dumpster at the back of the theatre so no one could see him sobbing in Jamie's arms, repeating "It's just a cartoon." Afterwards they'd smoked their first joint together – Hux had swiped one from his mom's stash. They'd skipped the bus and walked all the way home, gloriously high, discussing how every American home could be improved by the addition of a goodhearted dog.

"I'll see you tomorrow Hux," she replied because that was the response, even if it wasn't true.

She hung up and angled her face to the rotating fan on the carpeted floor which blew warm air. Her bedroom faced north, and she kept the blinds perpetually closed, but it was eleven am and the room was already an oven. It reeked of suntan lotion, Shalimar and soul-searching.

Reluctantly, she pulled on a crop top and shorts over her bra and panties, and slipped on her espadrilles. Before she left her bedroom she stood with her hand on the metal doorknob and inhaled a deep breath.

The living room was gloomy since the velvet curtains on the large windows were pulled shut. A thin, blinding white rectangle framed them, hinting it was another blistering day outside. It was cooler in here since Pop ran the AC in the evening, but it wouldn't last. Already the air felt as if it had been breathed in and out by the giant lungs of a cigarette demon.

He sat at the dining table, wearing a white undershirt and boxer shorts, with the tall lamp on for illumination, going through stacks of bills. The ashtray was full, but maybe he hadn't emptied it the previous night.

She said nothing as she walked past him into the kitchen to get a bowl of cereal. Outside's glare leaked through the white slatted shutters in the kitchen windows to provide enough light to navigate the space. She knew better than to turn on the light switch.

"I made coffee," he said without looking up.

"You mean you turned on the machine." She had set it up with grounds and water before going to bed. Just like Mom used to.

He slammed his clenched fist into the table and everything hopped.

"I paid for that coffee!"

Jamie ignored the urge to freeze and adopted her mask of jaded indifference. She poured herself a mug of Joe and could smell that it had been sitting there for hours. He'd probably been up since five am. The time he used to rise for work.

She opened the fridge and lingered in its deliciously cool air. There wasn't much food but at least there was a full carton of milk.

Jamie splashed a generous dollop in her mug to cut down on the bitterness of the stewed coffee, and poured the last of the sugar from the glass and chrome dispenser – a sentimental artefact from when Mom waitressed in a diner when she was a teen.

She held it in her hand and looked at her reflection in it. Her mother was once her age. That did not seem possible.

She raised the dispenser so her dad could see it through the partition in the kitchen wall. "Hey Dad, I think we should get rid of this piece of junk."

He narrowed his eyes and frowned as he did when he was giving a subject deep thought.

He returned his gaze to the paper in front of him. "Sure," he said.

Jamie slam dunked it into the garbage pail. Seeing it resting in the leftovers of last night's mac and cheese gave her a surge of satisfaction.

She made her breakfast special: half *Franken Berry* and half *Count Chocula*, swimming in milk. The carton was a lot lighter when she returned it to the fridge.

Suddenly cheerful, Jamie hummed the catchy hook from 'The Hustle' and grooved her way the table with her bowl, spoon and mug. Pop looked up from under his black bushy eyebrows. She expected him to moan about it but instead he joined in. He had a natural crooner's voice, with his version of Sinatra's 'My Way' being a speciality at parties. It was weird hearing him sing a disco track.

She flopped down in a seat and picked up her spoon. "Didn't think you knew that. It's new."

"I got ears," he said, indignantly. "And it's what all New Yorkers gotta do now. The Hustle." He gestured at his array of paperwork, and the copy of the *New York Post* with a screaming headline condemning Mayor Abe Beame's handling of the city's financial crisis.

Jamie eyed her dad over her spoon as she dug into her cereal. He looked older. In the space of three months he started looking a hell of a lot like granddad Rob. He was a grouchy, mean bastard (Mom's exact words when she left), but it was the two of them now. Without him, she'd be on her own.

A wave of nausea rose up. The cooked coffee and the sickly-sweet cereal had hit her stomach with lethal force.

She placed her hands on the table. "I'm gonna barf."

He was on his feet and at her side in a blink, checking her pulse and giving her the professional once-over.

"When did you last drink water?"

He was half-lifting her and guiding her toward the kitchen. Her head was woozy and the floor seemed to shift. She leaned into the strength of his big body, inhaled his Old Spice smell, and she remembered a trip to Coney Island with her parents when she was eleven. He'd gone on the Cyclone with her because Mom had refused to climb into that 'death trap'. Jamie was full of hotdogs and cotton candy, which she regretted the instant they barrelled down the roller coaster's first incline. She became a rocketing mixture of elation, panic and queasiness as they roared up and down the tracks, her fellow riders squealing in excitement, and for one clear moment she spotted her mother looking up at them, her arms crossed in front of her chest, with an expression of desperate loneliness.

Dad had put his arm around her halfway through the ride, when terror seized her heart as tightly as she gripped the restraining bar. "I'm proud of you, Imp," he shouted into the maelstrom.

Her childhood nickname. At thirteen she'd insisted they never use it again, but now she yearned for that title and the happy ignorance of a kid.

They stood together in front of the sink as she rode out the cramps and he gently rubbed the small of her back. She braced her hands on the cool surface and summoned every atom of willpower to subdue the urge to vomit.

"I think I'm okay," she mumbled. Hoping it was true.

He poured her a glass of water, threw in a couple of ice cubes from the freezer, and handed it to her.

"Drink," he ordered.

She held the glass against her forehead first, and it steadied her.

"Slowly," he warned.

She sipped and the world evened out again.

He stepped away. "You're dehydrated. That crap you eat didn't help."

"Thanks, Pop," she whispered. The water helped.

"You're not pregnant again?"

The words dropped like an ACME anvil into the room, and she was Wile E. Coyote, hammered into the floor from its impact.

She shook her head, and kept drinking, forcing the liquid past the new lump in her throat. Tears burned her eyes and she willed them back, just like the nausea.

They never talked about her 'mistake' in the spring, or the abortion, which he had arranged. All legal and safe, and terrible too.

Mom had been stridently against it, but Jamie had just turned eighteen, and had been accepted into Stony Brook University. She couldn't fathom having a baby. Her dad, with his paramedics training, had taken it better. He'd known what to do and had taken her to the appointment. He was always like that in an emergency: calm, rational, dependable. But give him a languorous afternoon with no obligations and he turned into a prickly jerk.

And a couple of months later, the day after her graduation, Mom had left.

Jamie had wept in her parents' bedroom while her mom packed, pleading with her to stay, but she had said in her measured, practical voice, "If you're old enough to get pregnant you're old enough to be independent."

Mom had continued folding her clothes in her methodical fashion. "I need to find out who I am again. Nothing has worked out the way I expected."

Jamie had retreated to her bedroom, blasted David Bowie's *Young Americans* on her portable turntable, and refused to say goodbye when the cab came to take her mother away.

A flame of rage sizzled in Jamie's heart at her dad's words. How could she have gotten pregnant? She was trapped in this hell house until the fall semester.

"I'm going to my room," she said. The heat was preferable to the judgement.

"I'm swinging by the Paxton place later this afternoon."

She paused in her storming off.

"Are you opening it up?"

He shook his head. "Barnaby isn't coming this summer."

"Is he okay?"

Her dad shrugged. "I cash his checks and don't ask questions."

"Can I tag along?"

He scratched the thick curly hair on his forearms. "Keep hydrated."

That meant yes.

At five the doorbell rang. Dad was already in the hallway with his car keys in his hand. From her bedroom, where she was applying a sweep of colour to her lips, she could hear him muttering, wondering who it was.

As soon as the door opened she heard the too-loud *"What's happenin' man?"* It was Randy.

She swore softly and lingered in her room, hoping her dad would get rid of him.

She couldn't hear her father's side of the conversation, but Randy's every word was audible to the Reds listening in from the Soviet Union.

"I brought Coors!"

That was it, the illicit brews. He was here to stay.

She left her sanctuary, and there was Randy in the living room: short, stocky, and with a face only his grandmother could love… and he lived with her. He wore his beloved Knicks shirt over shorts, striped tube socks pulled up mid-calf, and sneakers. The gold crucifix he never took off gleamed around his neck on a gold link chain – it had been his dad's, who'd died in Okinawa.

"Lookin' good, Jamie!" he bellowed.

She restrained the urge to shiver. Randy said whatever was on his mind, but he wasn't a mean guy.

"Hey Randy," she said in a lacklustre fashion.

Her father was easing the beers into the fridge. They had cracked two open already.

"I thought we were going out…" She nodded at the cans.

Her dad closed the fridge and picked up a beer to clank it against Randy's. "Don't worry, we'll sink these and be on our way."

The men didn't dawdle. As usual, Randy chugged hard to finish first and ended with a thunderous triumphant belch.

"Classy," she said.

Her dad wiped his mouth. "Randy's coming. He's never seen Paxton's."

"Cool."

Resentment attempted to hijack Jamie's thoughts, but she let it go. She was getting out of the house, and Randy, with his high-speed rabbit brain and Sports obsession, would chatter continuously to her father throughout the journey.

So, she sat in the back of her dad's beat-up Oldsmobile, and let their conversation sweep over her just like the warm air washing over her from the rolled down car windows. Her dad and Randy smoked incessantly as they debated games and coaching strategies.

She relaxed into the leatherette seat, no longer lava hot, and watched a succession of yellowed lawns and suburban houses whip by, until they were on the back roads and sailing past the larger estates of the wealthy commuters.

A half hour beyond that they were on the outskirts of Latiksville, a hamlet with a Main Street so cute it looked like it had been boosted from the Magic Kingdom.

It took a minute to drive through the clean, deserted town and it coincided with a break in the conversation.

"Creepy," Randy said as they hit the town limits. His tanned arm was braced along the open car window. "Not one bar."

"But two churches!" Her dad laughed. "I guess that's their entertainment."

She leaned forward and raised her voice so they could hear her over the car and the wind. "They hanged people for witchcraft in the town square in the 1600s."

Randy turned to look at her, his expression incredulous. "That's nuts!"

"I did a project on local witch trials last year."

Her father shook his head, and said with tangible anger, "Fucking holy rollers. To get their perfect world they'll kill everyone in it."

Randy shifted in his seat and reached up to touch his crucifix as if to apologise to it. He didn't like it when her dad got into one of his anti-religion rants. Randy's grandma was an old school Italian Catholic with a passion for icons and statues. Randy never talked about it, but Jamie guessed he was a quiet believer.

Luckily for Randy the rest of the trip was down snaky, narrow roads through woods so her dad had to concentrate more. It was cooler and darker in the tree canyon, the heat of the day had mellowed out, and the sky was taking on an orange tinge.

They finally arrived at huge black iron gates with an elaborate swirling design, decorated with gold stars and burnished feathered faces blowing trumpets.

Randy whistled to indicate he was impressed and ground his cigarette out in the ashtray.

Her dad jumped out and unlocked the big steel padlock on the thick chains keeping the gates tightly closed. The padlock was new, clean and worked well. Her dad took his job of keeping an eye on the empty estate seriously, especially as it had become an important line of income.

He even locked the gate after them before they drove the last mile to the house. "Can't be too careful," he said, checking his mirrors. He'd always loved his crime and spy novels, but the Watergate Scandal had heightened his belief in the world of covert surveillance. The movie *The Conversation* had left him paranoid for weeks.

"Far out!" Randy exclaimed as they saw the first glimpse of the building.

She let her dad give Randy the spiel about the Paxton family obsession with travel, and how they carted back sections of buildings to create their own replica of a French manor and filled it with antiquities from all over the Old World.

"Where'd they get their money?"

Jamie replied before her dad. "Oh you know, railroads, oil, banking… racketeering. Fine American industries."

Her dad glared at her in the rear-view mirror. "Fine American entrepreneurship, you mean."

"How come there's no staff? Won't it fall apart?"

He parked the car. "It's the first summer Barnaby missed. Normally he opens it in the spring." He shrugged. "He's getting on. I don't think his daughter cares for the place."

Randy opened the car door and for a moment he leaned on it to take in the grandeur of the building. "Imagine being so loaded you have a spare mansion."

Jamie got out and stretched. Other than birdsong and a distant buzz of traffic it was quiet. The woods surrounded the house, giving it complete privacy, with only a short breather between the shadows of the trees and the ivy-covered three storey building. The various windows – tall and skinny in the turrets, wide or arched in the front – were shuttered behind their panes of glass, lending them a blank feeling. The house was contained behind its barriers.

The giant terracotta urns placed at regular intervals outside the house only sprouted skeletal twigs. Most of the flower beds had gone wild in the spring and languished in the heat without water. The small border of lawn had devolved into a tangle of tall grass and weeds. Clusters of rose bushes that were partially shadowed had survived. Their large, messy heads drooped, scattering thick scarlet, yellow and white petals under their thorns.

A pleasant cooling breeze wafted from the trees. Jamie inhaled a deep lungful, tinged with the scent of overripe roses. Her movements felt easy and loose, as if an invisible weight had slid off her shoulders. Here she was released from the oppressive heat and the bondage of mistakes.

She suddenly remembered what she loved most about the house. "Wait 'til you see the pool!"

Her dad waved her off. "I'll check everything's secure. I'll see you round back later."

She pelted along the curved gravel path but halted to wait impatiently for Randy to catch up. Despite his love of Sports he was no athlete. He ambled after her with his head cocked up at the house.

He pointed at the gutters. "What're those weirdo creatures?"

"Gargoyles. Barnaby told me they were modelled on demons in Hieronymus Bosch's paintings."

A succession of open-mouthed hybrid fiends stared down at them.

Randy looked away. "Huh. All that money and they put ugly crap on the building."

She glanced up at a squatting man-bird with jutting limbs, furious eyes and a gaping beak. "He said his granddad wanted a reminder that a perfect paradise existed only in heaven."

The darkness in its mouth yawned at her. "Down here devils abound."

They circled around until they came to the striking layout at the back of the mansion. An ornamental garden with an Olympic-sized swimming pool at its centre was the first jewel. As she hurried Randy along she explained that the treelines, outbuildings and hedging system allowed each section to have a sense of its own space. The long building with the changing rooms at the back of the pool hid a tennis court on the far side.

"And there are stables!"

Randy was beginning to look uncomfortable. "Horses? Who takes care of them?"

"Oh they don't have any now. But Barnaby's dad used to play Polo."

Randy dug out a paper napkin from his shorts' pocket and dabbed at his forehead. "You think Walt's gonna be much longer?"

His disinterest deflated her. "I don't know. He's got a system."

Jamie ignored him and walked to the pool. Randy trailed after, reluctantly. He kept looking back at the house as if hoping for her father's return.

She loved the colourful mosaics that edged the pool. Mermaids with purple eyes combed their turquoise hair with coral combs. Seals frolicked through foaming waves and crabs scuttled across rocks. Octopuses slipped among them all – their trailing tentacles connecting all the images. At the top of the pool, visible behind the diving board, was an elaborate mosaic on the wall of the changing rooms. It depicted a giant Poseidon, with curling beard and trident in hand, bursting out of the ocean. From the distance everything looked rather pretty until you saw the details. Were the combs made from coral or human bones? Why did the mermaids have such sharp teeth? The seals had beseeching human eyes, and the crabs' claws looked like fused human hands. And were those loops of tentacles containing the images or were they chains retraining them?

Once or twice, when Barnaby was in residence, she had been allowed swim in the pool, but it had not been maintained well this summer. Someone had rolled back the pool cover and a film covered the surface. Normally the pool was a startling aqua blue, but the floating layer of seeds, bugs and leaves made it seem murky.

Jamie walked along its length until she reached the top corner at the deep end. Poseidon glared at her, trident poised to fling. She considered a trip to the tool shed to fetch the skimmer to clean off some of the murk, but she regarded the sheer size of the job and dismissed the idea. That was her dad's problem.

Randy had not followed her. He lounged on one of the carved stone benches on the border of the pool area, in the shade of a cherry tree, with his back to her staring at the house. From her vantage point she had impressive view of the entire building, bathed in the evening light. All the windows were shuttered like in the front.

Rows of cataracted eyes, unable to see out and forced to look inwards at their emptiness.

A breeze sprung up and slid though her, raising the fine hairs on her arms, and her body convulsed in a shudder. It was like standing in front of the fridge again.

Below her, the water skin stretched as if it were breathing.

She kicked off her shoes and revelled in the contact of her bare feet on the warm tiles. The day's antagonistic heat had shifted into a friendly balm, and below her the water pushed against the side of the pool in a slow tempo.

She shifted the weight on her hip and extended her pointed foot down to pierce the film and dip her toes into the water.

And then she was falling.

The moment extended, as if time slowed down, and the relentless consequence of her miscalculation took over. Her body prepared. She sucked in a breath and braced for the shock of the water.

Jamie crashed through the barrier and plunged deep into the drop until she was held. She opened her eyes instinctively.

She hung in a mottled world of grey and green light where others were suspended too.

To her right a horse appeared to gallop toward her but it didn't close the distance. Instead it cantered along a different vector: suddenly its flesh decomposed and its eyeballs melted, until it became a racing skeleton.

She tightened her lips on the bubble of air in her lungs, afraid she would inadvertently gasp and allow this place to rush into her.

To her left a man and a woman dressed in evening clothes from the 1920s were frozen in mid-Charlton. In a series of jerky flashes they devolved into babies. Their thin hair floated around their chubby faces but their eyes contained the wisdom of their adult selves.

Far in the distance Jamie thought she glimpsed Barnaby, older, frailer, lying on a hospital bed, alone. That scene didn't change. He was locked in one moment, his liver-spotted face slack with dread.

Some instinct prompted her to look below her dangling feet. Underneath, a graduated darkness fell away until at its inky centre she could *feel* the scrape of claws and spines.

A spike of terror jolted her. She sensed a chitinous line with a bony baited hook whip out, seeking. She was the unlucky morsel passing an eternal hunger.

Jamie kicked upward and tried to swim to the surface, but she didn't move. A wrenching vertigo and sense of dislocation seized her. Her lungs began to register their distress. There was no up or down, or back or front. Here the maps of her reality did not work.

A thought wormed into her mind: how easy it would be to let go and allow herself to be caught and consumed by that ancient voracious appetite. Its poisons would stupefy her awareness of her decline. She would be insensible to anything that could disturb her.

But her fury at the world exploded and she shot back: *Fuck you man!*

I'm no one's fast food.

If it could laugh, she thought it did, although its unnatural amusement numbed her mind.

It knew how to navigate to her, and she was stuck.

She thought of the horse, the dancing couple, and Barnaby and closed her eyes.

She remembered:

the crunch of sweet milky cereal in her mouth;

the sticky smell of suntan lotion;

her toes wriggling on hot ceramic tiles;

the tight hug she gave Hux at LaGuardia airport, before he boarded the flight to San Francisco;

the bittersweet heartache when he whispered fiercely in her ear, "We'll always be friends;"

waking in the clinic's bed, groggy from anaesthesia, and crying with relief;

her mom's lonely face angled up at her and Dad speeding along the Coney Island Cyclone;

her father's voice singing 'My Way'.

Jamie broke the surface of the pool and opened her mouth to heave in succouring air.

She thrashed for the pool's edge, aware of some commotion beyond its boundaries. All she could think about were her body and legs below the water, vulnerable. She cursed seeing *Jaws* that summer.

Her wet fingers reached up and grasped the grooved edge tiles. She levered her body up so her forearms were planted on the poolside, but as she emerged the water's membrane of filth coated her, rendering her body slippery.

Jamie fell back in, her whole body dunking under the surface again.

She looked once and wished she hadn't.

The space was packed with people – maids, bankers, gardeners, socialites, and nannies – tearing at each other but also unaware of each other's presence. Their eyes had the sheen of blindness so they flailed in their limbo and harmed those caught with them.

And so many of them had taut lines thrumming from afar embedded in their lips, eyes, nostrils, or ears, feeding that endless, insatiable craving and starving themselves. The dappled prison churned with despair and fear.

Jamie sensed the ravening lure seeking her again.

Panic almost caused her to breathe in the water, but she funnelled it into imagining her escape.

She propelled herself out of the pool and onto her stomach, and quickly kicked her legs up to roll onto the surface.

Jamie lay on her back, her heart hammering as she dragged in more air.

Above her Randy's concerned face was silhouetted against the lowering sun.

"You okay?" he asked.

She heard her dad's approach before he appeared in her eyeline. Then he was sitting her up, asking her questions, and checking her responses.

She grabbed his rough hand, and surprised, he looked at her directly. Not as a patient.

"I just slipped and fell in," she said, and grinned. "I'm fine now."

He kissed her forehead.

"Glad to hear it, Imp."

He helped her to her feet. Water sluiced off her, leaving a spackled residue on her skin.

"At least my sandals are dry."

She laughed and pivoted to take in the full glory of the summer's evening. The sky blushed shades of pink, lavender, and tangerine, bleeding into an edge of indigo. The cicadas were starting their evensong.

Randy pointed. "You scraped your leg."

Above her ankle a thin red line curved toward her tendon.

Her dad frowned. "I'll clean that up when we get home. It could get infected."

Jamie glanced over at the pool, which continued to swell from her entry. The hole she had punched through the surface film was closing.

Her injured cells throbbed.

Far below the bait continue to arc toward her need.

It would keep pace with her always.

The Tamga

The drumbeat stopped.

Kulin's guiding spirits spun once around the darkened cabin – jangling the chimes made from bottle caps and squirrel skulls – and disappeared through the thatched roof. Kulin murmured a prayer of thanks to the departing *hlung* before he nodded at his nephew Pietr, whose hand stilled the drum's skin. The low fire popped like gunfire. The healing ritual was over.

They waited to see if Dina would wake.

Her flushed face was barely visible under the massive bear pelt that engulfed her on the bed. Andrei, her father, lumbered to his feet and kissed Dina's forehead. He shook her gently.

Her eyelashes blurred. "Pa?" she murmured, sleepy.

Andrei clutched her to his chest.

Pietr turned, stoked the embers in the hearth, and set a battered kettle over the flames to boil.

Kulin ignored the ache in his knees as he straightened. The metal discs, bones, and charms stitched into his quilted robe clanked when he shuffled to the door and banged it open. "She is cured," he boomed, half-blinded by the afternoon light that skimmed the tops of the pine trees.

Cries of thanks erupted from the band of relatives who waited. Before Dina's mother could elbow her way into the house Andrei emerged, carrying Dina bundled in a blanket.

After the family's glad clamour died down, Andrei rushed to Kulin and seized him in a hug that had Kulin's ribs creaking. Andrei released Kulin and slapped a wad of roubles into the healer's palm. He sealed the money with his meaty fist. "No protests, shaman. You earned ten times this amount." He paused, before he crushed Kulin's hand with compassion. "I know you understand a father's grief."

Andrei spun around and spread his arms wide to receive his smiling daughter. The babbling group detached from the cabin's long shadows and entered the forest that bordered the farm.

Once they were out of sight, Kulin slumped onto the long wooden seat by the kitchen window.

Pietr rattled pots inside the cabin and grumbled about preparing food over an open fire. In four days he would return to university in Tomsk, and Kulin would be alone for three months.

He shut his eyes. An image of Vikka's flirting smile behind the mist of her lavender wedding bouquet appeared, wavered, and dissolved into the memory of their son's dark frozen eyes. Oleg stared at Kulin from a frost-whitened face.

A wolverine yelped in the distance.

Kulin opened his eyes and shrugged off the past and a threatening depression. He rose slowly and stamped towards the corral at the rear of his house to check his herd.

The reindeer raised their heads at the jangle from his ceremonial garb, and exhaled clouds in the cooling air. Unused to his costume, some of them shied from the fence. His three favourites, Gull, Ptarmigan, and Lazy, allowed him to pat their thick necks without any nervousness. He smiled and whistled a small tune. Lazy tilted her head and flicked her ears. Kulin laughed and moved towards the house.

His skin prickled in warning. Kulin circled to face the darkness that soaked the forest's fringe.

Limned by silver, the gigantic Bear towered on his rear legs. Kulin crunched through the thin layer of snow as he edged closer to his clan's spiritual guide. When he was within range of the massive paws, he bowed. "Father," his voice hushed with respect, "I am honoured by your visit." He breathed in the damp musk of Bear's fur.

Kulin my son, the words rumbled in his head, *The Tamga is awake.*

"The graveyard?"

Bear nodded. *Prospectors entered the sacred grove of your ancestors. They ransacked the houses of the dead and removed many of the soul dolls. They scattered what offerings they did not steal.*

"How, *how*?" Kulin stuttered, trying to absorb the images that piled into his mind. "How did they get in? What about the defences?"

Bear cocked his head to one side. *Few heed their instincts any more.* Sadness permeated his voice. *Your ancestors are angry, Kulin. The Tamga must be appeased.*

"But, sacrifice is the only way! I don't know the proper chants and charms." His hands bunched into fists.

I will teach you the songs to bind it and soothe it back to sleep. Take Pietr with you, and I will aid you if I can.

Kulin bowed. As he straightened, he looked into Bear's luminous eyes. Kulin's sight darkened, the world receded, and there was only Bear, encompassing him completely. The words and melodies enfolded him, and Bear growled, *Listen well, Kulin, and learn.*

The cold startled Kulin from his vision.

Beware the dead, a final whisper in his thoughts.

Kulin stood in the same spot, but his clan's *hlung* had vanished. The stars of the Great Bear wheeled above him in the night sky, and the reindeer's tendons went *crack-crack* as they shoved closer to one another for warmth. The songs and charms that looped in his mind pressed against his skull and sought release. He staggered back to the house, desperate for warmth.

Pietr knelt by the fireplace stirring a pot when Kulin entered. Pietr's forehead furrowed, but Kulin held up his hand to forestall questions. His nephew shrugged and dished up rabbit stew into wooden bowls.

Kulin undressed and put away his ceremonial outfit with the proper care despite the loud demands of his stomach. He pulled on reindeer skin trousers and a thick red shirt, over which he zipped a hooded fleece. Kulin lit another candle from the fire and placed it in front of his altar. The stuffed bear's head sat in the place of honour among the statues representing other *hlung*: *eekva-pygris'*, the spirits of the forest, and the river Ob. Photographs of his family leaned against amulets and talismans: his teacher Grandfather Dimitri, his parents, Vikka, and Oleg. Kulin knelt and prayed. Candlelight flickered across the button-eyes of the statues and the faces immobilised by time.

After touching Vikka's image in parting, Kulin sat opposite his nephew. He smiled despite the background hum of the binding charms in his mind. Within a day they would become a deafening roar if he didn't unleash them, and madness would follow. Kulin surveyed the steaming bowls, hunks of bread, blueberry jam, and glasses of vodka. He grinned slyly at Pietr. "Still pining for your microwave?"

Pietr sniffed. "I got by."

"We'll see." Kulin spooned stew into this mouth, suddenly starving. Soon he scraped the bottom of his bowl and nodded his approval at Pietr. He picked up his glass of vodka, and threw some of it into the fire to feed its *hlung*. The flames belched in thanks. Kulin clinked his glass against Pietr's before knocking back the contents. He gasped in appreciation as the alcohol warmed his gullet. "I had a vision of Bear outside."

Pietr's brown eyes betrayed no surprise, but he stopped slathering jam on his bread.

Kulin splashed more vodka into his glass. "You remember what I taught you about the Tamga?"

"It's the protector of our ancestors' souls," Pietr recited as one used to regular tests of knowledge. "The restless dead – those who died in accidents, or with unsettled minds in life – are bound to their soul dolls. They remain in the graveyard where the Tamga watches over them." His knife, poised above the bread, dripped jam. Concern tightened his voice. "Has someone died?"

"Three surveyors for the oil company entered the graveyard today and stole offerings as well as many of the soul dolls." He gulped more vodka and watched incredulity and anger chase across his nephew's face. Kulin slammed the glass on the table. "The Tamga's pissed off."

The fire cracked and snapped.

Pietr's hand tightened around his glass. "Bastards! They steal our ancestral land, pollute it, and now they rob our graves?" His chair screeched across the floor as he stood, his face flushed. "We have to do something."

Kulin grabbed Pietr's hand and drew him back into his seat. "Bear taught me charms to pacify the Tamga. Tonight, I will walk in my dreams and scout the area. Tomorrow we will put things right."

Pietr's lips thinned. "But what about the men? They have to pay for this."

Kulin glanced at the altar, and the shadows of the statues leaped and danced. "They will be punished."

Pietr crossed his arms and leaned back in his chair. "Tell me what is needed."

Kulin flew in the shape of owl across the dream landscape of Urga. The forest and peat swamps stretched to the Yamal peninsula, penned in by the Ural Mountains on the left, where the sacred Ob joined the Kara Sea. Dark stains rippled from blots on the land, where cities like Khanty-Mansisk squatted, or where the oil and gas companies ripped into the earth, desecrating the hunting lands and rivers of the Khanty and Mansi. His people.

Kulin swooped low into the Ob valley, over-flying his tiny farm, and following the tremors of shock that radiated from the village's graveyard. From above it was a bruise on the landscape: purple and yellow contusions of anger bloomed against the vibrant green of the surrounding forest. Kulin bolstered his defensive charms, and landed at the outskirts of the graveyard. He transformed into his man-shape. The spirits of the forest, those of spruce and fir as well as grouse, wolf, and fox, were absent, or subdued. Hiding from the Tamga's rage.

Floating above the earth, Kulin checked the boundary around the graveyard. To his relief the hungry ghosts were contained, but the binding charms showed signs of deterioration. He cloaked his lifeforce so the dead would ignore his presence; a chill settled over his heart. He could not maintain the illusion for long.

He slipped into the sacred grove. The pallid forms of the dead, some still, other agitated, moved around the confines of the graveyard. The outlines of the grave huts loomed above them: little wooden cabins on fragile stilts, where the soul dolls resided. Underneath them lay the grave boats in which the bodies were interred.

Anger and grief saturated the atmosphere, and Kulin restrained the violent shaking that threatened to overcome him. The living were not welcome.

The Tamga stood in the middle of the cemetery. Its skinny arms stretched upwards, and its black hair flared out. Kulin shrank into himself and concealed his life's pulse.

The Tamga's eyes blazed and its maw gaped. "Bring them back!" it screamed. It folded into a tight ball on the ground, and its lanky arms and legs trembled with tension. With a piercing cry it exploded from the ground and dashed against the graveyard's boundary. The air sizzled and the Tamga bounced back, snarling. The other ghosts hovered around the border of the cemetery in anticipation.

Kulin moved backwards carefully. He had to retrieve the soul dolls, but first he had to find them. A plan formed in his mind. As he turned to leave a ghost slid in front of him: Oleg.

"Father," he whispered, "have you come to visit me?" Shock stopped Kulin's voice. Oleg's shape solidified and his handsome features sharpened. His resemblance to Vikka was stronger than Kulin remembered. Kulin opened his mouth to speak to his son, but the words, knotted with old hurt and sorrow, lodged in his throat and would not budge.

Oleg searched Kulin's expression. "Nothing to say?" He opened his arms. "Let us embrace as a goodbye."

Kulin drifted towards his son.

Beware the dead. The warning flashed across his mind too late.

Oleg's arms seized him. Ice froze Kulin's heart.

His son's bitter voice pierced Kulin like a notched knife. "I died alone. Too drunk to feel the snowfall." The tightness in Kulin's chest increased, and the distant connection to his body, lying on the bed in his cabin, thinned. "You too will die alone. No one will save you. No one loves you. At last you will understand my death!"

At last Kulin tried to speak, to explain the grief that blinded him to everything after Vikka's death, but the pain devoured the words of apology.

A flare of light blinded him momentarily, and the awful constriction disappeared. Oleg screamed, and Pietr, with the form of Bear flickering around him, dragged Oleg from Kulin. Hundreds of ghosts turned as one. Their dead eyes were famished black pits.

A howl tore through the air: the Tamga had their scent.

Kulin changed into owl and swept upwards as the Tamga lunged for him. Distracted by Oleg, Pietr failed to see the Tamga turn its focus upon him. Kulin dived, grabbed Pietr, and beat his wings upwards with all his power. The Tamga leaped high after Pietr, its claws scraping his ankle, but it fell backwards, blocked by the graveyard's boundary.

Jealousy disfigured Oleg's upturned face. "You always chose him!" he yelled, and the accusation bit deep.

Kulin bolted upright in his bed. Even with the fur around him he could not stop shaking. A cup of hot chai was placed in his hands, and he drank deep though it scalded his tongue. Pietr sat beside him in a chair and gripped another cup. His face was gaunt. "I know you told me to stand watch, but Bear insisted I follow."

Bone-weariness and heartache drove away all pretence at annoyance. "Thank you," Kulin said, and Pietr nodded.

Remorse and sorrow consumed Kulin, but the tears did not fall. His heart remained frozen.

They sat quietly for a long time. Pietr coughed. "It's not your fault Oleg died." He placed his hand on Kulin's shoulder, and the ice thawed a fraction. "You might have changed other things, but not that."

The tears came. In a soundless rush, heaved out of his body in spasms. Kulin wept for his son, for his guilt and failure, and for the love that never came easy between them. And he cried for himself: for the fear and loneliness that haunted him in his empty bed at night, with no wife to comfort him, and no son to carry his name.

Pietr's silent presence consoled him. Eventually, Kulin succumbed to a deep and dreamless sleep.

Kulin shook Pietr awake before dawn. They said little during their breakfast of raw fish and bread. The binding spells crowded Kulin's thoughts, and he longed to sing them free. After their prayers and a purification ritual, Pietr stowed their supplies in his backpack. They pulled on boots, reindeer pelt leggings and parkas, and strapped on a hunting knife each. Before they left, Kulin touched the photo of Vikka. He lifted a sprig of dried lavender from the altar and inhaled its faint fragrance. He tucked it into his pocket for luck. Oleg's eyes accused Kulin from his image. Kulin traced the outline of his son's face. "Forgive me," he murmured.

He ate two sacred mushrooms and entreated the mushroom *hlung* to gift him with spirit-sight.

Kulin explained his plan to Pietr as they locked up the cabin and moved through the dense forest towards the cemetery.

Pietr stopped, his face red from the cold and exertion. "You're going to release the Tamga!"

Kulin marched forward, hoping his pace would impart a sense of belief in what he was doing. "It will lead us to the soul dolls. It's better than any hound."

Pietr trotted to catch up with his uncle. "But it's enraged! It will kill the men before we can stop it. And us too."

Kulin shook his head. "I can control it with the charm Bear gave me." He stopped, and rested his glove on Pietr's arm. "With your help."

"You'd better teach it to me, then."

Kulin resumed walking and sang the controlling charm. Pietr joined in, and they repeated it until the spell was memorised.

The outskirts of the graveyard emerged from the trees. An oppressive silence weighed over the area. A wooden post carved with leering faces glared outwards from the place of the dead, marking its boundary. Kulin removed his glove and traced a pattern over their dark expressions. Without being told, Pietr began to sing.

Kulin focused and the image of the double world, the realm of dead and invisible spirits, slid over his vision. The energetic wall that contained the dead was dissipating. The Tamga's outline shimmered as it battered against the shield. He signalled to Pietr, and his nephew's voice rose in command. Kulin lowered the boundary. The Tamga surged through in an instant. Kulin slammed the shield up, and trapped the slower spirits inside. He joined his voice to Pietr's, and the shadowy form of the Tamga stalked towards them.

"Lead us to the soul dolls." Kulin intoned, and he willed the Tamga to agree. It was eager. "You must follow our orders and leave the men unharmed." At this it rebelled, and Kulin felt it resist the charm and his control. Together Kulin and Pietr's voice rose in harsh insistent tones as the Tamga struggled to lash out at them. Both men were sweating by the time the soul guardian submitted. It gestured to the north, impatient.

Kulin slipped his lease of control a little so the Tamga sprang forward. The soul dolls drew it like a magnet. Pietr and Kulin followed quickly, each of them singing the charm while ducking through the branches of birch and alder, and avoiding holes and roots underneath the snow. Soon they were exhausted. The Tamga strained against Kulin's control, and never failed to test his limits whenever he tripped or his breath grew ragged.

Finally they arrived at a collection of temporary wooden cabins, clumped together in a clearing, with rubbish and equipment scattered around the buildings. A generator hummed, and an old Lada Niva sat in the mud with one door swinging open in the light breeze. The Tamga gestured across the clearing and strained forward in anticipation.

A scream, high and insane, split the silence. A cabin door burst open, and a bearded man dressed in a dirty parka rushed out. Even from a distance he appeared deranged, but Kulin caught a flash of a tormenting spirit latched upon him. The man jumped into the Lada and closed the doors, but did not start the engine. Instead he cowered in the passenger seat, covered his ears with his hands, and rocked back and forth. The Tamga growled, and moved towards the vehicle, but Kulin willed it back, and urged it to locate the soul dolls.

It tugged Kulin towards a small shed. A younger man stood beside their goal. He swatted at the air around him and called on Mary and the saints for aid. Despite the cold he wore only trousers, and his thin chest and bony arms were covered in cuts and bruises.

The flickering form of the Tamga bounded to the man's side in a single leap and hissed as it sunk its wispy arm into his chest. The man's eyes rolled upwards, and he collapsed, wheezing, on the ground. Kulin whipped the line of control to the Tamga so fast there was an almost audible *snap*. It jerked back, its snarl of anger heard only by Kulin. It turned and dove towards him. Kulin's voice rose with Pietr's in command.

The Tamga's face, frenzied with anger, came within a finger's breadth of Kulin's, but it halted, and bared pointed teeth in frustration. It loped over to the shed, but stopped and moved in circles, waiting for permission to enter.

Kulin hunkered to check the young man lying in the mud. A quick examination indicated there wasn't permanent damage.

Pietr stopped singing.

A man in a long grey overcoat held a rifle to Pietr's head. Like his comrades his face was pale and slicked with sweat. He questioned Pietr in panicky Russian. The Tamga dropped into a crouch.

Before either could act Pietr snapped his forearm up and knocked the rifle from his face while moving his hand to grab the weapon by the barrel. He yanked it from the startled man's grip and used the momentum to swing the rifle at his attacker. A loud *crack* echoed across the camp as the rifle's stock connected with the miner's jaw. The man crumpled to the soggy ground. The Tamga jumped towards Pietr's attacker, but Pietr stepped in front of the man and began to sing again. The Tamga skidded to a stop and scrambled back to the shed.

Kulin ran to Pietr and examined the unconscious man. He glanced up at his nephew, who was breathing hard. "He'll live. Well done." Pietr smiled tightly but kept singing. Kulin nodded at the figure of the other man lying in the mud. "Get them indoors."

Pietr dragged the men into a cabin as Kulin took up the chant, and entered the shed with the Tamga. In the small dark room the angry spirits swarmed around the abandoned bag of soul dolls like hungry mosquitoes. The Tamga crooned and reached its hands out in supplication. The spirits stilled and hovered in the air. Pietr appeared in the doorway, and Kulin gestured at him to take up the controlling song. Pietr sang in his strong baritone as Kulin reverently examined the contents of the bag. The hand-sewn dolls, representing the dead of his community, did not appear damaged. Neither Oleg nor Vikka's doll was present.

"Are they all here?" he asked.

The spirits spiralled around the Tamga's placid face. "I call the rest." A strange melody filled the shed, creating an eerie counterpoint to Pietr's tune. More spirits flew in and joined the circle of motes floating around the Tamga.

"The dolls?" Kulin pressed.

"All are present. Worry not shaman," it said, "your wife and son rest in the graveyard." Kulin shivered.

Pietr maintained the chant while Kulin checked on the man in the Lada, now unconscious, and hauled him to the cabin.

When Kulin returned he noticed the concentration on his nephew's calm face as he kept the Tamga in check. In a moment of prescience Kulin envisioned the shaman Pietr would become: powerful, honourable, and dedicated to his community. The tradition would continue. Kulin's eyes burned, but he refused the tears. "We must return to the graveyard," he said.

Pietr nodded and maintained the tune. Kulin picked up the bag and joined in with Pietr's singing. The Tamga, surrounded by its charges, moved with them as they set off for the cemetery.

Twilight had settled over the forest by the time they reached the edge of the graveyard. Kulin ignored his fatigue, and concentrated on the final part of his task.

He lowered the boundary so they could enter, careful not to allow any ghost escape. The Tamga appeared content, but Kulin kept an uneasy watch on the *hlung*. On its home ground it possessed more strength.

Bear whispered in Kulin's mind and told him where each soul doll resided, and he returned them to their original grave houses. The Tamga coaxed the corresponding spirit back into residence. Pietr placed new offerings of fresh meat, alcohol, flowers, and trinkets on the central altar in the cemetery.

Kulin signalled Pietr to stop the chant, and they waited to see if the Tamga was appeased.

No bird sang. The wind dropped.

Kulin shifted. He raised his hand to cue Pietr to begin the final song when he spotted the Tamga standing behind his nephew.

Before Kulin could open his mouth, it grabbed Pietr, pinned his arms, and gagged him with a hand. The Tamga glared at Kulin, and its feathery hair fanned out in warning. "A sacrifice, shaman. Those are the rules. No rest for me, no matter what you sing, until I am rewarded."

Kulin groped for his bundle of spirit items and seized his most cherished object: a bottle containing the soul of a rival shaman, the first he ever defeated. He held it up.

The Tamga's dark tongue darted out and tasted the air. "Not enough, shaman," it said. "Your nephew comes with me. To remind you to take more care."

Its teeth descended towards Pietr's neck.

Pain exploded in Kulin's shoulder. He almost fell backwards but remained swaying on his feet. Dully he watched the bottle fall from his hand.

The sound of a gunshot registered. Blood splattered across the white snow. He fell to his knees as the pain drained the power from his body. The Tamga dropped Pietr, and turned, quivering, like a dog with a new scent. The man wearing the grey overcoat, now sporting a huge bruise on his face, pointed a rifle at Kulin. Another shot *cracked* but splintered a branch to his right.

Kulin sank on his heels as his body numbed and his vision narrowed. He saw Pietr's anguished face as he crawled across the ground towards him, and Kulin wished he could tell him not to worry, but he couldn't remember how to move his mouth.

The Tamga leaped upon the man with the rifle, and plunged its clawed fingers into his chest. He screeched as the Tamga rummaged inside his body. It purred, ripped out the man's soul, shining and shivering, and sucked it into its mouth like a delicacy.

The body dropped to the ground, lifeless.

The Tamga turned to regard Kulin. It smiled dreadfully.

Pietr reached his uncle and pressed his hands against the wound. "The song, Kulin! We both have to sing it." Pietr glanced up and noticed the Tamga stalking toward them. He stood, between it and his uncle. Blood dripped from his fingers.

The scent of lavender filled Kulin's nostrils, and Vikka's breath stirred the hair by his ear. His heart throbbed. "Sing the words free Kulin," she said.

The words sprang from his lips, wheedling and strong. His lungs screamed in protest and yet the song flowed, reminding the Tamga to rest and take care of its charges. Pietr joined in immediately.

The Tamga slowed and faltered, its face confused, as if it had forgotten what it was doing. It swivelled its head from side to side as it checked upon the grave houses, and the souls tucked up inside. It frowned, and shook its head. The song lulled it further. It stretched long like a cat, curled once around the altar, and disappeared.

Pietr stared in disbelief. "It's asleep!"

Kulin slid sideways onto the snow. He closed his eyes. Time to rest.

Far away, Pietr pleaded.

A light touch upon his arm, and Kulin looked up at Vikka's radiant smile. Tears pricked his eyes. She was so beautiful. Oleg stood behind her, his arms crossed upon his chest in a familiar angry stance. Kulin's Grandfather Dimitri materialised behind Oleg and shoved him.

Oleg stumbled, and fell to his knees besides Kulin.

A drumbeat, an erratic rhythm, pounded in Kulin's ears.

His lungs were banded with pain, but Kulin gasped out the words that had burned within for so long: "I'm sorry, Oleg. I failed you."

The beat staggered.

Oleg placed his hands upon Kulin's chest.

The drumbeat stopped.

A hot pain jolted him. Kulin's back arched, he spat blood, and sucked in air.

Pietr's blurred face hovered close. His hands pumped Kulin's chest. "Come back, old man," Pietr raged, "Don't leave me!"

Behind Pietr the translucent figures of Vikka and Oleg smiled sadly, and faded.

The beat returned, thready, but stable.

Pietr choked, "Not yet, not yet," and hugged Kulin.

Not yet, thought Kulin, and he wept.

Spooky Girl

The first moment of video: Lindsay pushes open the hulking front door of Heath House, strands of purple and black hair seeping from the knitted cap on her head. The massive door scrapes open reluctantly so she pivots to shove her shoulder into its weight. She turns her face to glance at the camera, her forehead creased in frustration.

"Jesus, Jas, put down the phone and lend a hand."

Bright laughter and a shake of perspective to indicate no.

"Tania, will you help the weakling?"

Tania, taller, slighter, in a leather biker jacket and ripped skinny black jeans, steps into the shot, and touches the door. It slips open and Lindsay stumbles into the shadowed interior. A heavy, ornate staircase is suggested in the gloom beyond the rectangle of light impressed on the slate floor.

"You weren't kidding about this place, Tania," whispers disembodied Jas. "It's Gothic central."

Tania, her body in light and her face in shadow, turns to the camera. "It's revival, but you wanted a Hammer film vibe..."

From the darkness, Lindsay's tetchy voice. "Where's the shagging light switch?"

The image judders as Jas steps forward. The camera scales badly to adjust from the daylight to the shuttered dusk inside.

"It's perfect," she says quietly, her tone conveying awe and respect. The picture resolves into a dirty image of a large atrium, with the indistinct form of Lindsay patting down the wall under a huge framed landscape, and Tania standing at the bottom of the staircase, looking up.

"Pause it, Iris!" Matthew Wolsey barked at me, and stabbed his thick finger into my laptop screen. I wanted to slap his paw off my precious machine, but it's not considered polite to hit a client.

I checked out where he pointed. A grainy blur suggested a third figure standing at the top of the first flight of stairs. Perhaps a woman in a long skirt, or a person standing still with legs tight together. A gleam indicated polished, pointed shoes.

"And your expert couldn't clean this up further? That could be a suit of armour, or a piece of furniture covered in cloth."

I glanced up at Wolsey, who was leaning over my desk. His intense grey eyes under heavy brows glared at me. "You'll see when you get there. That landing is clear. It *must* be a person."

I leaned back in my chair, the tableau frozen on my screen. I'd read the police report, and all the newspaper stories over the past three years.

The girls had vanished. All that remained was this one piece of footage that had been uploaded to Jasmine Healy's cloud service a few minutes after it was taken.

They had hiked to the house from the nearby village of Lanslei that March afternoon, but not a scrap of evidence had remained of their visit: no clothes, no phones, no backpacks. A few scattered prints and footprints in dust. No signs of struggle, nothing to indicate that they had stayed there beyond a short tour around the house.

Wolsey was an obsessed cousin of Jasmine's. They were a year apart, and close. They'd gone to the same uni, and talked regularly. She didn't have much family other than him: her parents were separated and differently broken.

Lindsay came from a large, uncommunicative clan. They had hunched together, clamp-mouthed in grief, and waited for the police to solve the problem.

Tania was more elusive. She'd never been a registered student, even though the girls had lived together in a small flat near the university. Her name wasn't on the bills – they had all been in Lindsay's name, the designated responsible girl, from what I could tell.

I only discovered what was *probably* her name, Titania Molyneux, through my obsessive digital diligence: combing through texts, forums, and web sites that Jas and Lindsay frequented. I'd discovered they were all users of an occult forum called Dark Pathz, and with a little bit of cracking I'd gained access to Tania's profile, and from that to her email account. Surprisingly sparse. It had the hallmarks of an account opened solely to link to that forum.

After the initial rush of stories about the disappearances, the mystery lost oxygen after a terrorist attack a few days later suffocated the news agencies with pictures of actual dead bodies. Only the occasional local rag ran the obligatory 'What happened?' piece on them afterwards.

Three women vanished, and the world seemed indifferent.

Except Wolsey.

And me, I guess. They were a funny little band of girls, the kind that coalesce in their late teens when true personalities emerge once the weight of adolescent expectation eases. I examined their pictures frequently – Jas had the most selfies – imagining them going about their daily lives, and figuring out their dreams and goals; Lindsay had the most drive. Perhaps if they had been given another five years they would have drifted apart as jobs and partners pulled them into different directions.

But on that March afternoon they were united in a mission. And something had intervened.

"Tell me again what Jas said the day before they left."

Wolsey let out a long exasperated sigh. It's a familiar sound to me, made by someone who has said something so many times that it has become rote information he resents retelling.

"She said she was taking off with Tania and Lindsay to some grand old pile to take pictures. Jas was studying production design and had landed a gig with an amateur production of *Dracula.* Her and the other girls liked that whole *emo goth* business." He shook his head, but I spotted the fond remembrance that lightened his usual sombre puss.

"Jas was in it for the *style*, she wasn't into that black magic shite really. She did it to stir people. Lindsay seemed serious about it, but that was her thing you know, if you do something then all in. And Tania..."

He paused. "She was quiet. Like stillness gathered around her. People tended to lean in to hear her speak. She had this way of making you... take stock."

"Of what?"

He shrugged, and the perpetual annoyance settled on him again. "What do I know? It's been a long time. I forget what they were like, what Jas was like."

He paced away to the lone window in my cramped office to watch the rain slide down the filthy pane. "Is this what happens? You just forget those who die? Act like they never lived?" His tone was belligerent.

I placed my palms down on the table and slid them across the smooth polished walnut surface; my father's desk. Where he had read and written books.

"We continue after they have stopped," I said. "They're no longer part of our every day. It's a natural process of letting go so we can continue."

He turned, his fists clenched. "Well *fuck that!* Jas was like my sister.

And I'm going to find out what happened to her."

His anger sputtered at my raised eyebrow. "Well, with your help Ms Khouri."

I picked up an invoice from my printer tray. "First, my expenses so far. And once we've settled up we can discuss the trip to Heath House."

He smiled. It looked unnatural on him.

After he left I stood up from my desk, grabbed my battered white plastic kettle, and stuck it under the tap over the tiny sink in the corner of the room. The only space that wasn't bookshelves or a window.

I brewed jasmine oolong tea in my black dragon Yixing clay teapot. As always I rubbed the tips of my fingers over his arching tail that formed the handle. For luck, as my mother always said. The routine, the light floral fragrance, and the hot tea settled me. Wolsey tended to disrupt my space, like several of my clients.

I had to cast an oracle of some kind before this trip to Heath House. I'd read its history, and knew the girls had picked it for more than its vibe. They had planned to do a ritual there. Something the police dismissed as youthful delusion, and thankfully the press never had time to exploit. If the story had broken during a more humdrum period that might not have remained the case.

I stood in the centre of my office and closed my eyes, noticing the presence of my charms, and my more active artefacts. Inhaling, I centred myself and exhaled doubt and distraction. At once I knew to use my oldest tool: Aunt Frieda's tarot deck.

I opened the ancient biscuit tin decorated in skull stickers where I kept it, and unwrapped the silk scarf in which it lay.

I sat back at my desk and closed my eyes, feeling the rasp of the cards against my hands as I shuffled them, the bumps and small tears in the fading paper. Clearly, I gave my intention: what to expect from my journey.

Five cards slipped out easily, and I opened my eyes to a dangerous vista.

In the centre, the seven of swords, flanked on either side by the nine of swords, and the Queen of Swords. And alongside them The Moon and the High Priestess.

"Damn," I whispered, taking in the gleaming weapons at the heart of the spread.

I'd better suit up, I thought.

We set off early in Wolsey's car, a sporty blue Honda Civic, with gleaming surfaces and shiny instruments. He handled the car with the distracted finesse of a pro once we broke free from the congested roads around York and hit the clearer roads that swept over rolling hills stabbed with skeletal trees. The previous day's deluge had tempered the clouds into a dull, flat grey. It wasn't even ten and it could have been five o'clock in that perpetual twilight.

I'd taken precautions. A defensive amulet I'd created based off an ancient Talmudic design hung around my neck on a plaited white, red, and black cord. Sheathed on my belt, and covered by my denim jacket, was a small athame I'd fashioned years ago from the broken tip of an Anglo-Saxon sword Dad had kept in his office. My jacket bristled with a hodgepodge of plastic badges and decorative pins from favourite TV shows and films, which made me seem like a nerdy shut-in; always a good way to be under-estimated. They were blessed and bespelled in a variety of ways. Anything weird and wishing me harm would feel like it was grasping slivers of glass if it made a grab for me.

Plus stretchy jeans, and good old Doc Martens: 9 holes and cherry red. It made me nimble and able to get a good kick in if the trouble was more corporeal. Of course, I did have a 5 Yen coin embedded in each sole... just for luck. I'd also tucked away a couple of crystals and a bag of salt about my person, and had some extra supplies in my lightweight backpack.

I'd started the day with a lavender bath and scrubbed myself with Dead Sea salt – a great way to clean off the psychic muck, and keep your skin in good condition.

I felt strong, but not cocky. I'd seen enough weird situations go wonky as a result of big egos obscuring the potential danger of mischief by incorporeal rascals. And Heath House had a reputation.

It wasn't one of those loud and in-your-face thug mansions. Nope, it was the sly, persuasive kind that stole your soul while fooling you into thinking it was really on your side.

So, no splashy multiple murders and debauched parties. Unfortunate accidents were more its speed. The rotten branch that snaps as the toddler is on the swing, the pond that's deceptively cold and deep, which attracts the late night drunk or the bragging teen. The badly wired socket. A leaking gas stove. The crippling fall down the stairs because of that loose step.

Occasionally, the bald-faced move: a single death. Like Silas, the grand-nephew of Horatio Heath, who built the house. Silas committed suicide in 1916 while on leave from The Great War. He hanged himself from the banister of the first floor landing, using barbed wire. He was discovered when the family returned from chapel on Sunday morning. His neck was almost severed.

His sister, Eloise, was committed to an asylum a year later, and never returned to the house. A fact that might have given her some respite in her final years.

The house allowed some people to thrive under its roof, while like a huge, mean, territorial cat it singled out the sensitive and the troubled for its laconic, malicious mauling.

I knew to enter this space would be the equivalent of a priest kicking down the door of a brothel. The best I would get was the silent treatment, and the worst could be a violent attack. There was little I could do to affect such a systemic malaise. I could perhaps force a few secrets loose, or nail close its doors in a metaphorical sense.

I guessed that Lindsay and Jas were long gone. Tania, maybe not. She had led the others there. Perhaps sensing its nature and misidentifying it as a cool locale for spell casting, or she was bringing along snacks for her tame, monstrous building.

All I knew for sure was that the other trails were cold, except this dark path. I snorted sardonically at my poetic observation.

"You're not one for chit chat," Wolsey commented. He kept his attention on the road, his hands gripping the wheel firmly. "I like that. For a girl with a spooky occupation you seem pretty *real*."

"You'd be surprised how many people knock on my door positive they've got a poltergeist and are pretty peeved when I discover it's a case of subsidence or a bored dog."

He nodded, and I could sense the gears turning in his mind. "So how many cases turn out to be... unusual?"

"More often than not there's nothing strange going on, and it's family troubles manifesting. I know a few good therapists to recommend. Although I've had at least one business card thrown in my face with the accusation I was a psychic dullard."

He flashed a grin. "They called you a *dullard*."

"Maybe they didn't use that word..."

"So, what about the genuine cases?"

"Yeah, they're often messy and not my idea of a fun time. But you know, someone's got to clean up the spills on the dance floor." I shifted in my seat. He wanted juicy details of an exorcism or a spectacular astral battle so he could feel better about being forced to turn up at my door, and ammunition if he wanted to dismiss me later.

"I saw a ghost once," he said, matter-of-factly.

Now he had my attention. I watched his expression, and gave him a small psychic *prod*. His eyes squinted and he glanced about as if a fly had just bumped his forehead.

"Did it scare you?"

"It was my gran, and I was five. She sat on my bed, and I smelled the soap she always used. She smiled and I felt *safe*. I found out later she'd died that night in the nursing home."

I looked away to stare out the window of the car and the occasional thump of the wipers brushing away the scattershot rain. "That's a nice memory," I said.

He bobbed his head.

"Did you ever tell Jasmine?"

"No. That wasn't *our* grandmother... *Thank Christ*. She was a cow. I never told anyone that story. Jas was imaginative. And once she got into all that hippie crap I knew it would be chum in the water. She *claimed* she saw some things, but it sounded like bollocks to me."

We crested a hill and a sign proclaimed that Lanslei was five miles away.

"I rang old man Heath and said we were popping by. As far as I know he hasn't let anyone but me into the house since the girls... went away."

"Not that you know," I said.

He threw me a quizzical look. "What, you think he's holding out?"

"I think if that house hasn't been fed in three years it's starving."

"Psychic defence is like driving a car," my mum, the agnostic Jew who had been dealing with weird shit all her life, taught me. "Repeat the basics until they're muscle memory and keep refining your techniques. Once day you'll be driving a Jaguar doing handbrake turns while talking to Ganesha in the front seat and fending off a ghoul in the back."

I looked up from reading the prophecies of Mother Shipton and gave my mum a dead-eyed stare. I was sixteen and a know-it-all.

"Now you're being stupid. Who'd want to drive a Jag? Give me a Dodge Viper any day."

She dipped her head to return my glare over the tops of her red plastic glasses.

"Style, class, and grace my dear, they never go out of fashion."

"Tell that to the ghoul that's messing up the leather seats in the back!"

She laughed and returned to reupholstering an Art Deco chair she'd picked up cheap in a flea market. My mother did not like waste and loved the lived history of old objects. Some of them became the best wards in our house.

I frowned suddenly. "And what's that ghoul doing outside of a cemetery anyway?"

"I don't know, why don't you tell me? You're the one with the ghoul problem..."

And so we would go, back and forth, in our cluttered living room/library/workshop until Dad called us for dinner.

Arthur Heath looked as I imagined: a white-haired old man in a cardigan, tweed trousers, and brogues. He lived in a two-up two-down on the edge of the village, with a well-tended front garden.

He ushered us into his compact front room, which was decorated in a minimalist style, with a big flatscreen TV on one wall. He shuffled into the room with a tray bearing a cafetiere of coffee and a teapot, along with cups on saucers, a bowl of brown sugar lumps, and an astonishingly ugly china milk jug in the shape of a cow.

As he poured me a cup of tea I pointed at the creamer. "That's a striking object," I said.

"Oh Bessie!" He laughed. "She's quite hideous to anyone with taste, but when I was a child I loved her. I refused to eat porridge unless she was used to deliver milk on top. She's the only thing from the old house that I wanted."

I tipped Bessie over to pour the milk into my tea, and though she displayed a rather annoyed countenance there were no harmful energies attached to her.

"When's the last time you were in Heath House?" I asked.

Arthur settled himself into his black leather easy chair, with a cup of coffee in his frail hand.

"Gracious, let me think. I prefer not to go into the dreadful place of course. Three months ago." He nodded to himself. "Yes, when they were filming for that television show. The one that celebrates the old class system with queasy nostalgic romanticism." He made a disgusted noise.

Mum's parents were Hungarian refugees, and Dad was from Lebanon originally. They considered themselves resolutely British, but their calling as historians did not allow them to gloss over the more unhelpful vestiges of Empire.

I darted Wolsey a quick look to see what he made of this wrinkle, but he was focused on Mr Heath.

"I thought that would be right up your street, Arthur old boy," Wolsey said. He stuck his little finger up and winked at him.

"Don't mind his teasing, Miss Khouri," Arthur replied calmly. "He knows I've been a socialist all my life, much to my parents' horror. I wasn't supposed to inherit. But the duty has fallen to me now." The lines of his face set in a stoic acceptance. "The money from the production company has been a Godsend. It's allowed me some comforts, and to keep up the basic maintenance of the house."

I took a sip of tea to consider the implications of this information. "How long have they been using Heath House as a location?"

"For two years. Last year it was only exteriors, but this year they filmed in several of the rooms – they had to bring in the National Trust to oversee their work, but it all passed muster."

Wolsey placed his cup and saucer on the coffee table. "There's an opportunity there, Arthur. Plenty of people love to ramble around old houses, especially if they've been on the telly. You could organise excursions, parties. Breathe some life into the old place."

Arthur said nothing for a moment but gave Wolsey and me a sharp, penetrating look. I got a *gleam* off the old man. He was a sharp one.

"Thank you for the suggestion, Matthew, and a member of the production staff has already come to me with such a proposal. I declined."

I glanced between the two men. Clearly they had struck up a friendship over the years, and there was some unstated understanding hanging between them.

I always prefer the direct approach. "Is this because you feel that something untoward might happen if Heath House became active again?"

Arthur met my gaze. "To be the custodian of such a legacy and remain as I am has been difficult, Miss Khouri. It has been the result of distinct boundaries and a careful, guarded exposure to the house. I'm vigilant about who I allow onto its grounds."

He glanced over at Wolsey, who was contemplating the floor. "I truly regret that Jasmine, Lindsay, and Tania crossed its threshold. Tania had asked me for permission by letter, but I had refused. Unfortunately, for some reason I cannot understand, the house was unlocked the day they arrived. I have wracked my memory repeatedly, but I'm an old man. I cannot confidently state I remembered to lock it up prior to their visit."

I noticed a tremble in his hand, and without any special intuition I knew this burden lay heavily upon him.

"Tania was somehow familiar with the house. I got the impression she had been inside before. Do you know any of the Molyneux family?"

He started. "Why that's not a name I've heard in some time. Yes, my cousin who owned the house before me had a partner, Lilly Molyneux. They had not been married, so when he died she had no claim on the place." Arthur's face darkened. "I'd told Bertie to do the right thing, but the man was an idiot. And because of his obstinacy Lilly had to leave, cap in hand, and I was crippled by the family burden."

"There were no children?"

"No. I never saw Lilly again after the funeral."

Wolsey stood up and put his hand on Arthur's shoulder. "We'd better jog on. I want to be in and out before dark."

Arthur nodded. He rose slowly and patted Wolsey's arm. "I'll get the keys."

I waited in the car doing swift research on my Smartphone.

Wolsey opened the door and settled into the driver's seat, a large ring of keys jangling.

"What did you find?"

I looked up from my screen. "Lilly Molyneux had two children later in life, a girl and a boy with a Simon Foster. The girl's middle name was Titania. Her first name was the rather more nondescript Mary."

"So any news on Mary Foster?"

"I'm searching right now. There are millions of them."

He turned on the engine of the car. "Let's get to the house while you're Googling."

I seethed with frustration at the slowness of my search with an erratic signal while Wolsey wrestled with the heavy chain and lock on the iron gates at the entrance to the estate.

He drove us into the driveway and got out to lock the gates behind us again.

I imagined what information I could dig up with half an hour at my laptop and a fast broadband connection.

"*Lófasz!*" I muttered as I slammed the door shut on the car.

Wolsey looked puzzled. "Come again?"

"My mum never cursed in English, but had some choice Hungarian phrases she used when I was a kid. My grandparents nearly had a fit when they heard me use them."

My distraction meant I hadn't paid attention to the house as we had driven up the long yew tree-lined driveway.

Now, standing before its bulk, I stepped back to take it in. Grey stone covered in swathes of green ivy, with battlements along the top of the walls, a round tower visible on one side, and a rectangular clock tower spiking from the middle. Dragon gargoyles jutted out at the corners. The Heath coat of arms and motto were carved above the enormous double doors.

"*Espere mieux*." I said. Noticing Wolsey's puzzled expression, I pointed up. "'Hope for better", the family motto."

He grimaced. "Glum bastards. But they must have impressed the neighbours."

I nodded, because the unnatural chill seeping from the house captured my attention. It was aware of my arrival and it was giving me the first rebuff. I checked my phone again – only one bar and no data available.

Wolsey noticed and said, "I can never get a signal up here."

Sighing, I put it away.

While Wolsey attended to the lock on the door I grounded and guarded in moments. It was reflex now, like hitting the start button.

The house did not have a single point of malice, but functioned more like a hive-mind: linking numerous active spots in the building to each other, all of which fed off the residual imprints of the pains and hurts experienced in the space over the centuries. It was composed of many tortured personality fragments working together.

Snapshots of people's face appeared in my mind. I did not engage with the emotions attached to them but allowed the images to scroll past like a carousel.

I realised the door was open and Wolsey was staring at me. His shoulders were tight, and his expression was of resolute determination. Clearly he had some sensitivity, which was why he'd searched for someone like me to investigate this problem after so many other dead ends.

"Imagine you are wearing a suit of armour," I said to him, locking his gaze to mine, and adding a bit of *oomph* to my direction. It was a simple image, but one that worked well for most people. I noticed his stance shift slightly as if he was slightly encumbered.

"And remember. There's no guarantee I can discover anything from this trip that will give you peace."

Peace, I thought, *must be blissful.*

I crossed the threshold and felt a pulse of glee. I was on its territory now, and subject to its rules. I inhaled a steadying breath: I was going to teach this outdated bully what happened when you tangled with a spiritual specialist.

Wolsey released the deadbolt on the other door and heaved it open so more of the grey afternoon light penetrated the large atrium.

I scanned the room, remembering the film, and the young, happy women who had entered here.

"Let's not pussy-foot about," I said out loud, moving further in. "I'm here to find out what happened to these girls, and then I'm out."

I clearly projected the faces of Lindsay, Jasmine, and Tania, like handing out snapshots of victims to witnesses of a crime scene. "If I have to start dismantling some of your vortices to get answers I will."

Then I broadcast my credentials. A mental burst like a résumé so it knew I could carry out my intentions.

The first wave of hatred came fast. A body blow expected to stun, and no doubt to be followed by an uppercut to knock me down.

I stood my ground and it passed over my shields. I glanced behind at Wolsey's pale face. He was just inside the doorway.

"Stay there. You are not to follow me. If you feel ill then walk outside."

A curt nod in response. No doubt his macho notions were being short-circuited by that older part of his brain which was sounding klaxons. It was unlikely the house had ever shown him the full force of its ability.

I started towards the staircase. My stomach roiled at the emotional miasma I moved through. The suicide and its discovery was an old scream stuck on repeat. I dialled down the input as much as I could but I couldn't block it all out.

I called upon an ally for help, and at once the ghostly image of a magpie sailed in wide circles above my head.

Dive, I instructed.

It shot like a bullet to the first-floor landing piercing through a figure coalescing as if it was a badly pixelated image.

I heard a muffled *mumph*, like a detonation, and the cackle of Magpie's laughter as it swept back up to perch on the cloth-covered chandelier.

The house recoiled in shock. The atmosphere in the atrium immediately lessened, and it seemed as if more light streamed in through the doorway.

"The girls," I said throwing their images at it again. "What happened?"

There was a sense of regrouping and conferring. This place was not used to direct challenges or outright attack. The cost of energy was substantial, even though its metaphysical batteries were well charged from its contact with humans over the past two years.

It was now aware it could be harmed.

I sensed the approach of an envoy – it looked like a scullery maid, dressed all in white, but with scarlet eyes in her pallid face, and her hands coated in red gore up to her wrists.

Her mouth never moved while she spoke to me, but she restlessly wiped her hands up her forearms, spreading streaks of red.

"They were an offering, so we did not decline, *Albi.*"

I refused to rise to the bait of my father's affectionate name for me, but I deadened any sympathy.

"Did all three die here?"

It smiled, displaying pink teeth, and a pulse of triumph escaped it.

"We supped upon them well."

I frowned, there was a deceit hidden in truth.

"There must be remains."

"Our agents disposed of them."

Magpie screamed a warning, and I dodged to one side. Wolsey thundered past me, but snapped out an arm and snagged my backpack.

I staggered but slipped it off immediately – this was a move I had practised many times.

Around me the house gathered for a full assault while it tugged Wolsey's puppet strings.

I scooped dust from the floor and dashed it into his face. He yelled and dug at this eyes.

The maid extended her fingers, now hooked with wicked talons, and rushed at me.

I drew my athame and lunged. My hand sank into her chest and it was like plunging it into icy water.

A shock wave exploded in my face and I was knocked back. Magpie screeched and I sensed it diving at Wolsey, as he stumbled drunkenly at me.

My head pounded with a sudden, vindictive headache. But I gripped the shaft of the athame tight to ground myself again, and transferred it into my left hand.

Wolsey seemed to be fighting off the effects of the house's influence, but I couldn't have him getting in the way again. I bent my legs slightly to brace myself, swerved out of his clumsy grab, and punched him hard in the solar plexus.

I heard a gratifying *whoosh* as the air left his lungs, and he toppled to the floor. The pain should have been enough to break the connection, but I wasn't going to bet on that. I slipped the pouch of salt out of my jacket and inscribed a quick circle around the man. Then I buzzed through a shorthand of a banishing ritual I use for stopgap situations.

Magpie flew above my head adding its force as I intoned the words of cleansing.

At the final phrase the atrium fell silent, and all sense of presence withdrew.

Wolsey moaned. I backed away a few arms lengths toward the door in case he came up swinging.

"Stay in the circle," I snapped at him.

My knife was back in my right hand, held up. Threatening, sure, but I don't take chances.

He got up on one knee, his hand over his stomach, wheezing.

"Did you hurt those girls?" I asked, watching him carefully on all levels. Magpie circled above his head.

He raised his head and devastation was written all over his crumpled features. "Jas was the only one who ever stood up for me when we were kids. I would never have hurt her on purpose."

"But you know something."

He looked past me, lowered his face, shameful. "Tania."

I spun around, and there she was: older, better dressed, her hair cut professionally. Radiating power and assurance.

"Let me guess, Mary Foster, you now work in television?" I sent Magpie to circle above her and also sent out a careful probe to take stock of her abilities.

The dead wall I encountered indicated a person with considerable skills. Suddenly the chain of events made more sense.

I offered up a prayer to my Guardian spirits. It had been some time since I'd had to battle an adept in person.

She smiled with the smug satisfaction of a queen. "Tell your little birdie to fly away or I will fry its feathers."

Magpie drifted back but chattered curses at the woman.

Tania's gaze flickered to Wolsey. "Get up, Matt, and beat her to a pulp."

I scooted to one side so I could keep both them in my view as much as possible.

Wolsey stood up straight, his hands protective of his stomach, and shook his head. "No."

She narrowed her eyes slightly and I sensed a whip of influence cracking between the two of them. She must have him under thrall in some fashion, but the circle in which he stood also protected him from her.

"Don't move, Wolsey," I said. "She can't sway you while you're in that circle."

Tania's pretty crown slipped and I spotted the malevolent, greedy, darkness at her core.

"You!" she spat, "Think you can take *me*?"

Half a dozen bolts of pure energy zipped at me. I went down on one knee, placed my knuckles on the ground, and bolstered my defences. They hammered at my shields but did not penetrate. I knew it was a test. After this, she would have a better sense of my capabilities.

But of course, that worked both ways.

"My turn," I said, as I slipped my black tourmaline crystal out of my pocket. As I stood up I used the momentum to whip the stone at her head along with a piercing spell.

There was a satisfying *crack* as the stone smacked off the side of her forehead. I was already running at her as she staggered and I tackled her to the ground. I quickly rolled her into a hold, with her neck in my elbow. Carefully, I watched her eyes flutter as she fell unconscious.

Once I was sure she was out cold I dashed to my backpack and got out the plastic ties I kept there. As I cinched up her wrists behind her back I glanced over at Wolsey. He looked relieved, and anxious.

"What hold does she have over you?"

"She had some charm. I can't resist any of her orders for very long."

I quickly searched her, removing all objects – she was wearing an extremely potent necklace of lapis lazuli beads with a jewelled scarab pendent, and a cantripped ornate silver ring.

"Let me guess," I said as I continued frisking her, "you slept with her when you first met. And you've been doing her bidding since."

He nodded.

"Hate to tell you bud, but semen is very effective if you want to bespell someone." Deep in her coat pocket I found it: a glass vial with a stopper sealed in wax. Inside I saw hair, nail clippings, and a few herbs. The thing radiated cruelty and lust.

"Yuck," I said, and fished a blessed white linen cloth out of my backpack. I rolled the item up in it, and stamped on it with my Docs.

As it shattered Tania woke up. Good job she didn't have lasers for eyes or I'd have been a smoking ruin.

"What was the plan, Tania, bringing me here for your house to get a supercharged morsel? So confident your hold over Wolsey was impregnable?"

She sat up, her wrists behind her back, and glared at Wolsey.

"If you set me free now I will forgive you. Otherwise I will tell the police that you killed your cousin and Lindsay, and have been threatening me so I would remain silent ever since."

I laughed. "How about I tell them that you have been working to get control of the legacy that your mother felt she was cheated out of all those years ago? They'll also wonder why you inveigled your way into the girls' lives under a false name."

I looked at Wolsey. "You'll have to come clean for your part in this. You owe Jasmine and Lindsay that."

Tania pushed herself up on her feet, and her face was twisted into a furious visage.

"Even if I'm in jail I can curse you both. I will twist all who love you against you. Instead of comfort you will only ever know hatred."

I walked over to Wolsey, who seemed both looser and smaller, and kicked the circle of salt so it scattered wildly.

The house had been watching, I could sense it coiled up and waiting to strike at the weakest.

I indicated to the door. "Close one of the doors."

He hesitated and looked between Tania and me. I locked my gaze with his. "If you want to be free, then do as I say."

He moved quickly to the doorway and slowly pushed closed one of the big doors. The shadows increased in the room.

I backed out of the remaining open door and crossed the threshold to the other side.

Tania tottered toward us. "You can't leave me in here."

I thought of Jas and Lindsay and hardened my heart.

"You wanted to be Lady of the Manor," I said. "Enjoy your time together."

She attempted to rush out but we swung the door closed on her frightened face. Wolsey locked it on the faint thumps as Tania threw her body against the door.

I could feel the house seeking her out.

"What now?" asked Wolsey.

"You're going to the local police station to explain, and in a few hours they will come back here to collect Tania. What's left of her."

As we left I could hear her imperious commands through the thick doors.

I fancied they turned to screams before we departed the grounds.

The Hanging Tree

We're all told a story about our birth: the panicked drive to the hospital, or how long your mother suffered, or if you're lucky, how smoothly it went. Beginnings matter. No matter how difficult or easy, we like to recount them to each other.

Over time I gleaned the story of my birth from my grandmother, a few cousins, and even some of the kids at school. My Mam never talked about it. Just like she never made a big deal about my birthday. That's because my dad died the day I was born. So she was always conflicted about it, and I guess that's why she was always conflicted about me.

The story I pieced together is that late in her pregnancy my mam woke from a nightmare just after midnight, and my dad was gone from the bed. She told Gran she'd seen a vision of Dad walking down the road from our housing estate into the woods. It's a mean, dark tangle of trees and brambles, and it has a reputation. Few go in, except on a dare. And they always leave quickly afterwards.

Except me. I've been there a lot.

Mam heaved herself out of the bed, and stuck on wellies, and a raincoat. She had a terrible foreboding, and despite the darkness and the empty streets, she followed her instinct, and walked down to the woods. The one thing about my mam: she's brave, and she will risk anything for the one she loves.

She found a path into the woods easily enough, which was strange as the place always resisted entry. There was no moon, but she'd brought a torch with a fading battery. She had to jig it constantly to keep the light alive. The flickering spotlight led her to a massive, old tree. And Dad was hanging from it, still warm and kicking a little.

She screamed for help, and she tried to get him down, but she had no knife, and she couldn't get to where he had tied the rope far above her head. Then her waters broke, and from the story I have heard her labour came on fast. All she could do was squat down in the damp earth, and rake her fingers in grief and fury against the scaly bark of the hanging tree.

She had no mobile phone, and no one heard her cries. She gave birth to me, weeping in the gloom, with my father dangling above our heads.

Gran raised me for the first few months, as Mam couldn't cope for a while. And when I was sixteen I moved in with Gran because I couldn't cope with my mother. But I'd turned wild, hating myself and the ruin that lay between us. Our fights were spectacular.

Once she said to me, her face contorted and red, and her fists clenched, "Return to the darkness from where you came." It was a hammer blow to my heart, and I saw regret stain her eyes as soon as the words left her lips. Secretly, I wanted to throw myself at her, and beg for forgiveness for my cruel birth, but instead I curled my lip and said, "I wish you were dead." Soon after I packed my bags and moved a few streets over to my Gran's house.

I'd long realised that something hung over me, just as my dead father had once swayed above me the day I first drew breath. People nudged each other when I passed and whispered. I bent my head and avoided their looks. I felt weird so I dressed and acted weird. I grew to love giving people a shock or a scare. At school I was always asking questions and starting trouble. Teachers disliked my impertinence, but a few other kids were attracted to it, like Tom and Lizzie. Everyone called us the creepy three. We stuck together and fended off the real headcases in the school, the ones with the good homes and the cool clothes, who wanted to hurt us because they could get away with it. No one ever believed we weren't the instigators.

We weren't even stupid – well, Tom was a bit dim – but we preferred if no one had any expectations of us. The only class I cared about was art. I never missed it, and I kept quiet during the lesson. Ms Kilroy encouraged me, but never tried to be my friend. Sometimes I noticed her watching me, and in her appraisal I sensed a recognition. As if there was something in me she knew first-hand. But she never gave me 'the talk' or asked me to smarten up. She allowed me to be who I was because she seemed to trust I would come into my own in my own time. I respected her for that.

She even defended me when I created a big papier-mâché model of the hanging tree and pissed off a lot of people.

It happened a short while after I moved out from Mam's house, when I was angry all the time. Even Lizzie, who was the most easy-going of our trio, laid into me after I snarled at her and called her Lezzie, her most despised nickname.

"Fuck off and come back when you want to be my friend," she'd yelled. So I'd stomped off in strop, whipping my bag about, deeply ashamed and trying to figure out how to apologise without actually apologising.

Under grey skies I slunk down to the woods. I wrapped my anger and guilt around me like armour and burst my way through the heaps of wet leaves and barriers of wizened briars. I stood before the hanging tree, the one that had killed my father. It was huge, old, and the many outstretched branches made it look like the centre of a spider's web. The place reeked of rot. I dug a lighter out of my school bag and flicked it open. The click sounded dull in the space. Like an empty threat.

"You deserve to die," I told the tree.

A light breeze swayed through the woods setting off a cacophony of creaks and snaps. A shower of droplets fell onto my head from the branches above and soaked my hair. I felt I was being mocked. The wood was saturated with rain.

"I could come back with petrol," I warned. I knew Gran kept some in the back shed for her lawnmower. Not much, but enough to start a fire. I visualised it in my mind: the cleansing fire licking up the body of the tree, and the gouts of smoke. I imagined Mam's happiness at its demise.

A gust swept through the tree, rattling twigs and dashing more water at my face.

I grinned at it, and snapped the lighter shut.

Then I pulled out my phone and snapped photos of the tree's enormity. The idea formed in my head to recreate it as my end of term project for art class. Afterwards, maybe I'd burn it.

Or perhaps I'd present it to my mother.

I spent weeks making the bloody thing. Gran was happy I had a project and collected loads of newspaper for me. She wasn't too pleased about me stealing coat hangers for the wire. Grumbling, she picked up all my clothes I'd dumped at the bottom of my closet and put them on plastic hangers instead.

She also didn't like me using half the kitchen table, but the light was best in there, and it was easy to clean up afterwards. For a couple of weeks we ate side by side at one section of the table, and that closeness felt nice.

I loved the mess, and the feel of the wet sticky strands against my skin as I layered them into shape. As I built it I sensed something ease in my head and in my heart. The anger slipped out of my fingers and wove itself into the tree's lines. It grew into a strange and weird beauty.

Near the end, when I was painting it carefully, trying to make it as realistic as possible, Gran stood behind me watching my efforts. Finally, she said, "Good work girl, but I'll breathe easier when it's gone from the house."

The evening I finished I stepped back and admired the result. It looked like the tree had taken root and sprouted from the centre of the kitchen table. The knotted trunk gleamed with varnish, and the clusters of red, green, and gold silk leaves stirred in the slightest draft.

That night I dreamed I walked into the woods. A sickle moon offered a sliver of light, and thorns like razor wire rolled away at my approach. Shrubs and trees moved aside, offering a clear parade to the giant tree at its centre. I stood in front of it, and instead of hatred or anger I sensed love and affection. Branches stretched down and stroked my hair, leaves brushed my cheek. And in my mind I heard, *Child of mine, I offer you a gift.*

A gnarled bough in the shape of a hand swept up and pointed.

Mam hung by a rope from the tree. Her eyes protruded, and her fingers were frozen in their last position: trying to claw the noose from her neck.

As I sucked in a breath to *scream* I noticed the man standing beneath her: his arms open and wide, and a delighted smile lighting up his features. Shock bottled the cry in my throat.

Jump, my darling, he said to the corpse. *Then we'll dance together always.*

And my mother rictus-grinned and jerked the rope from her neck. She landed clumsily beside him, and he took her in his arms.

They danced in shambling circles, their necks lopsided, as the branches clattered a beat.

I fled.

Lizzie helped me carry the tree into the school, and up the stairs to the art room. We didn't pay attention to the groups of parents in tight knots by the gates, because we ignored their judgments daily. It was only when I noticed Ms Kilroy's reaction to the model that I knew something was awry. I was certain she would love it, but instead her brow knotted.

"Deirdre," she began, a careful tone to her voice, "have you heard the news today?"

I blinked. I never listened to the news. Gran always gave me a rundown of the goings on in the world and in the neighbourhood at dinner every evening, whether I wanted to hear it or not.

Ms Kilroy did an unusual thing. She laid a hand lightly on my arm, as if to brace me. "Leo Montgomery committed suicide last night. He hanged himself down in those woods..." and she trailed off, but I heard the intended words: *where your father died.*

I said nothing, but the dream from the previous night replayed in my mind. Leo was two years above me, popular. I'd never spoken to him.

Lizzie stepped forward, defensive.

"She's been working on it for weeks! She didn't do it on purpose."

"I know –" Ms Kilroy started, but it was too late. The first class for the morning was pushing in the door. They all saw the tree, fixed on a table by the large window. In unison their gazes swept over to glare at me.

In my mind I heard the low growling of a pack of wolves.

Later that day, while I waited in the principal's office, someone hung a doll from the branches of my tree and snapped a picture of it on their mobile phone. Soon it was online. Eventually it made the newspapers.

SICK JOKE OF TROUBLED TEEN, ran the headline beside the photo. I was lucky I was sixteen, so I wasn't named, but everyone knew it was me.

I was suspended for two weeks, despite Ms Kilroy's intervention. The text messages began to roll in immediately. WITCHES HANG!! shouted one. U'LL JOIN UR DAD IN HELL!!! screamed another.

Mam came over and conferred with Gran behind closed doors. A social worker with a kind demeanour had a long, earnest conversation with me over a cup of tea, using Gran's best china service.

I had to stay offline, because it was too upsetting to read the threats and abuse. I refused to go out. The world became a small, suffocating place, made worse by the concern being pumped at me in between the barrage of hate. Lizzie and Tom were not allowed to visit. I understood. They had to survive.

One night a pebble clipped my window and I peeked out, fearful of what I would see. Lizzie stood there with a sign on which she'd drawn a heart. She was crying. I nodded. She smiled in a broken fashion, looked about, and ran.

"It'll blow over," they kept saying to me. "Some other scandal will take over the Internet and they'll forget about this," but I had no doubts that this was the end of my life in this place. In fact, I didn't know where I could go where the online breadcrumbs wouldn't eventually lead people to my door.

Mam recognised it too. She scraped together money and began the process of relocating us. Gran was staying put. It was too hard for her to move. I saw the strain etched upon her lined face, and I *wanted* to leave. I had wrecked her life, and all she'd ever done was show kindness to a wretched girl.

One day the doorbell rang, and I heard a murmur of voices. My Gran sounded upset. "No!" she said loudly. "Take it somewhere else!"

I crept down the stairs so I could spy on the hallway. A delivery man was trying to push the model of the tree into the doorway, blocked by Gran. The model had been crushed in places, but it was mostly intact.

I took a deep breath and forced my legs to move. "It's okay Gran," I said, willing my voice to sound neutral. I smiled at the delivery man, but he averted his gaze, as if too afraid to look squarely at me. "We'll take it," I assured him, and I heaved the difficult form into our kitchen where it had first taken shape.

Mam was sitting at the table, a mug of tea in hand. I hadn't heard her come in, but I later discovered she'd often drop by using the back door to get a progress report about me from Gran.

I nodded at her and pushed the tree onto the table. It sucked all the conversation out of the room. Nothing swung from the branches, thankfully.

Mam stood up, the mug in her hand. She moved to the same side of the table as Gran and I, and we all regarded the tree.

"You made it look beautiful," she said, finally.

Gran sniffed. "They cut it down."

"What?" My nerves jangled, upset. I stared at the small model of the tree and remembered its vast presence.

"I understand," Mam said quietly. "I wanted to."

"Sean Montgomery, his father. Went at it with a chainsaw. He didn't get it all. It's that big. But the branches that you could..." She sighed. "They're gone."

"Such pain," Mam whispered. She moved back to her chair and sat down heavily.

"I'll get rid of it," I said, pointing at the model.

Gran raised an eyebrow.

"I made it. It's my responsibility."

My mother and grandmother exchanged a look. They seemed pleased in an indefinable away, which grated.

"Later," I grumped, and stamped up the stairs.

I waited until Gran was snoring, and the lights were out along the street. I was well wrapped up, wearing a reliable head-lamp, with my mobile phone charged up fully. I slipped downstairs and edged the model off the table. It was awkward, but I took my time getting it out the front door. I closed the door carefully behind me and hauled the replica of the tree down the street. I crossed to one side to avoid passing the Feeney's gnome-infested garden with the yappy dog.

There was no traffic, and soon I was off the road on the short muddy path to the woods. It was churned up and hard from a light frost. I switched on the lamp strapped to my forehead. Its LED light cut through the night in an unnatural way and turned my breath into puffs of white mist.

Someone had hacked a route into the woods. Frozen sap gleamed pearl-like in the darkness. The ripped and torn branches were arrayed like distressed hands, splayed in protest. I arrived at the centre, and the sight of the ruined tree.

Sawdust shone in the dark grass. Chunks of wood lay tossed about. The giant tree had shrunk: its limbs lopped off, and its force diminished.

Now, it lingered as a punished object.

I dropped the model to the ground in front of the mutilated tree. An awful grief rose up in my throat and transformed into a furious shriek. I lifted up my leg and smashed my boot into the model. I could not bear to remember what had been here before. Shouting curses I kicked and stamped until it was a mess of pulp and jagged wire.

Exhaustion curbed me eventually.

I stood up straight. It was eerily quiet, except for my panting breath.

The light streamed upwards into the topmost branches, mostly untouched by Sean's crusade.

Something shifted again the light. The sound of wings, a bird flapping perhaps.

Anger soured into fear.

I stood still, desperately slowing and quietening my breath so I could hear clearly.

A wind sprung up, and the branches rattled a beat.

A bright, high-pitched cry pierced the night.

I was born here, I thought. *That must count against the death.*

The bone chill of the deep night closed in. Moved by instinct I reached up and switched off my light. Darkness enveloped me, but at the same time the expanse of stars sprang into existence above. The ground seemed to shrink away.

Is this what he saw last? I wondered. *Did he regret the rope in that moment?*

Tears streamed down my face.

I hope he did not look down. I hope he focused on the stars through the branches of the hanging tree.

I waited until the dawn bleached the stars, before I walked home, stiff-legged.

The Diet

"We've nothing in common any more," Lucy said.

The pepperoni calzone in Frank's stomach congealed into a mixture of acid, fat, and fear. "But..."

Lucy raised her bronzed hand in an imperious demand for silence. A waiter with slicked-back hair interpreted the gesture as a cry for condiments and glided to their table with a massive pepper mill.

"Three years, Frank." She paused to smile up at the waiter. "No thank you." She revolved her attention back to Frank, her tone frosty. "Haven't we wasted enough time?"

Frank shook his head at the waiter, and thought he detected a flicker of fraternal sympathy in the server's face as he departed.

How many men had that waiter seen humiliated?

"Frank!" her tone was sharp and exasperated. She rose – her red curls flounced – and the chair screeched a protest. A neighbouring couple frowned at the noise. Lucy hauled her coat from the back of the chair.

Wedged into a corner, his belly trapped by the table's lip, Frank struggled to stand. "Lucy..."

"Don't bother getting up," she sneered. The waiter materialised and held Lucy's Burberry overcoat so she could ease into it. "You're so helpful," she murmured to him.

"Anything for such a *bella donna*."

Lucy's cheek's pinked.

Frank hated the waiter's mismatched Dublin-meets-Milan accent, smooth movements, and queasy charm.

Lucy opened her purse and extracted enough euros to cover the bill with a generous tip.

Frank protested. "Let me pay at least!"

Lucy pressed the notes into the waiter's eager hand. "*Grazie mille*," her Italian accent was crude, but sexy. The waiter's smile smarmed wider.

"Please, Lucy, don't leave." Frank despised the whine in his voice. At least the waiter had the manners to vanish. "I'm sorry. I'll change."

She was already angled towards the exit. When she turned her lovely face towards him it was stripped of masks. Brutal contempt glared at him.

"Change? You've changed enough. Look at you, Frank. What happened?"

He bent his head, and noticed the straining buttons on his striped shirt, the sauce drips on his Homer Simpson polyester tie, and the buckle that tugged on the final notch of his belt. Frank could not meet her gaze or respond to her question.

The bell over the door jangled.

She was gone.

"Christ, Frank, you look like shite." Mattie's sing-song Cork accent rose to new heights. He shoved his chair away from his workstation.

Frank slumped into his swivel chair. "Lucy dumped me." He slipped on his phone headset.

His friend switched from concerned to outraged. "The bitch! Why?"

"Something about different directions."

Mattie ignored the blinking light on his phone. "I bet the only thing going in different directions were her legs, boyo."

Jack, their supervisor, bore down on them, a pissed-off expression on his face and a heavy folder in his manicured hand.

Mattie zoomed back into his niche and gestured with an imaginary pint glass in his hand. "Consolation drinks later?"

Frank had no time to answer before Jack launched into a tirade about the evils of long lunches. Throughout his supervisor's lecture, during which Frank nodded at the appropriate moments, Mattie's insinuation looped in Frank's mind so his thoughts circled around one question.

"Do you think she was cheating on me?"

Mattie pushed one of the two pints of Guinness sitting the mahogany counter at Frank. "Get that into you." Behind the bar, hanging between arched mirrored alcoves, the mounted Stag's head stared down at them with its small black glass eyes. Frank averted his gaze, sucked a mouthful of creamy stout, and tried to avoid being jostled by the thirsty punters calling out orders to the barman.

Mattie wiped white foam from his moustache and sighed before his expression turned sombre. "I saw her with someone."

Frank swallowed more Guinness. It tasted bitter.

"Last Thursday. On Grafton Street. They looked friendly – too friendly." Lucy told Frank she was out with her girlfriends that night. He didn't inform Mattie; dignity was scare enough.

"You're better off without her," Mattie added, "she was a stuck-up cow."

Frank regarded his reflection in the slick dark surface of the pint glass. A tiny head and massive body stared back at him: a fat clown.

He pushed the porter away. "I'm going to win her back."

Frank marched towards his apartment. His arms pumped with the force of good intentions. As he passed the brightly lit window of a travel agency he slowed. In a diorama an Egyptian pyramid loomed over a svelte couple: the tanned man in trunks had perfect abs, and the athletic woman in the swimsuit resembled Lucy. She always wanted to visit Egypt, but Frank loathed the idea of the heat and foreign food and put her off until she gave up pestering him.

He was going to get back into shape. He'd join a gym or return to rugby. On Monday he'd talk to Jack and change his attitude about his job. Maybe change career. He'd scrape together enough cash for an adventure holiday: Egypt, Peru, China... somewhere exciting and exotic.

Frank wheeled around a corner and into a narrow side street, the location of his favourite bakery. Every morning Marco the barista brewed Frank a grande cappuccino and sold him a *pain au chocolat*. The smell of baking bread and freshly ground coffee prompted a grumble from his stomach.

Most of all he needed to go on a diet.

Frank crossed the road to elude temptation and noticed a tiny shop bright with fresh paint. A luminous sign pasted to cardboard leaned in the bare window.

"The Diet never fails!" its gaudy headline blared. Frank read the rest of the neatly printed page. It boasted of a diet plan that guaranteed dramatic weight loss within a month. The old pie-loving Frank would have dithered, then walked away. Instead, Frank opened the door, and approached the chrome counter.

A gaunt man wearing glasses with tinted lenses glanced up from a book. The florescent light shimmered off his marble skin and bleached his blond hair white. His nostrils flared as if he smelled something fragrant. "May I help you?" His voice had an east European burr.

"I want to lose weight."

The man smiled and offered his hand. "You're in the right place. I'm Goran." His limp handshake was moist, and Frank itched to wipe his palm on his trousers. "Our product is a mixture of freeze-dried herbs, plants, and minerals, fashioned from an ancient recipe." Goran reached under the counter and presented a round plastic container with a lurid purple label. "You take two heaped tablespoons a day in water, instead of food, and for your third meal you can eat whatever you like."

"That's all?" Frank picked it up. Hypnotic yellow letters boasted that the ingredients were "All Natural!"

"We also offer a support meeting once a week for our customers, free of charge."

Frank nodded. "How much?"

"That box costs 100 euros."

"What?" Frank almost dropped it. "That's outrageous."

"What price tag do you put on your health?" Goran's long fingers stroked the container. "If you follow the plan exactly, and you are not completely satisfied after a month your money will be refunded."

"Do you take it yourself?"

Goran's thin lips peeled back from his teeth. "Oh yes."

Frank dug his wallet out of his pocket. "I suppose you have to say that, eh?" He counted out two fifty-euro notes.

Goran placed the container into a brown paper bag and offered it to him. "The next meeting is 6pm, this Friday. Please come."

Frank took the package. He needed motivation. "See you Friday, Goran."

Frank paused on the threshold of the shop for a moment. He was making a change. Soon his life would be different.

In his kitchen, Frank eyed the glass doubtfully. Shredded moss-like clumps floated within a dark bilious liquid. He sniffed it and yanked it away from his face. It stank of stagnant pond.

He inhaled a quick breath and gulped a mouthful.

Frank made it to the sink before he spat it out. The taste of rotting fish and a slimy texture coated his tongue. He picked up the glass and held it over the plughole, ready to toss it.

"100 euros," he said. He smelled the concoction again. It wasn't as bad as the first whiff. He imagined Lucy, supple and tanned, lounging in a bikini on their cruise down the River Nile.

He knocked it back and willed his constricting throat to accept the goop.

It would be worth it.

The next morning's drink wasn't as bad, although Frank had a couple of dodgy moments when he thought he would vomit it back up.

He didn't grab a taxi or ride the bus to work but walked the whole way. He passed the bakery and waved to Marco through the window.

When he arrived in the office he was sweating and red faced, but he tackled his backlist of calls and by lunchtime he was ahead of schedule.

Mattie peered over the partition. "You angling for a promotion?"

At lunch, Frank polished off a bowl of soup, and a steak with mashed potatoes. He tried not to contemplate that it would be his last solid food for twenty-four hours.

Mattie's eyebrows rose when Frank refused after-work pints but didn't comment. Frank even walked home through the lashing rain.

That evening the mixture didn't taste any better, but Frank gagged it down.

He remembered the first night he'd made love to Lucy, when his waist was thinner and he didn't mind leaving the light on.

Soon, his former body and girlfriend would return.

The water was salty, warm, and dark. Illumination came from the phosphorous glow on the talons of rock that clawed up from the black void below.

Far above Frank sunlight sparkled on the surface.

The pressure changed. Something waited below. A chill seeped into his bones, and a primitive terror seized him.

He was naked, and underwater!

Panic flooded him and he trashed up towards the light. His lungs shrieking for air.

Frank woke, choking.

On Friday evening when Frank opened the shop door Goran was sitting in the same spot as if he never moved.

"Welcome, Frank." Goran rose, and pointed to an entrance behind a curtain of beads. "How are you getting on?"

"It tastes vile you know."

Goran inclined his head. "Your palate will adjust."

The beads clicked as Frank walked into the dim stuffy room. Three people sat on plastic chairs arranged in a circle. Against the back wall a table covered in a white paper tablecloth held a kettle, cups, a box of tea, a jar of instant coffee, a carton of milk, and jugs of water. Candles provided soft lighting.

Frank nodded at the two women and the man and joined them in the circle. He coughed. They watched him. A plain stocky woman smiled at him and flashed dimples.

"Um, I'm Frank," he said.

"Dora," the taller, darker woman.

"Maeve," said the dimpled woman.

"Brian," offered the huge man. His arms were crossed across his chest like a barrier.

Goran walked in and sat among them. "We'll begin with a meditation for relaxation, and then we'll discuss your progress. Now, if you will close your eyes please..."

Afterwards, Frank sipped his coffee and listened to Maeve. "My last boyfriend joked about my weight all the time. He'd compare me to other women in public, and in front of friends or family."

"What a tosser," the words slipped out.

Maeve's dimples made another appearance. "I might have low self-esteem, but I'm not an idiot. I broke up with him." Her voice crumpled at the end.

"My ex didn't like my weight gain either." Frank swigged more coffee. "I played rugby at college when we met. But, when I started working I found it hard to make time for it. She encouraged me to join her gym, but..." he shrugged to imply his disinterest.

Behind him he heard Dora speak to Goran. "I'm always submerged in an ocean. But there's something in there with me. Something that frightens me."

Maeve laid her hand on Frank's arm, so he didn't hear Goran's murmured response. "As long as you're not losing weight for her, Frank." She paused. "Once I tried to change for a man... my ex-husband. He left anyway, and I gained even more weight." She laughed, but her eyes brimmed.

"I don't think you need to change."

She smiled up at him, before she checked her watch. "I have to go. See you next Friday?"

"Looking forward to it." And he was.

It became natural to breathe underwater.

At first Frank stayed close to the surface, but over time he explored further. He swam between the needles of rock, and examined the carbuncles and growths that glowed white, blue, and pink.

Once he thought he saw the flash of a body, but it vanished below.

The water cooled the deeper he went, and it was harder to see.

The first time he sank far below he spied a mammoth shadow. Dread paralysed his limbs and he drifted helplessly towards its monstrous darkness.

He woke screaming, his heart pounding, and could not close his eyes until dawn.

That morning he skipped the drink and stopped at the bakery. Marco, delighted to welcome back a wayward customer, gave him the pastry for free. Frank was starving by the time he arrived at work, but when he bit into the light pastry the sugary taste sickened him. He offered the rest of it to Mattie. Frank found it hard to concentrate, and a mug of coffee didn't help or satisfy his parched mouth. His stomach cramped, and he longed for the satisfying texture of his morning tonic.

By lunchtime he was shivering and sweaty. A taxi carried him home, and when he measured the tablespoons of supplement his hand shook – from anticipation.

After the drink was ready, Frank hesitated. What was in that stuff? What was it doing to him? He closed his eyes and thought of the solace of deep waters. When he opened them again he noticed the red light blinking on his home phone.

He pushed the button to retrieve the voicemail. Lucy spoke in the brusque tones she used with tradesman: "Hi Frank. I dropped by and picked up the rest of my things. I left my key on the hall table since I won't need it again. Bye."

Frank slammed the handset on the counter and the plastic case split in half. He flung it across the room and it shattered against the wall, inside the ghost square where their shared photograph used to hang.

He grabbed the drink and gulped it back fast. Immediately he felt stronger, in control.

Lucy hadn't seen the new Frank yet, so of course she still thought of him as a pudgy loser. He stuck his finger inside the rim of the glass and wiped the gooey residue off. It tasted delicious.

When she saw how much he'd changed, she'd come back. His finger dipped into the glass again and snagged a wet clump. Frank sucked it into his mouth like spaghetti and licked his lips.

Or maybe...

"There are plenty of fish in the sea," he said out loud, and laughed.

On the morning of his third Friday meeting Jack invited Frank into his office.

Jack stabbed his finger at a graph on his desk. "Whatever you're doing, don't stop." A mauve line spiked upwards on the chart. "Your sales are climbing, you're on time, efficient, and ahead of schedule. If you remain at this pace we're going to discuss the terms of your promotion by month's end."

As they shook hands outside the office door, Jack paused to reappraise him. "Have you lost weight?"

Mattie pounced on him by the cooler as Frank drank a large cup of water. "Are you joining us for drinks tonight?"

Frank bent and poured another cupful. He shook his head.

"Have you become a hermit or something?"

"I'm going for a swim and then I've a meeting..."

"What meeting?"

Frank stood up and swirled the water in his plastic cup. He checked to see if anyone was within eavesdropping distance. "I'm on a new diet, and there's a support meeting..."

"I thought you'd lost weight. Hey, maybe I could try it." Mattie patted his modest waist. "You can never be too slim."

Frank hesitated. He didn't want Mattie to go to the meeting. He'd make fun of it and being such a cheap bastard he'd whine about the cost of the supplement. Plus, it wouldn't work for him.

Mattie wasn't *suitable*.

"Did you just sniff me?"

Frank frowned at his friend. "What?"

"You just sniffed me."

"I don't know what you're talking about!"

"Look, it's called Brute Force."

Frank's bemused expression elicited an explanation.

"My aftershave. I'm assuming you're too afraid to ask what it's called. The birds go mad for it."

"Thanks for the tip." Frank returned to his desk, glad for the diversion.

During the meeting, Frank could not pry his attention from Maeve. She glowed. She smiled. She'd slimmed down.

Their ranks had climbed to ten. Dora, Brian, Maeve and he were happy to encourage the newcomers to stick to the regime.

"I like the taste of it now," Dora said. Frank nodded. The newbies were sceptical, but the testaments of weight loss were impressive.

Afterwards the four of them refused tea and coffee and drank water from the jugs Goran supplied.

"You're even off the tea?" a hefty middle-aged woman asked Frank, aghast.

He placed his empty glass on the table. "It's important to keep hydrated, and water is better, purer. I can't get enough of it." With his peripheral vision he watched Maeve offer advice to a spotty bespectacled youth.

Jealousy surged in him, hot and sudden. He turned and touched her arm. A strange noise vibrated in his chest. The young man stepped backwards. Maeve tilted her face up and responded in a similar manner but at a higher pitch. The boy retreated.

Frank and Maeve joined hands and smiled.

His swimming improved. He darted in between the pillars of rock, and dove deeper. His eyes had adjusted to the gloomy waters. Now, so much more was visible.

The previous night he had discovered the wreck. It was covered in growths, shells, and cankers. Iridescent sediment drifted upwards from its gnarled surface, which curved down into the darkness. Huge masts, like spines, erupted along one side. He could not discern what kind of craft it had once been.

He floated towards the crust, and a flash of white between the masts attracted him. He moved closer.

She was naked.

Bone-white hair floated in tendrils around her ghostly face and huge eyes. Her movements possessed the grace of one born to this place. He swam closer. Her presence was magnetic, alluring.

When he stared into her eyes the shock of recognition electrified him.

Maeve.

She kissed him hard, and it inflamed him.

Pain lanced through his tongue, and he pulled back. She smiled at him. Her sharp teeth tinged pink.

His tongue wiggled in an odd way. He touched his fingers to it, and felt its new bifurcated form.

He seized her and plundered her mouth. Their tongues separated, tiny serrated edges slid out and their interlocking tongues sealed together. Pain and desire mounted.

They wrapped their limbs around each other, drifted down towards the hulking wreck, and thrashed and squirmed in ecstasy upon its cancerous hide.

The following evening Frank saw Maeve at the swimming pool. Her pale figure, encased in a swimsuit with a scaled pattern, was a beacon among the clumsy bodies that churned and wallowed in the water. He swam to her, nimbly, and she turned before he could touch her.

For a long moment they stared at each other. Words were superfluous.

His fingers encircled hers.

A whale of a man surged past them towards the steps. "Out of the way!" He brushed against Frank and recoiled. "Freak," he muttered under his breath.

Frank didn't care. He climbed out of the pool and offered Maeve a hand when she followed. They paid no heed to the whispers that trailed after them.

That night Maeve moved into his apartment.

"Is that you Frank?"

He turned in the crowded street, his hand still linked with Maeve's.

Lucy stared at him, her expression shocked. He smiled and walked to where she stood transfixed.

"My God, you've lost so much weight." Concern wrinkled around her eyes. "You're not ill, are you? You seem... pale."

Frank lifted his sunglasses over his forehead, and squinted in the mellow evening light. "I'm fine, I've been on a diet. Lucy, this is Maeve," Maeve's hand tightened in his grip. The women nodded at each other.

"I want to thank you, Lucy," Frank said. Lucy leaned closer. "If you hadn't been honest with me I wouldn't have changed." His lips pulled back from his teeth in a smile, and Lucy stepped back. "I wouldn't have met Maeve."

Lucy clutched her Louis Vuitton handbag to her chest like a shield. "I'm glad, Frank, that you're... Are you sure you're well?" She reached out to touch his arm, but Maeve stepped between them. Frank raised his hand and stroked the sensitive ridges on the back of Maeve's neck –

hidden by the collar of her shirt – and she relaxed.

"I've never been better." His hand dropped down and Meave's hand found it instantly. "We must be going. It was good seeing you again."

Lucy nodded, her face tight with suppressed words, and walked away.

Maeve looked up at him, and Frank marvelled at the fine cheekbones that sculpted her face now The Diet was erasing her excess flesh. She had dyed her hair platinum blond, and in the sunlight her complexion seemed dusted with frost.

"How did I ever find her attractive?" Frank said. "She's so tanned, and muscular."

Maeve grimaced in agreement. "And that red hair!" She thrilled low in her throat and kissed him on the cheek. Her tongue darted out to lick his skin. "She was a fool."

He shivered, and pulled her body close to his. "Let's go for a swim," he muttered into her ear.

The new office had a large window, real timber desk, and an ergonomic chair. Frank adjusted the slatted blinds to cut the glare of the morning sun into a more agreeable light. He removed his sunglasses.

Jack knocked on the open door and strolled into the room. "If you continue to accomplish in six months what you did in six weeks then I'll have to watch out for my job."

Frank sank into the chair behind his desk and slid his hands over the surface. He felt the texture of his desk and stroked the metallic sides of his sleek monitor. His list of calls glowed on the screen. "I must get to work," he said. Frank turned the new headset over in his fingers and touched its shiny contours before he placed it in his ears.

Jack grinned at him. "My favourite words. I won't interrupt." Jack paused at the doorway and turned. "Sorry to mention this, Frank, but Susan in HR said there'd been complaints about a health shake you've been making in the kitchen?"

"It's an old herbal recipe. It speeds up the metabolism and promotes well-being."

"Yeah, well Susan says it stinks like hell. Actually, I think she used the term fish guts."

Frank smiled. "It is pungent. Now that I have this office I will prepare it here."

"Fantastic. You're looking great by the way. I'm not sure about the blond hair, but I wish I knew your secret" Jack pinched his waist, which hinted at middle-aged doughiness.

Frank inhaled but did not taste the correct *need.* "A healthy diet, plenty of exercise, and a loving girlfriend."

Jack raised his hands in shock. "Whoa! How easy. You forgot a strong work ethic, Frank."

"That too."

His boss shook his head in amazement. "You're a saint."

"I'm committed." Frank looked down at his paperwork, and Jack took the cue to leave and bother less dedicated employees.

Later, after the office was empty and quiet, Frank opened his desk drawer and removed the boxes of supplement. His fingers traced the label and he wondered how he ever thought it was garish. Now he could see the lines of blue and red that underlay the purple and etched a star that enclosed a staring eye. It was attractive and vibrant.

It watched over him.

He unfolded the list Goran handed him at the last meeting. He touched the headset by his mouth and tapped in the numbers. The phone rang, and a woman's voice answered.

"Your friend, Dora, recommended you for a one-time offer that guarantees weight loss in a month, or your money back. Do you have a few moments to discuss the revolutionary weight-loss regime, The Diet?"

A dozen of them floated in a circle above the knotted surface of the wreck.

Maeve glided by Frank's side. Goran hung opposite them. Soon there would be more.

They opened their mouths, and the glorious vibrations that emerged were a hymn to the deep and the creatures that slumbered in its shadows.

A movement beneath him. Frank glanced down and noticed a leprous growth crumble off and sink into the void. Elated, he squeezed Maeve's hand, and intoned the song that would wake the slumbering giant.

A corrugated shelf of rock and shells cracked, and slid off. Underneath, a gargantuan eye glistened. A wicked black pupil the size of Frank's head darted under its scabrous lid and fixed on his adoring gaze.

What remained of his puny human faculties fled – unable to bear the regard of a creature that had witnessed the birth of stars and the demise of countless civilisations.

Frank joined with the chorus of dirges, and prayed for the time when their numbers would be enough to shake their ancient master truly awake.

Involuntary Muscle

Lilly wakes to the taste of ash.

Immediately she checks: Dave, asleep beside her, their tidy bedroom, and the tang of citrus rising from the crisp sheets. Serenity and order exude from the taupe walls, soft carpets, and framed photographs of flowers.

Home. *Her* home.

Quiet. Peaceful. Clean.

Relief buoys her into her morning routine. She spends extra time scrubbing her teeth, and gargles twice with mouthwash before she dresses in her classy but practical suit, and kisses Dave goodbye with spearmint-fresh lips. Despite being five minutes behind schedule she arrives at work early, because she values her reputation for punctuality and always factors in extra time for traffic hiccups.

From her office, Lilly continues her impeccable job as geek-wrangler – her private term for her job as project manager of a variety of incredibly smart but socially awkward software engineers. She marshals their genius in productive ways without invoking their contempt, despite her disinterest in the trappings of tech culture: Lilly doesn't blog or boing-boing, she sings along to sappy country and western tunes, and she prefers to play tennis on a court than on a Wii. Yet, she is a balm for their highly tweaked geek nerves, and she always coaxes the code from their exacting fingers on time and bug-free.

She begins each conversation with a smile so automatic she can no longer ascertain its authenticity.

Lilly returns home as the evening rushes towards night, to cook a meal with Dave – salad on the side – and maybe watch *The Daily Show*, or a movie they recorded that's cluttering up the queue. She hates leaving shows in limbo. Their expectation of attention creates a vague anxiety in her mind. Every two weeks she erases them, cleans them all out, seen or unseen, and every time she wishes she could point the remote at the caged memories in her mind that stink of smoke and hate, and click 'delete all'.

If she could just do that, Lilly knows she could tear off the pinned-on smile, and loosen her tight throat so she could say something *real*, rather than squeezing out sterile, safe words.

Another headache throbs at her temple. Stress, her doctor diagnosed, because there's nothing physically wrong, and what has she to complain about? Sometimes Lilly chases back an Ambien with a glass of Shiraz at night to help her sleep, because if she's still staring at the ceiling at 3am, listening to Dave's soft snores rising up beside her, the quarantined thoughts will rattle the bars and demand attention.

She and Dave make love. Unlike her mother's generation Lilly's always known about her clit, and isn't afraid to ask for and expect pleasure. She loves the taste of sweat on skin, the tangle of limbs, ecstatic breaths on half-parted lips, and the urgent thrusts towards bliss. It is her favourite way to dissolve into sleep: liberated by the glorious white-out of post-orgasm. Exorcised, her mind slows, stills, and she eases into a comfortable slumber with Dave's arm snaked around her waist and his breath warm upon her dewed neck.

But the next morning she wakes with a parched acrid taste in her mouth. As if the brackish well of discontent brims across her tongue and is stopped only by her teeth. She checks her calendar, and at lunchtime makes a trip to the pharmacy. The prospect is unthinkable. She has always been so careful.

She cannot wait, and at work locks herself in the bathroom cubicle, pees on the stick, and waits three minutes. "Pregnant," it declares. She laughs – a brittle unfunny sound – at technology's blunt truth. Lilly can almost hear a siren wail as the imprisoned thoughts in her mind riot for release.

For a couple of days she resides in a state of shock, and seeks comfort in details of beta tests and employee reviews which she can schedule and rate. Her doctor confirms the results, so she breaks the news to Dave and accepts his joy with a smile she believes must be genuine. After all, it's the logical next step, the relentless evolution that swept her and Dave from girlfriend/boyfriend, through live-in-lovers, joint homeowners, and finally to marriage's secure shores. She knows Dave will be a wonderful father.

Her mantra becomes 'We're so happy!', even though every time she says it she wipes her tongue across her teeth to erase imaginary grit. It is the effluent of Lilly's involuntary muscle, which pumps assurances and breathes evasions.

Fear begins its assault. The physical changes are difficult enough – she endures puking with white-knuckled forbearance – as are the endless horror stories that women cheerily recount in the smug fashion of battle-scarred veterans, but she can't shake the awful realisation that the baby is growing inside of her, residing in the same space as her unfiltered corrosive past.

She fears the baby will be infected by it. Lilly dreams of birthing monsters, babies with claw-like limbs and lopsided faces, who attack her as soon as they gush from her lumbering body. When she hints at this to a friend with two curly-haired miracles, the flicker of repugnance makes Lilly swallow the words back, to join the crowd of unuttered wrongness jostling inside of her that she never dares set free.

At the first scan she squeezes Dave's fingers so hard he makes a joke about how she maintains the programmers' attention at work, but the baby is deemed perfect, normal. Lilly relaxes a little. She sings to the child, listens to meditation tapes, and tries to breathe out the anger and allow only positive thoughts to halo them both. Everyone swears she will be an outstanding mother, but Lilly has never shown anyone, not even Dave, the ugliness battened down inside. If they glimpsed its raw unrefined fury she knows they would wrest the baby from her at birth. Another reason to beam, admit nothing, and corral worry with books, doula interviews, and childbirth plans.

At eight months they decide upon a name – Siri – for the girl pummelling Lilly's ribs and bladder. When the baby kicks so hard that Lilly staggers, Dave lays his hand upon Lilly's belly and says, "Be nice to your mother, Siri, she loves you." Lilly cries at that, and excuses it with the oft-repeated, "it's just hormones."

Only the most irresponsible of pregnant mothers indulge in wine, Ibuprofen, or sleeping pills, so at night Lilly lies awake besides her slumbering husband, her hands sliding over her skin, and whispers plans to her daughter: how she will read her *Winnie the Pooh*, and allow her to play piano if she wants, but not force it upon her if she doesn't, however Siri should at least try it.

Siri's life will be secure and loved, Lilly pledges. No missed bedtime stories or forgotten lunch money. No crying apologies or shrieking blame. No empty seats at the school recital.

Lilly's a week late when her doctor suggests inducing the birth. She resists and says her family has always been stubborn. Siri will arrive when she's ready. "Better not force her," Lilly laughs weakly, "because she might dig in her heels."

It's 4am, and Lilly sits on the couch in a splash of light cast by a single lamp in the quiet living room, a glass of decaffeinated iced tea numbing her hand. She raises the wet glass to her forehead, relishing the chill against the deafening pulse beating in her head. The unyielding surface slips against the dent in her temple that Lilly's mother always insisted was a result of Lilly's forceps delivery.

She squeezes her eyes shut as if that will block out The Story, the one her mom repeated every year on Lilly's birthday: about Lilly's drunken whoring absent father, the agonising labour, the tearing, the blood, and Lilly ripped from her mother's half-dead body, screaming an angry protest.

Lilly whooshes out a long breath, hoping to release that narrative from her body, like a valve on a pressure cooker made of drum-stretched skin. Her eyelids are hot, heavy, but she knows she is not tired enough for sleep. She reaches for the remote, but it lies across the impossible gulf between her and the coffee table. The Netflix queue is empty anyway, and the squawk of late night television will agitate her jangled nerves.

She has no distraction from the thoughts in her cramped skull, or the restless movements of her daughter against her organs.

"I had such dreams for you when I was pregnant," the words, slurred by time and alcohol, swim from the shape standing in the rough shadow of the kitchen doorway. A cigarette tip burns red for a moment, casting a dull light across a face cratered with bitterness.

Lilly's fingers grip the glass so hard she's afraid it will shatter, just like her eggshell façade. She breathes in the grit of Luckies, the signature scent of her childhood.

"I did my best, Lillian," the familiar self-pitying whine distorts her Mom's voice, "considering my problems." She puffs again, brutal. "You'll understand soon enough."

Lilly whispers, the smoke scratching her throat, "I won't make the same mistakes."

Her mother's laugh is a light bulb pop, and darkness blots everything out except for the intermittent glow of the Lucky Strikes tip. "I swore that too," she says between asthmatic gasps, "every time."

Lilly heaves out of the yielding cushions, scrabbles at the lamp for leverage, and clicks the useless switch multiple times. The wire of pressure cuts so deep she raises shaking fingers to her forehead and expects them to touch blood.

"I'll never be like you!" Lily swears.

Her mother's voice fades like a curl of smoke. "You'll see."

Lilly lurches to the light control embedded in the wall and smashes the button with her palm. The glare of the overhead light banishes the past, and she winces at its clarity. Nothing. Of course not. Her mother died five years ago, alone in her ashtray apartment.

She turns the light off again, unable to bear the harsh illumination, and in the dark she wraps her arms around her daughter and promises it will be different. "Please forgive my mistakes," Lilly murmurs, and Siri moves lazily, stretching against her cocoon.

Exhaustion tackles Lilly. She shuffles to the bedroom and trails her hand against the hall wall to guide her to the doorway, blind.

A final whisper – an echo, a prediction – is the rasp of sand tumbling in an hourglass: "Forgive my mistakes."

Lilly settles into bed beside her husband. He shifts to accommodate her, and drapes his arm over her stomach, cradling their daughter. Lilly covers his large hand with her swollen fingers, but she doesn't close her eyes.

Instead, she watches the ashen morning light seep through the blinds until the first contraction shakes her with its irrevocable signal of change

Family

Her call came, as it always did, at the yawn of morning, when the mind drunkenly staggers through the tatters of dreams into the awful glare of wakefulness.

The tune of Björk's 'Violently Happy' announced her.

"Do you know what time it is?" Oisín croaked, prone on the bed, phone misaligned against his face. His anger wasn't even awake. An indigo hue suffused his bedroom and familiar shapes bled into the walls.

Orla said something, her breath loud as if her mouth was mashed up against the receiver, her teeth clicking against plastic, but the rasps overwhelmed the quiet words.

"... he returns... light fades..."

"What? Are you pissed?" He fiddled with the phone so it slid correctly into place over his ear.

She snapped into legibility. "I'm outside."

"For fuck's sake!" Irritation burned off the dregs of sleep.

"Can I come up?"

He fumed, knowing there was only one answer, but let his sister stew. He heard a car rumble past her in the street. One other mad person up and awake in Dublin.

She slid into a soft, American stoner accent with chameleon expertise. "Don't hit me with them negative waves so early in the morning."

A smile slipped past his resentment. For a moment he remembered her vividly as a girl in their cramped living room, her wild hair sticking out in tufts from under Mam's black bra lopsided on her head, enveloped in Dad's leather jacket, as she rolled around in her cardboard box 'tank' and quoted Oddball from *Kelly's Heroes.*

He sighed. "The bridge is still up."

"Put the kettle on."

It was whistling when he opened the door to the apartment. Orla held up a litre of milk in one hand, and a package of digestives in the other as a peace offering. Her soaked hair clung to her face, and the bones of her skull seemed to press tight against her skin. In the dim hallway her eyes glinted amid deep shadow. Beads of water rolled off her battered leather satchel slung over her drenched trench coat and splashed into a little pool on the floor.

"Christ's sake, Orla," he whispered, checking up and down the corridor to see if anyone was about, "did you swim here?"

She gave him a pouty sad face with puppy eyes.

"You'd get the Oscar for best seal impersonation, but you're a bit too rough to play the ingénue today." He opened the door wide to avoid her wet flounce into his apartment.

"That's not what my director tells me," she said, chin up, squelching past him with damp dignity.

"Yeah, but that's what's trending on Twitter. Hang your coat in the bathroom, but gimme your supplies first." He unburdened her and hurried to the kitchen.

"There are clean towels in the spare bedroom," he added, voice raised over the clink of china and the scraping of butter over toast.

She returned, a red towel twisted into a turban on her head and wrapped in his favourite brocade dressing gown. Not for the first time, he was struck by her effortless way of drawing beauty about her in every circumstance.

He handed her a cup of tea.

"Hmm, milky perfection." She slurped, smacked her lips with comic vulgarity, and winked. "You'll make a lovely wife someday."

He snorted, then sipped his tea daintily with his little finger stuck outward like an exclamation point.

Orla picked up a slice of toast and wandered from the kitchen into the living room. Water sluiced down the two giant glass windows. Outside, dull light seeped through the low grey clouds, signalling the timid advance of morning. From their vantage point the car headlights of the very early commuters were hazy dots of light reflected in the slick roads either side of the River Liffey.

"Tea, toast, and cosy inside," she said, quietly, the expression on her face distant, as if she was looking through the veil of rain onto a different vista.

He finished their mother's mantra: "All's well, worries outside."

Instinctively he moved to her and wrapped his free arm around her. She leaned hard into the hug, and he tightened his grip. Her skin smelled of sea foam.

A chill transferred from her into his bones. Her stillness alerted him. Tenderly, he spoke to the top of her head. "What's wrong?"

"I went back," she replied. "I saw him."

Orla sat in the passenger seat of the car, her boots up against the dashboard, her body curled defensively as she meandered through topics as varied as her dress disaster during her last trip to Cannes, and the intricacies of the Appalachian accent.

Oisín noticed the tightness of his grip on the steering wheel and tried to loosen it. Ahead the motorway to the West of Ireland undulated across the patchwork of green fields in an almost direct path to the sinking sun, now a blinding orb in a clear blue sky. In his memory, trips back to the West were uncomfortable bus jaunts down bad roads through gridlocked villages while whipped by torrential rain. He'd been a student then. The last time he'd taken this route it had been for his gran's funeral just before he graduated from art college. Obligation had forced him onto the bus that time, but the apocalyptic row with his grandfather afterwards had been justification never to return.

This smooth journey in clear weather seemed to want to prove everything had changed.

"What's he like now?" The words came out gruffly, he hated that he even wondered if the old bastard had decided to join the human race. He wanted to squash that tiny spark in him that yearned for some Hollywood breakthrough, which would launch a new relationship.

"Older."

He cast a withering glare at her, and noticed she was chewing the ends of her hair, an old childhood habit that always made him feel vaguely ill. Familiar words of censure rose up. He refused to say them. He was the big brother, but she was a grown woman. It was hard to unlearn rote expressions, but she had demanded freedom from his stewardship years ago, and he was determined to honour that even when he suspected she was incapable of responsibility.

"Calm down! He's... shrunk. Remember how big he was when we were kids? He seemed to fill every room he was in. Now, he's smaller, white hair, and walks with a cane." She paused and narrowed her eyes. "He's harmless."

"Pity he wasn't harmless when I was eleven." Oisín clenched his jaw.

Orla reached out and stroked his arm. He wanted to bat it, and her sympathy, away, but didn't.

"What prompted you to visit?"

"Lots of things. I've got a new part, and it's a bit gruelling." She hugged herself as if she was suddenly cold. "I needed to remember something... comforting. I wanted to go back to the cottage, and to do that I had to see him."

Oisín remained silent under the onslaught of too many conflicting emotions.

She glanced over and judged his mood, before she continued. "After all, he's our only link to..." Oisín guessed she wanted to say *Dad* but was afraid that word would be too much for him on this reluctant journey. "... our childhood."

"What there was of it after Mam died," he said, barely able to get the words through his gritted teeth.

She loosened a long sigh. "But before that we had good times in the cottage with her. We were happy."

He nodded, curtly. "Maybe. I was older. I noticed things you didn't after Dad left."

Orla removed her hand from his arm and lifted a lock of her hair back up to her mouth.

He scowled, and she noticed. She dropped it, guiltily.

She laughed suddenly, grinning. "Do you remember the plays we used to put on for Mam in the evenings? And the mad outfits she used to make for us from the likes of sheets, plastic bags, and egg cartons? She was a genius with a pair of scissors, cloth, and thread."

"I remember we couldn't afford a telly, and she had to distract two kids from hunger and a cold house."

She turned her face to the window, and he barely heard her mutter, "... his cloak, shredded, flapped around his vile visage..."

Oisín's foot hit the brake, instinctively.

"What?" His voice too loud.

Her face turned to him, dispassionate. "You remember. The play."

A fragment, shrouded, flitted across his mind, and associated with it: paralysing dread.

An exit loomed, and he wrenched the steering wheel towards it.

Orla clutched at the door handle, and the car in the lane beside them blared a warning.

He was still breathing hard when they pulled up to the petrol station.

"We're losing the light," she said, munching on a chip. Across the table Oisín nursed a large cup of coffee and stared at it as if expecting answers to appear in its surface.

"Good. You're not the one driving into the sunset."

Nearby, inside a play area constructed around a large, custard-yellow plastic castle, a child wailed.

"Once we're off the straight roads it's a twisting drive. Are you sure you remember the way, in the dark?"

The cry escalated into a hysterical shriek. Oisín glanced over at the ugly structure, wondering where the parents were hiding. Huddled over tea and pastry, perhaps, wilfully ignoring their infant's tantrum, and preparing for the final push home in a car full of squabbling siblings.

The pitch of the child's scream notched upwards. "I'm the king!" he screeched, "Obey me!"

"Where the fuck are the parents?" Oisín wondered, frowning. The tables closest to the stronghold were deserted. He looked around, trying to spot the guilty party.

"Maybe they're tired," Orla replied staring out of the station's window across the fields at the setting sun. "Maybe they don't care."

The noise increased to a pitch Oisín did not think could be made by any human throat. He stood up, hands clamped over his ears. Orla didn't pay attention. Outside the sun dipped under the horizon.

"The light fades," she whispered.

In an instant, beyond the glass, darkness reigned.

The gaudy squat castle shuddered.

The eerie scream halted.

The ensuing silence held the ponderous weight of awful expectation.

Smiling, Orla drew a sign upon the glass, and cracks cobwebbed across its surface instantly.

"No!" he yelled, but the glass exploded inwards and the night invaded the room.

He dived to the floor, arms covering his face, but not before he saw a phosphorus glow spring up around the castle.

Then, in the booming voice of a victor: "Prepare for his return."

Oisín jolted awake, heart juddering, as Orla grabbed at the steering wheel. Before them the twin headlights of the car revealed a grassy verge. The car bounced over the soft ground. He pulled the wheel, hard, and the car skidded badly in mud, until it regained the road. He spotted a space by a gate to a field, and pulled in, gasping.

Orla panted beside him.

"Shit! I'm so sorry!" memory rushed back. They had left the station an hour ago and had been driving down quieter country roads ever since. "Micro sleep."

She punched him in the upper arm. "You nearly killed us!"

He turned to look at her face, so fearful, so precious to him.

"You've all I've left," he blurted out.

Orla placed her hand upon his cheek. It felt like a benediction. "I'm here. We're okay. Can you stay awake or do you want me to take over?"

He kicked open the car door and staggered upright. The wind ripped at his coat, and water from the hedgerow dashed into his face. His mind was so clear it felt cruel.

Orla sprang out of the car and came around so she stood in the wash of the lights, a spectral being.

He reached in and turned off the headlights. The night sky of his youth, awash with stars, crashed upon him. He grabbed the car door, dizzy from the majestic immensity.

"Were there so many back then?" he murmured.

Orla removed the keys from his frozen hand. "I'll drive the rest of the way."

He nodded, stumbled around the vehicle, and fell into the passenger seat, glad to be hidden from the dispassionate heavens.

He woke again, in darkness. His neck ached. Orla was gone. His first sight through the windscreen: the square outline of the white farmhouse gleaming in the dull starlight. Their hated home after their mother passed away. His stomach knotted in response.

No lights graced any of the windows.

A cold welcome, he thought, followed by, *same as usual.*

Oisín climbed out of the car in discordant movements, his body protesting his cramped, interrupted sleep. The mixed-up clean and nasty smells of a farm assaulted him and he wrinkled his nose in protest. The gravel crunched under his leather brogues, and he imagined the first comment his grandfather would make would be on how inappropriate they were. He stood before the blue door and braced himself for contempt and indifference, while reminding himself of his achievements and successes.

The door opened easily, and the stillness of an empty house greeted him. The long, dark hallway disappeared into a void where the kitchen lay.

"Hello?" he said, not too loud. "Orla? Fintan?" Oisín had begun calling his grandfather by his first name when he was thirteen, as an act of rebellion.

He didn't want to enter the house. It was the repository of bad memories and old hurts, and he felt they would consume him if he stepped over the threshold.

Instead, he leaned in and flipped the light switch just inside the door: nothing. Oisín turned it on and off several times before stopping. Now, he could smell a faint odour of mildew, and sense the coolness unique to a deserted home.

He turned away, shuffling his feet against the invasive chill, and buttoned his overcoat tight to his chin. As he moved, he noticed the spark of light gleam between the hawthorn trees, up the *boreen* which lead to the cottage he had lived in for two years with his mother and Orla after their dad disappeared.

Oisín fished his mobile phone out of his pocket and turned the flashlight app on. The bright LED was a tiny point of ease against the immensity of the blackness surrounding him. He gazed up at the sky bursting with stars and wondered if each of the minute lights above him marked another being stumbling about, lost in a dreadful place.

We are alone, together, he thought, and there was a doubling effect. As if he had heard that phrase before but said in his father's rich timbre.

A faint memory coalesced: his father in a chair tipped back in front of the fire at the cottage, reading through lines for his last play. Orla stood beside him, barely eight, and speaking the part of the opposite character. Then: his mother, raging, yanking the pages from Orla's hand.

"She's not speaking these unholy words, Miles!" she'd reprimanded.

And the mocking laughter in response. "You're never too young for great art, Ellie. And this will be my masterpiece. They will remember me forever after this is staged."

Bitterness blotted out the recollection, and Oisín hunched his shoulders against his father's egotism. Miles had always chased fame, and despite his talent – which everyone acknowledged, even critics who loved to disparage him – he had never found the right role, the right director, or the right theatre big enough to house it. There were always excuses and reasons for his failures. Until he abandoned them outright after his last play was stopped during its debut performance.

Oisín moved quickly along the grassy path, framed by rough, limestone walls, which led to the cottage. He was angry. Baffled at being left alone by his sister after taking this long voyage with her into their turbulent past, and most furious at himself for letting the shadows in his mind roil up so many emotions. He had never understood why Orla threw herself into a profession that required her to tap into the raw root of life's experiences again and again. Sure, the results were luminous. Orla inhabited her characters on the screen in an exhilarating fashion, but he had also witnessed the cost she paid for her mercurial shape-shifting. He preferred to keep his emotional life under wraps and guarded.

As he rounded the final bend before the whitewashed building his steps slowed. He had taken this road so many times before, every bump remained familiar. He wasn't sure if he knew the street he lived on for the past five years as well as this ramshackle path to his childhood home.

Welcoming light blazed from the windows. He'd expected the small house to be almost a ruin, since it had been dilapidated when they'd been forced to live there after being chased out of Dublin by debt collectors. Instead, it appeared renovated.

He approached the door, painted a bright red, and the top half of it swung open in the traditional style of meeting a passer-by.

"Surprise!" Orla said, leaning on the bottom half of the door. Inside Oisín could see a sympathetic restoration that harkened to the older period of the house while adding modern amenities.

"What on earth...?"

Orla unfastened the bottom half of the door and swung it open to admit him. Oisín walked in, confused. Before he knew it Orla had removed his coat and put a crystal tumbler containing whiskey into his hand.

With a cheeky grin she raised her glass and clinked it against his. "Oh yes, the irresponsible sister has grown up a little."

"You..." he glanced around. Traces of the past lingered, but the overall impression was of a new, tasteful history.

He sat down in a comfortable armchair by the crackling fire and downed a gulp of alcohol. Its fiery path down his throat woke him up.

"I've made money you know. Enough to pay someone to tidy this place up. A nice retreat for when I need to remember who I am."

"Why didn't you tell me?"

"Where's the drama in that, Oisín?" She laughed and sipped the whiskey. "If you could just see your face... I'm taking notes of that expression!"

He frowned, an unpleasant realisation surfacing. "Were you putting on a pretence in Dublin, to lure me down here for your big reveal?"

She stood up to stand by the fireplace, and drank a bit more, but he noticed the irritated swish in her step. Perhaps that was part of the spectacle. A weariness settled on him, mostly borne from the relief that the ugly scenes he'd anticipated had not materialised.

"So, where's Fintan?"

She arched an eyebrow. "I didn't think you'd be eager to meet the old devil again."

"Not exactly, but what's been going on here?"

"Fintan has been in a nursing home for a year. Great Aunt Nora contacted me. Everyone knew you didn't want to be bothered about him."

Protests crowded into Oisín's mouth, but he choked them back. He'd not contacted his grandfather in ten years, after all. What concerned him most was this disclosure exposed the gulf that lay between him and Orla. So much of daily life excluded from each other. All her travel, and his investment in his job. Their different social circles, and her growing fame. Their connections now seemed more fragile than he'd imagined.

A sadness at the rupture between them overwhelmed him. Once, they had been each other's only shelter against the world. He missed that conviction in her love.

"You're right," he admitted, defeated. "Is he okay?"

"Better cared for than we were by him." She winked and drained her glass.

Her glibness rankled, and yet he would have said the same an hour ago. The map of his universe had been altered, and it felt as if he was scrambling to chart his bearings.

"I have another story to tell tonight," she declaimed, in a theatrical fashion. Dad had called it the *Getting the Punters' Attention* voice, and it was eerily reminiscent of him.

"I think I've had enough surprises for –"

She flicked a switch and the main lights extinguished, leaving a couple of candles and the fire as the only source of illumination. "I've engaged with a new collaboration. One of the most challenging of my career."

Oisín withheld his questions. He was now cast in the role of audience, not interrogator. If he wrecked the moment he would fuel resentment for years. It had been one of his earliest lessons: the show takes priority. He settled back and prepared for Orla's announcement of her next grand adventure.

"I've been approached by my first teacher, to take on a part in a play that has been banned from live performance in every country for years. We've assembled a cast in secret, conducted rehearsals, and we'll live-broadcast it over the Internet from here, in the outer lands crushed against the Atlantic Ocean."

The shadows in the room flickered with the candlelight. Outside the wind rose. Oisín shifted, and glanced behind him, but there was only darkness. Yet, he felt as if he was part of a gathering witnessing a grave event.

Surely, he heard whispering?

Orla continued. "Soon everyone can marvel at the mysteries it divulges. All masks will be discarded, and our revels will reshape the world."

And she drew his symbol in the air.

It burned a dire mustard glow and hung there.

It would always remain, now it had been inscribed, even after its light had faded. And Oisín would never forget it. It lived in him now, stamped upon his cells, and all those he would ever pass on.

The building shook, but its foundations were set fast in ancient ways, and did not falter. It was forever marked as a way in for a receptive audience.

The atmosphere seemed denser, and Oisín struggled to breathe. Around him the shadows materialised into other forms and they leaned forward in anticipation to observe the first performance.

Everything vibrated to Orla's voice.

She held her hand out to Oisín, and before she spoke he felt the compulsion, and the love, pull him to her. "Tonight, we will have our first reading featuring a new performer."

He jerked upright, not in control of his limbs, terrified to see the assembly. A wave of applause coursed through him and spun him around.

Their expectation paralysed him more than their cruel faces.

Orla's tone turned exultant. "And, the oldest actor, the original. Our father who was before and who has returned. His guises are never false, but we rarely see him true."

She gestured to the left, and Oisín did not turn his head, for he knew once he looked upon that face, Oisín would be no more, there would only be the façade, and the performance inscribed upon his DNA that he would be compelled to act out.

The glowing sign vanished at the approach of its master. No longer necessary when its originator appeared.

Oisín heard the flapping of his tattered cloak, like the beating wings of crippled angels furious at their banishment.

Orla placed her hand upon Oisín's back, to guide him to face the artist.

The heat of his gaze removed all of Oisín's doubt.

Tears streamed down his cheek and he grasped his sister's hand. Family, reunited. Communion restored.

Together they spoke the opening words, and gladly unleashed the play.

Wake the Dead

"If you're running from yourself you'll always come in second."

Donnacha didn't understand this cryptic statement when he'd heard it as a kid, impatient and bored, in his Gran's kitchen. She'd been counselling his father about his restless job hopping. Yet a haunting vision lodged in his mind, despite his desire to return to his Mam's house and his unfinished Zelda game. He imagined his Dad being pursued by a better, fitter version of himself in a long race, but dream-like, his father's faster self outpaced him, and drew away until he disappeared into a hazy horizon. Uncatchable.

Red-faced and panting, his father slogged on, alone. Too proud to admit defeat.

In the car ride home, Donnacha puzzled over it, and concluded Gran was implying his Dad was a loser. And looking at him, compulsively wringing the steering wheel, crumpled, unshaven, and permanently broke, Donnacha reckoned she was right.

Now, after a month of driving around rural Ireland, trying to evade his cracked adult life choices, Donnacha had a grudging new insight to her meaning, and unexpected empathy for his Dad.

But he wasn't ready to admit he couldn't dodge his demons.

"I'll run them ragged first."

He glanced guiltily around his car. Talking out loud wasn't a good sign.

He signalled, and drove into another small town that existed half in the past and half in the present. A shabby, boarded-up hardware shop cringed next to a shiny Thai street food restaurant. A statue of the Virgin Mother and Child cast a shadow over the town square that pointed at the lingerie store opposite. Teens loitered together on a street corner with their individual faces illuminated by their mobile phones, while a tractor motored past them and the auld fellah in a cap driving it waved at the older locals.

"He even has the sheepdog on the passenger seat," Donnacha marvelled. The collie lolled his tongue at him as Donnacha pulled his car around the slowpoke driver.

This was typical of his impromptu tour of the cultural blindspots of his homeland. Ireland had emerged from its colonial chrysalis, but its new form was not yet set. It was malleable and shifting. Underneath the wet flesh some of the old bones were resistant to change. They could establish the new form from their obstinacy.

Perhaps there were even more ancient shapes that might re-emerge. From when people chanted to stone and paid respect to trees. When blood was spilled for nature's tribute. And primordial forces responded to such offerings...

Donnacha blinked rapidly, surprised at the strange direction of his thoughts. Luckily he spotted the B&B he had booked for the night, and made a quick turn into its driveway. This owner had a quixotic array of statutes and potted plants in the small garden. A gnome wearing sunglasses held court with a duck dressed in a raincoat. A hedgehog in a Hawaiian shirt lounged beside a dancing, piping satyr.

It was another in a series of cheap, unassuming B&Bs he had picked for his wandering. He avoided hospitable homes with cheery fireplaces, chatty guests, and reminders to review the premises kindly online. He preferred the old-fashioned, reserved host, who took money without questions and offered a spartan experience.

Donnacha craved their cell-like rooms. He read books, anything abandoned in the lodgings he occupied briefly, and never turned on the TV. Perversely, the world continued to turn without his attention. He heard snatches of news via the radio in his car, but he thought of them as stories. Fantastical yarns of tyrants, villains, and beasts, wrangling in distant kingdoms.

Each day he got up and drove, over drenched rolling hills, past indistinct villages, through tangled, black-boughed woods, and over swollen rivers. Dependable Ireland rolled out a sepulchral chill as October deepened, and around him every dark rock and huddled glade was damp and glistening.

His funds had ebbed. What remained from his share of the house – Mairead had done well out of that showdown between solicitors – had paid for petrol and a frugal month of roving around a landscape he had never explored.

He could get work as a barman. That well-honed skill was ever needed. He wasn't the best at feigning interest in customers, but his supply of sardonic commentary was limitless, and there was nothing his countrymen liked better than banter, especially if it skewed bleak.

That evening Donnacha fired up an antique computer in the beige living room of his current residence. He browsed through job ads on local towns' forums, and noted some likely contenders. It meant he had to log into his email account, and endure the few concerned messages from old friends. The ones that knew him from his happier days in Boston, before he and Mairead returned home, or those childhood mates who stubbornly believed there was some spark of that original kid left within his chest. The most difficult was the patient reminder from his younger brother Fintan that a room was available at his home. He responded with a one-line thanks, but he knew that Juanita wouldn't welcome him. She and Mairead has always been tight.

He scrawled a couple of addresses and numbers on the complimentary notepad by the asthmatic PC. His pay-as-you-go phone was a primitive plastic savage. His address book was slips of paper in his wallet.

Donnacha didn't notice the lady of the house enter the room until her shadow obscured his writing. He startled and turned.

She could have been in her twenties or her fifties: a tall, thin grey woman with big plastic spectacles, and a smile that hung on her long face like a titled picture. She wore some orthodontic contraption that gave her a slight lisp and added to her indeterminate age.

"Buster Mahon needs a hand."

He blinked at her, a variety of interpretations crossing his mind, including a joke about prosthetics.

She pointed at his scrawl. "You're looking for work?"

"Depends on the job."

"Pub. Town's so small if you sneezed while passing through you'd miss it." She snorted a laugh. 'It"s the pub, and the grocery shop, *and* the funeral parlour. They used to do petrol too, but gave that up when the big companies took over. Traditional place. Old men in wellies and caps. Young people go elsewhere."

"And I'm not young?"

"You'd fit right in there. They want pints pulled while they read papers and complain about the weather or the price of sheep."

"Is the pay is as attractive as the company?"

She shrugged. "Buster has a room above the place. It could be right for someone minding his own business."

Donnacha stood up. She was half a head taller. "You've come to some conclusions about me."

She met his direct look without any caginess. "I know people." She held out a piece of paper with an address.

His bitterness rose like addictive bile. "That's impossible. We're all pretending."

But he reached for the paper anyway. She held onto it for a moment longer than necessary, and he met her gaze again.

"I see you Donnacha Sweeney."

Her knowing stare pierced his bravado. A shiver rippled down his back and his hand jerked back involuntarily with the paper.

She smiled, and the row of metal bands covered her teeth so completely it was as if they were fashioned from iron. "I'm away early tomorrow. Busy day. I'll leave a cold breakfast for you, and you can let yourself out."

He watched her leave the room as soundlessly as she entered.

It was one of the occasions he cursed not having a smart phone. The town wasn't on the map, which lay in a crumpled mess on the passenger seat. He had been circling through a series of winding boreens at a crawl because of the silvery rain shroud. The car clock said it was 1 pm, but he had set out at 11 am, and the place should only have been 30 minutes away. Through the haze he spotted the smudged shape of the apex of a stone church he was sure he had passed twice before.

"Fuck's sake!" he shouted, and gripped the steering wheel to knuckle-white tightness.

He pulled the car into a scrap of earth by the barred gateposts, beyond which lay the outline of a church after a long, gravelled path. Listing headstones and ivy-strangled vaults studded the mist.

He hoped some farmer's son in a souped-up Honda Civic wouldn't bash into him while he consulted his map. His finger traced along the creased page for a tell-tale cross that would indicate the church, but there were only a squiggle of lines. They met in a crossroads where he suspected the town was located.

A bell tolled, oddly muffled. He glanced up. A figure moved down the path toward him.

Donnacha reached over to roll down his passenger window, and plastered on a bewildered smile. It appeared to be a man in a dark suit, who walked steadily but didn't get any closer.

He squinted. The mist had already seeped into the car, and a fine film of water beads clung to his face, obscuring his vision. He wiped at his eyes, trying to focus properly on the approaching person.

It walked, but it gained no ground.

Warmth leeched out of him, along with his enthusiasm to meet the person. The bell clanged again, dully.

At this the figure blipped forward on the path. Donnacha could make out a translucent face with black voids for eyes that radiated malevolent triumph. Long-figured hands hung loosely from the sleeves as if the suit was badly fitted. A costume for an intruder.

There was no other sound. No crunch of gravel, or the complaint of crows.

Again, the bell rang out strangely.

The manshape was almost at the gatepost. His pretend mouth was a vicious slash, curved up in the delight of the predator. His arm reached up as if to hail him –

Donnacha put the car into gear and slammed his foot on the accelerator.

The car caught on the mud and the back swerved slightly, to scrape against the stone post. The grind of metal merged with the bell. Donnacha refused to look at the path despite the freezing gust that swept through the window causing his rapid breaths to materialise before him.

With an anguished shriek his car surged onto the road and sped forward quickly, but he had to slow immediately because of the mist.

Donnacha glanced in the rear-view mirror for any sign of his pursuer, but all that was evident was the concealing rain.

His heartbeat slowed down again, and he broke into a stuttering laugh, mocking and congratulatory.

Then, he spotted the signpost, at a drunken angle, pointing at an obscured road, and the name of the hamlet: Rathdearg.

He turned the car, and heard the protest from the back wheel, relieved he was only a couple of miles from his destination.

Rathdearg was a collection of houses, rather than a village, yet the road widened to accommodate a small green area with benches and a saint's statue. Everything was tidy, with walled gardens up front. The pub/shop was called The Haunt. Next door what looked like a home also had the green flash that indicated it doubled as a post office. A bus stop pole punctuated either side of the street.

He parked the car in a small concrete space at the side of the building and got out. He wilfully ignored examining the damage. What did it matter when he couldn't afford to fix it?

At the entrance to the pub sat a collection of turnips, carved with deranged faces, and with a light flickering inside each one. The hanging sign depicted a revenant dressed in a 19th century black suit, sitting inside the pub holding up a pint of porter in a perpetual toast. A skeleton in an apron grinned from behind the counter.

He pushed open the door which had wavy glass inset, and it squealed loudly as if griping about its use. Inside, the dimly-lit room was narrow due to an ancient counter running along the left-hand side. It was composed of glass and wood, and displayed a variety of canned goods, including baked beans, peas, and spam. Behind it were shelves with toilet paper, washing powder, and giant boxes of tea. A small fridge containing juice and milk hummed. An old-fashioned register sat unattended. A rack of newspapers, containing national and regional publications as well as *The Farmer's Journal* and *Ireland's Own,* finished off the row.

After the shop a swinging half door opened into the pub itself.

It's the Wild West, Donnacha thought as he entered.

This space was roomy, with a smoke-stained counter at the back, which looked like it has been worn smooth by generations of elbows. The array of tall stools didn't have padding or cushions. *The townsfolk have hardy backsides*. The usual pumps for the dominant breweries were on display, but he was surprised to see a craft beer from a nearby town given a prominent spot. Glass shelves behind the bar displayed the selection of spirits, and rows of glasses. He noted the lack of dust on the bottles of Babycham – someone had professional pride. A turf fire blazed in the large stone fireplace on the right. In front of the hearth lay a grey, grizzled hound. It raised its head at Donnacha's appearance, and watched him with wise, brown eyes.

A faded, hand-written sign pasted on the back of the bar proclaimed, 'No Cappuccinos!', but underneath that it offered a WiFi password.

He crossed the tiled floor toward the counter. The dog stood up, revealing its height. It was a cross but with a strong wolfhound pedigree.

"Hello," he said, and cautiously extended his downturned hand.

The dog sniffed from a distance. A tag dangled from his collar, and

Donnacha sank down on his hunkers to read it.

"Joxer," he read out loud. The dog's ears twitched.

"I'm Donnacha."

Joxer walked right up to his face, licked it once, and returned to his post by the fire.

Donnacha straightened, and looked around, but no one appeared. He walked to the counter, leaned on it, then coughed politely. An old clock hanging among black and white photographs ticked loudly.

After another minute crawled by he noticed the black door at the back of the room. No doubt it led to the toilets and some quiet room where people retired for the lock-in.

He walked to it and placed his hand on the old-fashioned metal handle, but before he opened it he glanced back at Joxer. The dog regarded him placidly. He clicked the door open.

The short corridor beyond was icy cold, and he was glad again for his parka. A fragrance of lilies and beeswax lingered. He cautiously opened another black door, and formed his mouth into a "Hello?" as he entered.

The word died in his mouth when he took in the tableaux before him.

It was the funeral parlour, and it was in session.

The first thing he saw in the rectangular room was a huge, ornately-framed picture of the Madonna hanging from the wall facing him. It was painted in a modern – or primitive – style. Her radiating halo – perhaps gold leaf – glowed in the subdued candlelight cast from four huge wrought-iron standing candelabras positioned in the corners of the room. Her skin was blue, and her raiment red, but her yellow eyes contained compassion despite their eerie, direct gaze.

A plain, wooden coffin, painted black, sat in the centre of the room on top of a plinth covered in maroon velvet. Donnacha could not tell what was in the open coffin from this distance, but a skin-creeping horror of dead people shivered through him. He could still remember the waxy, lifeless features of his grandmother when she had been waked, in the old way, in her home. Donnacha had been eleven, and his father insisted he kiss her goodbye. He had practically dragged Donnacha to the coffin in her old living room, where the gathered neighbours drank cups of tea and glasses of whiskey. His lips only grazed her forehead, but he'd had to choke back a retch.

The old revulsion, and the shock at intruding in such a private ceremony, paralysed him.

The room was lined on all sides by seats, and they were occupied by people wearing traditional black. Their faces, grey with grief he supposed, turned to stare at him.

A wide man in a coal black suit emerged from a darker part of the room and walked up to him.

"I'm so sorry," Donnacha began in a whisper, "I was looking for Buster Mahon. I had no idea –"

"I'm him," he said in a quiet tone, and held out a square hand.

Donnacha took it, and Buster gave him the shake that implied with one extra pulse of pressure he could crush his hand. Buster had the gait and carriage of someone who used to be a rugby player, or a soldier. Someone not afraid to apply force if provoked.

"You're Donnacha Sweeney I'm guessing?"

Donnacha nodded to cover his surprise.

"Connie warned me you might be dropping by."

"Ah..."

"Constance Harte. You stayed in her B&B last night."

"Yes, of course!" He never remembered the names of any of the people he stayed with. "Tall lady," he added, idiotically.

Buster smiled in a neutral way, and titled his head back slightly as if appraising him. "Yes she is. Good judge of character."

Donnacha looked about, unsure what to do. The people in the room were standing now but remained fixed on him and Buster. He could not tell who the lead mourners were. They all seemed equally... morbid.

"You're looking for work?"

"Yes, but I don't have a CV –"

Buster waved him into silence. "Paper doesn't tell the tale of a man. Work does. Anyway, you got past the dog."

"I'll have to thank him."

This time Buster's eyes crinkled along with his smile. "He likes avocado."

Buster gestured to the door back to the pub. "Let's see how you handle yourself. After that we'll know what you can deal with."

"Now?"

"There's an apron behind the counter. A tradition of my father's. He always liked us neat."

"Okay."

Buster nodded at the door. "We'll be coming through in a minute, and you can begin."

"Connie said something about a room."

"No matter how it goes tonight, you can stay in the flat upstairs. Tomorrow we can assess."

Donnacha inclined his head, glad he'd thought to wear his black jeans and shirt, which he considered his uniform for bar work. He turned his back on the room and felt an unnerving vulnerability. A sibilant drone began, but Donnacha could not make out the words or even the language. He imagined it was a decade of the rosary or some other chanted prayer. He was relieved to depart and return to the vacant pub. Joxer didn't even raise his head from his paws when he entered.

A black apron hung from a peg behind the bar, He swapped it for his coat, and tied the apron around his waist. It hung to mid-shin, and he felt more like a European waiter than a barman. He spotted a dishcloth by the sink and began a wipedown of the counter even though it looked perfectly clean. It was his ritual for getting into the right mindset for the job: clean down the space and prepare for the array of mad ones and saints: always in proportion of ten to one.

Joxer got to his feet and gazed at the door. Buster walked in and the dog gave him a tail wag before he sat down, looking like a regal stone statue.

Buster noted Donnacha's final polish of the counter.

"Good habits," he said with approval.

The sea of mourners washed in behind him, and soon Donnacha had no time to think. It was a pints-of-stout and balls-of-malt crowd, with a sprinkling of shandys, and white wines. A tab was established – no one's hand was allowed near a wallet. All the seats were full, and people milled around the bar – none obstructing orders. A buzz of conversation built up, but even illuminated by the cheery fire, which Buster kept feeding, the customers' faces retained a greyish cast.

After an hour a sturdy woman in an old-style housecoat and a crocheted cap knocked through the swing doors with a big tray of sandwiches in her muscled arms.

"Delores! Just in time," declared Buster. A muted cheer rang out from the assembly. He relieved her of the tray, and set it down on the nearest table. Hands grabbed the offerings in moments.

"Two more trays, and cake coming," she told him, before she swung out again.

Within minutes most of the bar were chewing contentedly. Buster snagged a few for himself and for Donnacha. He deposited a plate bulging with ham and cheese sandwiches and moist tea cake behind the counter for Donnacha.

"Get these in you boyo, quick. They'll call for another round once they've scarfed that lot."

At the same time Delores returned with two china plates covered in tin foil, and left them on the corner of the counter. Nobody touched them.

"Delores, my beauty", Buster began, and curled his arm around her shoulders affectionately. She beamed at him. "Meet Donnacha Sweeney. Tonight's attendant. Connie sent him to us."

She eyeballed Donnacha the way a farmer appraises livestock.

"You seem competent."

Buster laughed. "Steady on, Delores! Such praise. It'll be offers of matrimony next."

She raised her eyes in an exaggerated eye roll. Clearly they were old friends.

"Delores is our hamlet's postmistress, professor of all the town's legends and gossip, and our establishment's provider of pub grub when required."

Buster was opening his mouth to say something else when a disturbance from outside the pub slipped in between the mumble of conversation.

Drumming; whistles; chimes.

The pub hushed, and the cacophony drew closer.

Nobody moved, or took their eyes from their drinks.

Joxer stood up.

Donnacha glanced at Buster, ready to ask a question, but the expression on the man silenced him. Buster looked like someone with a sombre duty. Next to him Delores had her hands stuffed in the pockets of her housecoat, and her lips tightly held, as if holding back an alarm.

Three knocks hammered the front door.

"You!" Buster said with quiet urgency to Donnacha. "Come with me."

A path through the bodies opened, and the two men pushed through the swing doors.

Through the wavy glass of the front door Donnacha could make out three figures.

"What –?" Donnacha started, but Buster clamped a big hand on his wrist and the pressure quietened him.

Buster opened the door.

Outside waited three capering characters, resplendent in suits of gleaming straw, wearing rough animal masks of straw: a goat, a hare, and a bull.

The goat played a battered tin whistle in an eerie melody that stuck to the minor keys, while the hare shook an old-fashioned tambourine, and the bull banged an ancient, stained bodhran drum.

They danced in the light cast through The Haunt's windows, and the flicking candle light from the carved turnips in front of the door. Behind them, darkness and fog. It was as if the town had melted away, and nothing existed except for these players and Buster and Donnacha.

The trio became stock-till, and struck up a folk tune that sounded familiar in a warped way. They sang a chant:

"Hungry we stand before your door
No food nor drink since the year before
Give us whiskey, give us bread
Open the door, *let's wake the dead!*"

They performed it three times, increasing their volume after each turn, until their last version was a shouted demand.

Silence again except for their excited breaths through the masks. There was only darkness behind the eyeholes.

"Welcome to our hearth Mummers," Buster said. He carefully handed each one a coin.

He jerked his head at Donnacha to indicate he should open the door. Donnacha stood inside and held it. The three Mummers swept past him, bringing the smell of a field of barley bending to a wild wind under starry skies.

When Donnacha pushed through the swing doors after the entourage, he froze.

They had brought the coffin into the pub. It stood on six stools, parallel to the hearth, but not close to the fire. Joxer had vanished. The three Mummers stood in a half-circle around the head of the coffin.

Everybody was standing. Delores was stationed on the left of the coffin with a plate of cake, and Buster was at the counter collecting the other plate. He waved in an underhand manner to Donnacha to urge him to his side. Donnacha had to swerve by the coffin and Delores. This was his first chance to see what lay within. He darted a glance, and could only make out a dark shape. Something glinted into his eyes when he tried to see the face. Further unnerved, he almost hopped forward to reach Buster.

The big man picked up a china plate filled with thinly sliced pieces of meat, cheese, fruit, and soda bread. He pointed at a small silver salver, on which sat three glasses of whiskey. He pointed back at the coffin.

Donnacha picked up the tray, and followed his boss, who took up a position opposite Delores. Buster titled his head to indicate that Donnacha should stop at the foot of the coffin.

Donnacha kept his attention firmly on the glasses, concentrating on keeping the tray level, and halted where indicated. Immediately, the Mummers stuck up another tune, the weirdest disharmony so far, accompanied by occasional cries, squawks, and yelps that were more animal than human.

The sound bounced off the walls in the room and magnified it. Donnacha felt like he was *inside* the song. An updraft caught the flames in the hearth and they roared and leaped, pumping out tremendous heat. The din began to reach intolerable levels and at some unknow signal the crowd joined in, stamping, clapping, and crying out encouragement.

The clamour became a great beast whipping around the room seeking a prize.

Donnacha squeezed his eyes shut against the fear and the overwhelming sensory overload. A chilly breeze zipped past his neck and he nearly dropped the tray in shock.

He opened his eyes. The glasses were empty, the food taken from the plates.

Silence fell like an anvil dropped from a great height.

The Mummers spoke in unison:

"Look now, don't wait,
Learn your New Year's Fate.

One heartbeat: past
Two heartbeats: truth
Three heartbeats: dare
Four heartbeats: death."

Delores lowered her plate, and leaned forward slightly to stare into the coffin. Donnacha found himself counting a slow beat, and it seemed to him that she pulled back after two seconds. A line of people formed behind her, and they repeated her action.

Most only attempted a moment or two. One man slumped after three, and staggered away helped by a friend in the crowd.

Donnacha remained motionless, the tray of glasses balanced on his hands. His mind stalled; the black eyeholes of the goat, hare, and bull remained fixed on him, unwavering throughout the parade of questers.

Finally, Buster stood in front of him, his solid face serious. He removed the tray from Donnacha's hands and gestured to the coffin.

Everyone else had looked. They waited on him.

He moved forward stiffly, and his trembling right hand clamped on the side of the coffin. He could almost smell his grandmother's perfume, and feel his lips brush her lifeless forehead.

The shape of a body, wrapped in a black shroud, lay in the coffin lined with black silk. An aged oval mirror covered the face. Its surface was dully reflective, and splattered with ink blots of tarnish.

Donnacha leaned forward so a dim version of his face appeared in the mirror.

One heartbeat: *he was with Mairead, dancing and laughing at the Irish Cultural Centre in Boston.*

Two heartbeats: *he staggered, blindfolded, after a version of himself dressed in gleaming white who walked arm-in-arm with an ethereally happy Mairead.*

Three heartbeats: *he stood behind the counter in The Haunt, Joxer by the fire, with a small group of contented customers; but once a year the Mummers would call...*

He tried to pull his gaze away from the mirror, and he sensed the moment stretching into what came next. A memory of the grinning spectre in the graveyard reaching out to him rose in his mind. A cool mist settled against his face, numbing it and blinding his sight. A dreadful bone-deep understanding of the constant proximity of death settled into him. During this night, as the tissue between worlds became as soft as dandelion down, the illusions of life were easily rent, and the reality of time's quick passage revealed.

The race existed to be run, not won.

He tried to say something, a gasp, a grateful cry for the unbearable beauty and doleful duty of living, but his body was locked as if bracing an anticipated blow... until a sudden pain at his ankle yanked him out of that vision, and he fell, clutching his leg.

"I've got you lad," he heard Buster say, and his hands held Donnacha's shoulders, offering support and comfort.

Under the coffin: Joxer watched him alertly.

"It's over," Buster said, and he drew Donnacha up.

The Mummers were gone. Delores and the crowd had departed.

The coffin lay empty.

Donnacha heaved in a ragged breath.

By the counter, Connie saluted him with a glass of whiskey. "Happy Hallowe'en," she said with a solemn expression.

Donnacha turned to look at Buster.

"I want time and a half for that."

Buster slapped him on the back. "Let's talk terms and conditions. But first, how about a drink?"

Donnacha shook his head. "I need to get that dog some avocado."

Both Buster and Connie laughed, and Donnacha lurched forward, his feet awkward and unsteady. He could not sprint yet, but he could shuffle to the counter.

Around him reflections abounded: in a copper coal scuttle, the mirror over the fireplace, in the glass case of the clock, and the glint in the eyes of his patrons.

And in each one a hazy hand stretched to seize him.

Y

"Why is the world wrong?" five-year-old Ygraine asked her mother for the first time.

Nerthus didn't respond for a moment. She was perched on the edge of the couch in the darkened den, an intent crease in her forehead as she watched a lurching black and white film on the telly. Old chiaroscuro dreams sculpted her features.

She blinked, picked up the remote, and froze the image.

"What did you say?"

Ygraine flapped a free hand to indicate the entire shadowy space (her stuffed rabbit Zepher was clamped in the crook of her other arm). "Why is everything… *wrong*?"

Nerthus sat back and regarded the serious expression on her daughter's face. She drummed a slow beat with the pen in her hand across the notepad balanced on her knees. It seemed to Ygraine that this was the first time she had ever captured her mother's complete attention.

"What's wrong with everything?" Nerthus asked.

Frustration spiked Ygraine's belly like one of Mikael's ugly cacti in the conservatory. She didn't have words for the wrongness. It was a bone-deep knowledge that she was misplaced. Every morning she woke up expecting to be *someone else* and *somewhere else*. All Ygraine knew was that she and the world were out of sorts, and the pain from this mismatch had become a constant numbness in her heart.

"It's not *right!*" she cried. She twisted her bunny's head, and a black desire to rip it off rose in her. *That* would demonstrate her feelings.

Nerthus patted the cushion to her left, and with sullen, reluctant steps, Ygraine moved to her side and plopped down. Nerthus placed her arm around Ygraine's shoulders, but Ygraine did not relax into it like another child would, seeking comfort. She suffered the touch.

Nerthus did not act offended. "The world is a difficult place to live in, Y."

It was the first time Nerthus abbreviated Ygraine's name, and she pronounced it *ee*.

(A *click* registered in Y's mind. This name felt *almost-right*. An approximate of what *should be*. She instantly claimed it as her own.)

"It doesn't make sense half the time," Nerthus said. "It's a confusing place even for adults." She bent her head and looked directly into Y's eyes. "You have to unlock the puzzle of life on your own terms. Don't believe what other people tell you. Most of them make up their solutions and pass them off as truths. Find your own logic to the nonsense."

The one thing Y liked about her mother is that Nerthus spoke to her as an equal, but that meant she didn't always grasp everything she was told. She frowned.

Nerthus broke her gaze and sat upright. She gestured at the books, papers and photographs spilled on the coffee table, and the DVDs stacked around the TV in the corner. "This is how I decode the messages of the world. I break them down and reforge them in a way that approximates my inner landscapes."

She straightened her spine a little. "Just don't expect people to like it if you show them unsafe territories."

She tapped Y on the head, and Y knew she was dismissed. She returned to her bedroom, sat on her bed, and stroked Zepher's head roughly. She thought about her mother's words until Mikael's deep voice called her for dinner.

It took two decades for Y to realise that it was the best conversation she would ever have with her mother.

The landscape outside the bus window rolled past desolately. Y considered how it mirrored her experience of the world: an observer separated from people and places by an invisible barrier. Rarely connecting with anyone truly, never feeling at home in any place. 'Distant' is what most people called her. 'Aloof' if they were being passive aggressive. "A fucking psychopath," was Levi's summary at their last meeting. The fatal shot in their breakup duel.

What a mistake, Y thought and adjusted the seal of her headphone ear buds, so the music of Sigur Ros pushed out the thrum of the bus engine and the chatter of the two schoolgirls in front of her.

The stench of warm egg sandwiches left half-eaten on the seat across from her was harder to ignore. She wanted the view and the swell of the music to overwhelm all her senses. The bleak landscape and the slate skies soothed her in a way that was unusual. She sensed she was coming close to the next place she needed to live – somewhere isolated and surrounded by rock and sea. She'd felt this urge coming upon her for a year and had finally given away most of her possessions to travel in Europe and find the location that drew her.

Things meant very little to Y, apart from her laptop and smartphone. They were tools for her work, creativity, and social interaction: the online articles she wrote for income, her social media personae, and the obscure discussion boards she moderated. All her photographs, articles, and notes were stored on encrypted cloud servers, so even if she lost her devices, the data would remain. Those intangible files were her tether to her ongoing attempt to decipher the signs she had relentlessly followed since she spotted her first clue at age sixteen.

That initial marker had been an unassuming concrete wall in an underground car park at a supermarket. Nerthus and Gawain were loading up the car with groceries, and Y noticed a strange pattern out of the corner of her eye. Plain square pillars lined up like a colonnade before the wall splotched with abstract grey shapes. A pool of black water slicked the floor before it, reflecting the cold white strip of the overhead light.

All those elements, seen in a moment, *clicked* in her mind. The same way her name, Y, had fitted some unconscious lock. It was the first time a piece of the puzzle presented itself.

She drifted towards the space, feeling as if she was floating. The screech of car wheels and the clash of shopping carts receded. As she moved, her hand scrabbled in her satchel for her camera. It had been a birthday gift from Mikael the previous week – her first digital camera. Nerthus had *huffed* about it. She was a purist and preferred film, so she assumed Mikael had done it on purpose to annoy her. Instead, Mikeal had just listened when Y said that's what she wanted. Y had no ambition to be a photographer or a director like her mother. She just needed something to document the signs.

A week earlier, she'd had a dream.

The signs, a voice thundered at her from darkness, *follow them!*

She'd woken up shaking from both excitement and fear. The emotions were so raw and unaccustomed she felt woozy, like the time Mikael had given her too much cough medicine.

Y swung the camera up, flicked off the flash, and was snapping images before she thought about it consciously. At the same time, there was a pressure on her skull like a giant hand slowly squeezing. The *certainty* that she needed to photograph this arbitrary array of clean lines intersecting with grey stains was so strong she ignored the weirdness and kept clicking the button.

"What'cha doing, Y?"

Gawain had slouched up behind her.

She hated her brother for making her speak. It disrupted the connection. "What's it look like, jerkface?"

"You're photographing a wall, dumbass. Mum wants you to get in the car."

She could feel the moment slipping away.

"Come on!"

It was gone.

She whipped around, a fury boiling up her body in an instant.

Gawain stepped back from her anger. She took a photograph of him for spite. It neatly captured the surprise – and fear – on his amiable features.

She shouldered past him, yanking on her headphones, and climbed into the back seat of the car. She slammed the door, hard, and switched on her music, loud.

Y turned her face to the window and blanked her brother and mother in the front seats. She vaguely heard a mumble of conversation but steadfastly ignored it. Instead, Y stared at the wall, which no longer seemed possessed of secrets.

Yet that night, when she repeatedly scrolled through the odd assemblage of shapes on her laptop, it unsealed a conduit, and something *whispered* to her.

Bring Her back, it seemed to say. *Find Her.*

Who was Her?

Y still didn't know. Not after years of eclectic study at college, followed by a nomadic existence in three different countries and ten different houses and apartments.

At the arrival of each sign, Y could feel herself closing in on this mysterious person. It also signalled a change or a move. A week after she photographed the wall, Mikael died of a massive heart attack. Y did and said all the necessary things, but she found it difficult to care in the deep way everyone else seemed to feel about the death of her father. When they lowered Mikael's coffin into the grave, upon which lay the three white roses they'd thrown in, she only experienced the typical dullness in her chest.

Then Gawain grabbed and squeezed her hand, and she glanced up at him: his tousled hair limned by the sun, tears shining on his agonised face, and a throb swelled up. He had always been her lone, tenuous human connection.

She hugged him, and he cinched her so tight she gasped – it felt *real*, and a few tears escaped, followed by a scald of sobs because she'd always thought herself incapable of such sentiment.

The bus braked suddenly, and Y was thrown against the seat in front of her. Dust burst out of the cheap material. She coughed and pulled back in disgust. She was re-evaluating her decision to take this tour of the Clare coastline in Ireland. The vehicle rumbled slowly up a steep corkscrew road to a cliff overlooking the vast Atlantic ocean.

They would have had a good view of the fields of grass and folds of limestone rock separated by rough stone walls except for the silver mist that hung in the air. The higher they climbed, the more it closed in. Beads of water rolled down the outside of the glass pane, and a film of condensation built up on the inside until only smears of green and grey were visible through the window. A chill pressed in and enveloped Y.

Close now, some innate knowledge told her. She trembled a little, not sure if it was the cold or the coffee she'd been sipping throughout the trip.

The bus heaved up the final ascent and levelled out with a strained gasp of relief from the engine. A few minutes later, shapes of houses and shop signs emerged from the gloom. The bus pulled in at a dingy petrol station, and its door wheezed open.

"Half an hour stop," the driver announced. The passengers disembarked and streamed through the mist towards the dim light of a neon café sign that advertised CHIPS.

The driver stretched and strained the buttons on his navy rayon shirt as Y paused, ready to alight.

"Where are we?" she asked.

"Kilcailligh. It's a hole of a town. I don't normally stop here, but the weather's shite, and I need a piss."

"Kilcailligh," she said, enjoying the way it rolled on her tongue. She stepped into the damp, turned away from the café, and followed the narrow winding street.

Pale two-story houses hunched against each other on either side, but after a minute they thinned, leaving only a country road that merged with the haze. Unseen seagulls shrieked in the murk. She tasted salt on her lips.

She noticed a stile cut into the stone wall and climbed over it. Her boots crunched on a gravel path as the mist pushed in. A dark, hooked shape began to materialise: a hawthorn bush, no doubt hammered into its crooked contour by constant storms. Y drew abreast of it and considered how the branches resembled a woman's hair rippling in a perpetual breeze. She reached out and touched its slippery, black-brown surface. Its gnarled roots clamped into the rocky ground in an obstinate fashion. *It could be eternal*, she thought idly.

An owl hooted to her right, and she swung around. The outline of a derelict building hung like a watermark in the moist veil. She moved towards it, and the curtain pulled back to reveal the roofless shell of an early stone church.

Weathered, listing gravestones littered the area around the bare walls. Humps of grass hinted where nubs of stone had been overgrown. Ivy-choked tomb slabs dotted the area – some of which were broken as if those interred had smashed free of their confines. Only a pair of Yew trees seemed to thrive there. Twin green guardians of the ruin of people's faith.

The owl perched at the apex of the church walls and stared at her. She nodded at it, and the woozy feeling slipped over her.

This place was significant.

She almost tripped over a mossy lump and staggered into a semi-circular wall built of smooth stones. It protected a massive granite boulder, the top of which was sheared off to form a flat surface. Five depressions were carved into it. Water pooled in them, so they looked like black mirrors.

She'd read about this in the guide book for the area. They were *bullaun*. In the past, people used to place polished pebbles in the indentations and turn them – for good luck or to curse. It was a strange practice thought to pre-date Christianity.

Y bent to examine the base of the boulder and spotted piles of stone lying about. She didn't consider her actions, merely moved on instinct. Over the years, she'd learned to trust the wisdom of the moment.

She dropped a stone into the middle pool and, for a fleeting instant, hesitated at putting her hand into the icy water. The notion that something might grab her fingers or cut the tips off flashed into her mind. She glanced over at the owl, but it had disappeared – there was no instruction except her intuition's urging.

She inhaled, bracing herself, and dipped her hand into the little pocket of water. Her finger tips numbed instantly, but she discerned the shape of the pebble below. She turned it five times counterclockwise and left the stone inside its well. She picked another stone at random and repeated the process until she had turned a stone in each of the pools.

"It took you long enough."

The woman's voice behind her was so unexpected Y yelped.

She turned and froze at the sight.

The woman perched on a low headstone that had been worn down with age. She was naked, sitting on her heels with her arms wrapped around her knees. Her skin was red, like brick. The first thing Y noticed were her bird-like feet: her toes were impossibly long and weirdly jointed. There was a ring of white bone around each one just before the curved talon. A ridge of feathers grew out along her forearms, and her hands were similar to her feet, except they looked more agile.

Her face was the most arresting: heart-shaped with a chin that came to a fine point, framed by a beard of feathers. Her eyes were large, upswept with yellow pupils and a black, reptile irises. They glowed. Her mouth curved into a cynical smile. A mane of scalloped white feathers edged in black flowed in a wide strip down her skull and back, between her glorious wings.

The woman's strange beauty dazzled Y, rendering her speechless. The void in her chest vanished as a warm familiarity flooded her. Y felt she knew this being better than her own family.

A soft breeze stirred the mist in eddies around them.

The woman jumped down from her roost. Her breasts were small, and the nipples pierced with the same bone rings. Her pubis was bare. She was shorter than Y, but Y did not believe she had a single advantage over her.

"You called, and I came," the woman said, her accent odd but melodious.

"I followed the signs," Y said. She wondered if this was a dream, and if she was still jaunting along in the bus. "Who…?" she couldn't continue.

The woman cocked her head. "You don't remember, sister?"

Y shook her head slowly.

The woman shrugged. "You never remember. I thought it might be different this time."

Y pondered this. "What should I call you?"

She laughed, an almost whistling sound. "There are so many names. I don't think I trust you with the important ones yet. How do you identify yourself?

"Y," she said.

"Then call me Aan," she drawled the vowels. "Who needs complicated names when you know who you are?" She laughed, and Y knew she was being mocked.

"What now?" Y asked, her tone sharp.

Aan darted forward, and it took all of Y's control not to flinch. She stood close and gazed up at Y. Y could smell her – a mixture of incense and sweat that was oddly arousing.

"Are you ready?" she said intently. Her bright eyes wide and mesmerising. "To bring Her back."

"Who?" Y asked, but in her mind, a shape had begun to form. A column of fire and black smoke and, roaring inside it, a heart forged for destruction.

Aan placed her hand upon Y's arm, and it electrified her.

Y dipped her head and kissed Aan, deeply, passionately. The pillar of fire in her mind erupted. Lust gripped her. It had never been like this before: not with Levi or with Alice or any of the partners she had sampled over the years.

"Nothing is forbidden, all will be made anew!" a voice cried joyously, and Y realised it was her voice.

Y pulled off her coat as Aan ripped open Y's blouse. Buttons pinged. Aan's fingers were remarkably agile, and sliced through Y's bra and were massaging her breasts in moments. Y groaned from deep in her belly. Her knees gave slightly from the intensity.

She wanted to rut in the grass with this woman-creature. To roll in the soil among the graves of the deceased. She wanted the dust-mouthed dead in the underworld to be stirred from their leaden existence by Y and Aan's cries of pleasure, to envy the flickering glory of life.

So she did.

Afterward she lay naked and panting beside Aan. Small cuts and bruises throbbed on her arms and legs, but she had never felt more alive. Over the years, she had sometimes wondered if she were merely a flesh golem, magicked up by her parents.

Yet the warmth subsided, the connection eroded, and dissatisfaction needled its way into her mind again. She sat up.

Aan stretched and preened and, in a flash, was perched on a headstone again.

"It won't last," Aan commented. "Not while you're in that body. Not while the world remains this way."

Y glared at Aan, suspicion slipping into her thoughts.

"Why?" she shouted, and the hatred at being *wrong* flooded through her again. "Why was I made like this?"

"You have a choice," Aan said. "To call Her forth and bring about a new world or to remain as you are, eternally unhappy in this one."

"What?"

"It was an ancient curse. We were separated, Her avatars. You, to be reborn, again and again, each time with the choice to bring Her back. Me, to wait, to offer you the choice."

"I've never chosen Her?" That seemed impossible, already the pillar of fire held Y's devotion.

Aan's expression darkened. "Nothing will survive Her return. Not even us."

"That's not…" she was going to say possible, but already she knew it was. The vision of the planet burned to smouldering pitch and prepped for another race's emergence resolved in her mind.

Gawain would be roasted. Her mother melted to slag. Her past acquaintances and lovers would be incinerated. She and Aan would be the last witnesses to the razing of the world before they too writhed in the final flames.

All for a promise that what would come after would be more marvellous – and even as she contemplated the notion, Y sensed the beauty beating at the edges of this world. It wanted to come into being so desperately. All that stood in its way was Y's decision.

The responsibility crushed her. It was too much to ask of any person. She pulled on her trousers, grabbed her coat, and buttoned it up. The mist chilled her again now the heat of passion had died.

"This always happens!" Aan screamed and sprang into the air. Great wings extended outward and beat, so she hovered above Y, her expression livid. Y's coat flapped in the gusts.

"By living with them, you become attached. You swallow their teachings about self-sacrifice and 'the greater good' and choose martyrdom rather than renewal." She spat. "And what do I have? Centuries of loneliness, interspersed by moments of hope. Always dashed. And sometimes you never come. Generations pass without any contact."

Aan darted high into the air, keening.

The thunderclaps of her wings buffeted Y. She grabbed onto an old stone cross and wished this had never come to pass. Hatred scored her heart. She craved death rather than to endure such pain and to cause it in others.

Aan dove down instantly and grabbed her arms.

"If you wish for the end, at least bring on transformation! Don't leave me behind, waiting again upon another choice and another rejection."

Y closed her eyes against the pleading. "Nothing will remain," she whispered.

Aan's talons tore into Y's coat sleeves and gouged Y's arms. She cried out.

"Choose!" Aan bellowed and threw Y away from her.

"I can't." Tears streamed down Y's face.

"You have," Aan replied, and her words were ice.

She leaped into the air and vanished.

Y lay crouched on the grass, sobbing. The emptiness inside her returned, worse than before. She welcomed it. The void would swallow confusion and pain. She had lived like this before: a meat shell containing a vacuum.

Calm settled upon her again.

Y stood, dragged fingers through her hair, and brushed grass off her coat. She was prepping the mannequin for display.

She returned through the mist, over the stile, and down the road to the bus station.

Stranger than everything else, the bus waited for her.

Y stood at the open door expecting the driver to be aghast at her appearance or chastise her for tardiness.

He sat with a newspaper draped over the steering wheel. He glanced up and gave her a nod. "You're early. No one else is back." Then he returned to his perusal of headlines and scandal.

Y climbed into the empty vehicle with leaden feet and plodded down the aisle. She dropped onto her seat and clutched her bag to her chest.

Outside the dewed glass, a line of ghostly figures approached the bus. Unreal forms moving through an unreal life.

The driver turned the key in the engine, and it growled and vibrated, awaiting the impetus to depart.

The smell of spoiled food filled her mouth.

She jumped up.

"I have to go!" she cried.

Y raced past the rows of seats and shoved through the protesting bodies.

The pillar of fire in her mind roared and exploded until she could feel the flames bursting through her bones.

She scorched a path through the mist, and behind her, there remained only ash.

Bone Mother

The house tilted. A thighbone rolled off my kitchen table and clattered onto the floorboards. I cocked my head and waited for a warning.

Silence. It was still sulking.

I whacked its bony walls with my hawthorn stick. "Out with it!" I demanded.

"A man approaches, you withered old crone!" The floor trembled with irritation.

"A fine house you are! Allowing a stranger to sneak up on me."

I pulled tangles back from my ears, which set off the rat skulls knotted into my hair. A tap from my stick shut their jawbones. The jingle of a horse's reins drifted through the half-open window.

I knocked my walking stick against the rafter fashioned from a mammoth tusk, carved with runes. All activity ceased. My servants – three pairs of disembodied hands – hung in the air above the table, paused in their task of sorting the stack of bones into animal or human. The spiders that infested the thatch stopped in mid-spin. Cobwebbed chains of nails and bundles of herbs swayed from the beam. The only sound was the breathing of the redbrick oven. It huffed out a ball of disgruntled smoke: "Ouch!"

I scuttled to the window, and propped my dugs on the sill as I leaned out to get a gander at the fellow. Despite the lingering sting of that morning's quarrel, I trusted the house to shield me from his eyes.

From my vantage point I should have had a fine view across the compound, past the skeleton fence, and into the breathless gap between the forest and my home, but my weak eyes only saw a blurred outline of a man on a horse leading a pack animal.

My long nose twitched. It makes drinking from small cups inconvenient, but I can smell yesterday's fart, and last night's nightmare.

I sniffed. "Mud from the mountains weighs his cloak. It was woven from wool in…" I inhaled again, "Moldavia. Underneath the sweat, and the reek of blood and death, is a memory of... cloves and cinnamon."

"Can I eat him?" the house whined. I caressed its bleached-white walls, and it leaned into my touch. The fire sighed.

"Cross your gutters that he doesn't know the charm," I said, and squinted for better sight.

The man halted at the gate, and glanced upwards, but the hood drowned his face in shadow. There wasn't a whiff of fear from him at the sight of the gateposts topped with glowing skulls. Leather creaked, and he rose in his stirrups. He brandished a wand that stank of borrowed magic.

The man wove a glyph in the air and I leaned back, wary. The sigil flashed like sparks from a smithy's fire. Even I could see it. My knuckles cracked as I tightened my grip on the window.

"House of Bone, lower your legs and rest. Gate of Skulls, admit this guest," he commanded.

"He knows it!" the house moaned. Its giant chicken legs creaked and the floor bobbed as it shuffled around so the front door faced the gate. It eased downwards.

"I haven't heard that version since the plague," I muttered, and slammed the window shut. With a snap of my fingers the hands sprang into action and tidied the bones into the oak chest where I kept leftovers. They blinked out of existence at another click. I picked up a file and sawed at my iron teeth for a moment. With the tip of my tongue I tested its edge – nice and sharp. I lowered myself almost double, and clawed at my hair so the matted weave trailed after me.

"Ow! Ow! Ow!" complained the rats skulls as they clacked off the floor.

The house crashed into the ground, and I grabbed a wall to steady myself. I poked it in the ribs. Smoke belched from the fire in apology.

The door swung open.

The man had dismounted and thrown back his cloak over one shoulder to reveal a pleated tight-fitting jacket, leggings, and splattered riding boots. His right hand flirted with his sword hilt, which smelled of Spain, hot fires, and whetstones.

I grovelled low. "Can I help you my lord?" I cackled.

"I doubt it, hag," he said. I stabbed my stick into the dirt path instead of skewering his eyeballs. "I seek the bone witch." He peeled off his gloves, and peered past my hunched back into the room beyond. His accent had a Wallachian base, with a Turkish flourish.

"Who wishes an audience with the Mistress of Bones?"

"Vladislav Basarab."

His ancestry sang in his name: ruthless and stubborn rulers of southern Transylvania. I saw the native Dacians of his lineage surge on horses against the invading Romans, then the Pechenegs, and later the Mongols, but most recently the Turks. His was a pedigree of resistance, and tyranny.

I unfolded myself slowly until my head brushed the lintel. He stepped back, and looked up. Wet black hair slicked his high cheekbones, but the twin dark wells of his eyes reflected nothing.

"Baba Yaga bids you welcome, young Vladislav, son of the Dragon." The rat skulls chittered my praise. "Do you come of your own free will, or did someone send you?" The house leaned in to hear his response. The wrong answer would grant us a meal.

From under his cloak he produced a blue rose.

How had I not sensed it?

I tasted the peppery tang of cunning magic I had thought forgotten in Christian lands. My eyelids lowered at the flower's intoxicating scent. It promised porcelain skin, clear eyes, and an end to aching joints. All I could see were the sky-blue petals that curled away from an indigo centre.

As if from a distance I heard his answer.

"I come to trade, Bone Mother, for the secrets of life and death."

The souls of the damned trapped in my house's walls screeched in frustration.

The flower lay on the table, and its perfume lulled me. It conjured memories: sienna eyes under copper hair; a spurned hand; a drop of blood, and the pact of Guardianship, which brought long life in a decaying shell.

I blinked the past away and did not stare at the rose, despite my desire. The infrequent potions I concocted from its petals were all that revived my body. When last I'd tasted its ambrosia Alexander had held Constantinople.

I summoned my servants, and at least Vladislav started in surprise as one wizened hand wielded a poker on the embers while the other held open the oven's door. The other two pairs bore blue-patterned china plates and wide navy glasses to the table.

Vladislav shrugged off his cloak on the back of a big chair with arms made of wolf's ribcages, and a seat covered in cured pygmy skins. He settled into it, comfortable, and stroked the curving bone. I perched on the three-legged stool made from Minotaur horns.

He leaned down, pulled a bottle of kvass from a greasy saddlebag, and placed it on the table. He was irritatingly well prepared.

"Where did you find the rose?" I snapped.

"My mother's people are from Moldavia." He picked up the rose by its black stem and twirled it slowly; the thorns had an evil curved point. "Some of them remember our heretical past." He laid it upon the table a little closer to me.

"You imperil your soul with such devilry." I restrained a smirk.

"The Lord guides my path. He delivered me from the Turks, and urges me to build a strong Wallachia."

I nodded at one pair of hands and they poured kvass into the containers. "I understand your younger brother, Radu, enjoyed Turkish company. The Sultan's in particular."

Vladislav's knuckles whitened as he gripped the glass. If he broke it I'd fillet him like a trout, and damn the rules of hospitality.

"Maybe he was wise to spurn women. They offer little beyond a dowry and heirs."

Once I'd stopped a man's heart with a glance, but his eyes did not flinch from my gaze. I grabbed my tits and gazed down at them. "Yes, still a woman." He pulled back in disgust. I leaned forward and hissed, "Still a witch."

"The lord protects me from your wickedness," and his hand crept to the crucifix around his neck.

"To faith," I barked, "however misguided," and knocked back the kvass. I smacked my lips as he swallowed the alcohol in one gulp. "Is your father well?" I asked, hoping for a lie, and a way to break peace. I dug my nails into the palms of my hands and glanced again at the flower, luminous in the candlelight. I had smelled his father's bones wrapped up in elk's leather on the back of Vladislav's mule.

"Slaughtered, by Hunyadi's army. Along with my mother." He paused and turned the glass in his hand so the light spun a shower of navy stars across the table and the rose. I smelled blood as my nails punctured my skin. "They buried my brother alive. I never found his grave."

"I heard you were routed from the capital, and ran to Bogdan of Moldavia squealing for sanctuary." I gave him a good view of my iron teeth as I smiled.

The glass vibrated when he banged it on the table. "I will take Tirgoviste again."

I gestured towards the rose. "What's your price?"

"I need the advice of my father to regain the throne."

I waited.

He moved the flower again, almost within my reach. "You are the Guardian of the waters of life and death," he said, "It lies within your power to resurrect him."

"The flower's not worth necromancy," I lied. "Mourn your family, marry, have children, and teach them to fight. There are always Turks and Christians to slaughter."

"Were you ever beautiful, witch?" His tone was cold like the earth under ice. "How many wrinkles could this flower erase?"

It was so close.

A sliver of brown edged a cerulean petal. He'd removed the charm that kept it fresh. Now it rotted slowly. I only had a couple of days.

"If you take it by force it will turn to ash instantly," he whispered.

The spicy taste of a spell lingered. Something akin to admiration sparked in me, or maybe it was fury. I've always had difficulty telling them apart.

"I have to gather the waters."

He nodded. "Tomorrow, then."

"You sleep in the barn," I added, "if you want to pass the night unmolested."

He grimaced at my leer.

I woke to the sound of the hands reviving the fire, and laying out food. I crunched the shells of the eggs they left me for breakfast, and sucked the wriggling embryos in one go. After some grumbling, the house lowered itself to the ground.

"Just kill him, Bone Mother," it said as it hit the earth, hard. "And feed his bones to my fire." The flames capered in anticipation.

I stretched out my hand and my birch broom swept into it. "He has the rose," I said. "Keep locked up tight, and high above the ground." I looked at my hands, gnarled with pain, and imagined them smooth. "Besides, who says I can't have him *after* I get the flower?"

The door creaked open and I inhaled the scent of clouds boiling over the snow-capped Făgăraş Mountains, a fox ripping into a hare's flesh, and the sweat of the young man who leaned against the doorway of my barn. Straw stuck to his clothes. "After all," I muttered, "when I'm younger again, I'll have needs."

I whistled, and from inside the barn Vlad's horse screamed in fright and the mule kicked the walls. He turned, and leaped out of the path of my huge iron mortar, which whizzed past him and across the ground to hover beside me. Aware of his appraising gaze I jumped inside the mortar's bowl and showed no trace of the pain the impact caused. I brandished the long pine pestle in my right hand. There was wonder on his face, and he smelled of excitement, but not fear.

I frowned. "I'll expect payment when I return, *voivode*."

I cracked the pestle against the ancient iron, and the mortar climbed towards the sky. The ground beneath quaked, and the trees around the compound bent and shook like they were whipped by fierce winds. The house straightened its legs and rose as I drifted upwards. I shrieked in delight, urging the mortar across forests and rivers, and swept away my trail with the broom. My hair streamed after me, and the rats skulls sang of dead cats and dunghills.

I returned to my compound at twilight, exhausted. Each time the trip took longer, but I could almost taste the honeyed infusion of blue petals on my tongue. The earth shuddered, and the trees flailed as the mortar eased downwards.

The house squatted on the ground. The door was open, and no smoke breathed from the chimney.

I hopped out of the mortar, dropped the pestle and broom to the ground, gripped the skins of water to my chest, and hobbled on my walking stick to the doorway.

My house was in disarray. Bloodied fingers from my servants lay scattered on the floor, the door to the stove was open, and the fire was dead.

A lone blue petal stirred amid the ashes scattered before the hearth, and the charred end of a rose stem lay in the cold oven.

The hawthorn fell from my grip to the floorboards.

A fingerless palm lay in the centre of the table, impaled by a dagger. The walls were streaked with soot.

He'd tried to burn my home. I glanced up. The runes of making on the mammoth tusk were intact. Mundane fire wasn't enough. Fury trembled my limbs.

"Mother!" my house babbled between cries, "He made me. I'm sorry! I told him where to go. I told him the source, from where the rivers spring."

I picked up the petal between thumb and forefinger. If I was careful, and brewed the potion well, it was good for a thimbleful: enough to ease the pain for fifty years, and to remind me of youth but not grant it. The process would take a week, and Vladislav would be gone.

Fatigue gnawed my body. "Why did you let him in?"

"I was so hungry, and he had bones!"

I leaned my forehead against a wall and stroked its filthy surface. My hand shook. Eventually hate and age weighed me down onto the stool as my house retold the story of its ordeal.

If I was careful...

I gathered twigs and paper, and muttered the charm that lit its flame, even though it cost me strength. Gently, I fed the fire with logs after it caught and burned.

"He is mad," the house whispered, and it puffed angry dark smoke.

"He has a mission," I said.

My home stank of fear and surrender. It was ravenous, and I needed servants.

I brushed the soft petal against my dry cheek and inhaled its perfume. It promised pain-free years to hunt for another rose.

If I was careful...

I was the Guardian of the waters of life and death. None could drink them without my permission.

I slipped the petal under my tongue. Saliva flooded my mouth at its sweet taste.

Strength returned, and I rose to my full height. I uncurled my hands and remembered my power. The rats skulls rattled like ivory dice.

The petal began to dissolve in my mouth.

Through the open door I stared at the night sky. The moon was the shape of an ox skull's horns.

I would spear the Wallachian prince upon them. I would girdle my home with his entrails and wash its walls with his pulp.

I bounded from the house, and leaped high as a mountain goat into the mortar as it rose at my command. The door to my house slammed shut and its legs quivered as it heaved the structure from the ground.

Vladislav would pay for that weakness.

I struck the pestle against the side of my mortar and it was a roll of thunder. The iron bowl thrust into the sky.

I shrieked my displeasure and every living being within earshot fell to the ground and pissed itself in fear.

He had already drunk from the stream of life by the time I arrived.

Trees snapped and broke under the force of my fury as I landed in the clearing before the cave. I hurtled from the mortar before it landed, and rock cracked underneath my boots.

Vladislav waited at the entrance, resplendent in armour. Charms etched into his breastplate glowed, and old enchantments misted his drawn sword blade. His belief had not stopped him thieving spells from the mountain folk who had gleaned their tricks from water, earth, and air.

I had been the midwife of such magic.

"I am now immortal, *old woman*," Vladislav's voice rang with faith and arrogance. "I am the instrument of righteousness. I shall crush the unfaithful, guide the humble..."

I snapped my fingers and the blade tore from his grasp and embedded hilt-first in a boulder of granite. Its edge shone in the light of the moon's horns. I clapped my hands and his breastplate fell apart and clanked on the ground.

Yet he crouched and grinned as I rushed towards him, my hands spread wide, my nails sharp, and my teeth bared.

"Come on," he goaded, and the crucifix around his neck glinted.

I punched him, broke his thin nose, and he flew back into the rock wall and his ribs shattered. He spat blood from his mouth, but did not moan. His dark eyes were wells of brutality. Within them I spied years of torture, and a glacial promise forged in a Turkish prison: he would visit horror upon any who caused him pain – family, ally, or ancient foe.

I seized the front of his tunic and threw him upon his sword. It impaled his chest. It was excruciating, but he would not die. Not now. Immortality kept him from death, but not from suffering, or decay. I knew the cost well.

He lay on the ground, the sword skewered through his broken chest, and blood splattered on his face. Yet he laughed... choked... sneered.

"You'll dry up like dust, witch. No rose will restore your bloom."

The sugary taste faded.

I stood above him, and uncapped one of the skins. I reached down, squeezed his jaws, and pried them open.

I poured the waters of death into his mouth, and watched his eyes widen as he sensed the change. His wounds healed, the blood flow ceased, and his heart stopped. I hunkered down beside him, my bony knees level with my ears, as he flopped like a landed fish.

"You are alive, Vladislav, but you are also dead. You will thirst for blood, but it will never satisfy you. Your victims will be legion, and my house and I will feed upon their corpses. You will drive your enemies from your land, but you will never know peace, or redemption."

I pulled him from his sword, and threw him across the clearing. Flesh sizzled, and Vladislav's limp hands scrabbled at his neck. He ripped the crucifix off and threw it to the ground.

I grinned. "Only the sun will unravel this spell." The prince shuddered, and gasped as he died and the red thirst gripped him. I reached down and ripped a chunk of hair from his scalp. He screamed and bared his teeth. They had a new sharpness. I showed him the bloody hank before I tucked it into a pocket. "My revenge upon you will be long in coming, and complete."

The sweetness died in my mouth.

He attempted to rise, and failed.

I hid my limp as I walked to the mortar, and climbed carefully into its basin.

With a strike of the pestle the mortar ascended into darkness, and I did not look back.

I sowed Vladislav's hair into a hexing doll to keep track of him over the years. Whenever my house and I were hungry I'd ask it where Vladislav had last visited. It would pull its awkward woollen body upright, and point its crude hand towards bloodshed.

Vlad the Impaler massacred thousands while he dined on foods that never nourished him, and consorted with women who never pleased him. He delivered misery and terror in his drive to slack an endless appetite.

We feasted well during his reign.

Always, I hunted for a blue rose, but it eluded me.

One night, as I whipped my mortar through the air I sensed a change in the hexing doll, which I kept in my pocket. It raised a limp arm. I followed its signs until I crossed the Danube, and traversed the lands of the Ottoman Empire where the white turbaned men shrank from my shadow. After a tiring journey the doll drew me to a city of spires, minarets, and gold domes, where prayers rang out as the sky pinked for the dawn. The scent of cloves and cinnamon wafted upwards.

There I found him, or what was left.

His head was stuck upon a spear, the spine and throat ragged and hinting at a long and torturous decapitation. I dropped the hexing doll, and watched it land with a spray of sparks in a charcoal brazier far below. I flew close so my failing sight could behold his death.

His eyelids fluttered open, and the thirst continued to rage in his eyes.

I smiled, baring my iron teeth. The muscles around his lips twitched into a rictus.

The first rays of sunlight touched his face, and seared it black. His mouth opened, but whether it was to howl, or laugh, I did not know.

As his eyes boiled I thought of the luminous blue flower, and the beauty he'd stolen from me.

He'd got off lightly.

I clacked pine against iron, and urged the mortar upwards. Sluggish, it lifted above the clouds, where my passing would go unnoticed. I slumped against the cold metal. The pestle and broom were heavy in my aged hands.

In the airless cerulean expanse, I tasted a burst of nectar.

My movements were fluid, and painless. The far mountains and forests of my birthplace sharpened and became clear.

I smelled gore from a recent battlefield far beneath me; fresh food for the pot.

The rat skulls chattered nonsense.

I floated towards home.

WATER

The pot lids hopped and fizzed when Mark's mother laid the wooden spoon down calmly, opened the back door of the kitchen, disappeared into the overgrown garden, and drowned herself in the river that flowed past their house.

Mark figured out what happened an hour later, as he scraped potatoes from the blackened scab at the bottom of the pot, when she *sloshed* back into the room. She didn't blink. Pools of water shimmered over her open, staring eyes. Her short hair plastered to her skull in thick tendrils; a curl of fern clung to one dull, grey cheek.

Mark gripped the spatula harder. "You all right, Mum?"

She turned to him, and opened her mouth to speak. Bubbles of air emerged from the river water that was contained, as if by a force field, behind her teeth.

"Yes, love." Bubbles burst, and her words emerged with a slight pop. "I needed some air." She stopped, her flaccid face showed no emotion, but foam churned at her lips and released shrill, staccato laughter.

Mark edged back to the hallway. Behind him sounded the brusque clatter of Dad's keys against the front door. Mum picked up the pot, walked with it to the counter, and scoured charred mush onto three plates. Dad dropped his suitcase by the stairs and sniffed in a dramatic fashion as he strolled to the kitchen.

"Did you burn dinner again, Liz?" he asked, and slouched against the doorway. "Hardly a homecoming treat." She shook her head slowly, her water-full face bent to the task. Thick beads slipped down her hair and splashed onto the plates.

Dad glanced at Mark and frowned. "Put that down," he said. Mark stared at the crooked plastic spatula in his white-knuckled grip, and twitched a refusal. His father reached over, tugged it from Mark's hand, and walked to Mum. He tossed the spatula into the sink and laid his hand upon Mum's damp shoulder. Mark shuddered.

"I'm not hungry," Mark said.

Dad tasted the mash. He winced. "I don't blame you." Absentmindedly, he rubbed the small of Mum's back. A little frog jumped from under her cardigan, and flopped onto his arm. It winked its gold eyes at Mark, and climbed Dad's suit sleeve like it would a tree branch.

Mark pointed. "Your arm!" The frog settled on Dad's shoulder, and nestled under his earlobe. It lifted its head and stared at Dad's open ear.

Dad looked down. "What?"

Mark felt as if the air was made of water, and he was suspended, breathless, unable to swim.

Mum handed Dad his plate of crusted mash, withered lamp chop and sodden vegetables, and they sat at the table. "Don't you have homework to do?" Dad asked, and he laid his hand upon Mum's limp fingers, and squeezed.

He leaned forward and kissed her, and the river gushed into Dad and filled him up. His fingers trembled a shivery beat against the tabletop.

They separated and raised their watery eyes to regard Mark. Their moist ashen lips stretched, and crescents of silver water gleamed.

Bubbles boiled in Dad's mouth. "What's wrong?"

Mark bolted from the room, gulping for air.

Author's Afterword

Years ago I determined never to explain my stories once they are written and published. At that point it's often months – or years – later and I'm caught up in the new worlds I'm imagining. The roads back to those old lands are dusty and dim.

Plus, a new narrative may emerge: 'the story of the story' which can veer into utter fabrication if you're not careful. Writers can't resist making things up for a receptive audience.

There are occasions when your story arrives at the right point in a zeitgeist and the writer can attain the glamour of the mystic. Mostly it's a combination of luck and timing. Stories are often gestated for years. They are scraps, fragments of lines, titles, or broad concepts listed in a file that wait until we are ready to poke at them.

Occasionally stories appear like Athena: a zap of inspiration and fully formed – perhaps prompting a migraine.

Yet I'd like to offer a selection of anecdotes and observations about some of the stories since context can be useful.

The oldest story in the collection is a flash piece from 2004 called "Who Hears Our Cries in Forgotten Tongues?" and it's an example of a question that pesters me often: *who is telling the story?* Since I've always adored mythology, folklore and fairy tales I'm often inspired by the spaces inside the traditional story where I sense omissions. Inside those gaps I intuit the overlooked people who have been silenced. I interrogate the conquering people and how they chose to describe their victories in 'their' narratives.

"Bone Mother" is a useful way to introduce a pivotal moment in my development as a writer: attending the Clarion West workshop. I am grateful for the six weeks I spent in a hot and labyrinthine sorority house in Seattle (serenaded by next door's fraternity singing karaoke) with seventeen other writers; reading, sweating, writing, and pushing myself very hard. I remember producing a terrible story for the delightful Maureen F. McHugh (not a relation!). I was deeply unimpressed with myself and resolved to do better.

I'd been a *Dracula* nerd since I wrote about the novel for my first M.A., so I'd come up with the idea of a meeting between Baba Yaga and Count Dracula, but I struggled to find a way into the story. I tried to write it from a third-person perspective, but it wouldn't work no matter how I tried to force it.

Finally, in a café with a cup of Seattle's finest caffeinated brew, Baba Yaga started dictating the story and I was off… It was her story to tell. That week's mentor Ian R. MacLeod offered me several wise and useful pointers. It was the first story I sold after Clarion West (many thanks to Ellen Datlow for a timely introduction) to editors Sean Wallace and Paul Tremblay. It later sold as a podcast for *Pseudopod*, and a young animator in Canada called Dale Hayward listened to it.

Years later Dale and his partner Sylvie Trouvé, and the National Film Board of Canada, optioned the rights to the story to make it into a stop-motion animation. Twelve years after I wrote the story the beautifully dark short film premiered at Festival Stop Motion in Montreal.

My choice was vindicated: *always bet on witch.*

Another Clarion West story, "Home", is in the collection. I wrote the first draft of it for the week Ellen Datlow mentored, but in a crisis of confidence I wrote another, completely different story, and presented that to her instead.

There is more than a touch of cosmic horror in "Home", and it is a story about Ireland, its long and difficult history of colonisation, and was prompted by the question: 'What causes a house to become haunted?'

I love haunted houses and the many things they represent. This collection contains an English haunted house story, "Spooky Girl" – a story I had so much fun writing – and an American haunted house story that's original to this collection: "Suspension" (although you don't see *inside* the house).

"The Light at the Centre" is set in a ghost estate in Ireland. I drove past so many of them during our country's bleak and deep recession post-2008, so that story was waiting in my mind until Brian J. Showers asked me for a submission for his *Uncertainties* anthology. It was subsequently picked up by Stephen Jones for his *Best New Horror #28*.

Sometimes we are haunted by events, or people, such as a random ghost on a train in "Moments on the Cliff", which was inspired by a train journey from Dublin to Galway. This was published in the Galway literary magazine *Crannóg*, and it was wonderful to have a story set in

Galway also published in a journal from Galway. Another haunting in "Involuntary Muscle" is more about we conjure from our past. And the weight of expectation.

"The Diet" focuses on the eldritch horrors of the diet industry, and "Beautiful Calamity" is partly a love song for New York, a crazy, beautiful city I adore.

I'm fond of my poignant *Frankenstein* story "Vic", which broke my heart in its writing, but I finally got it right. Thanks to editor Andy Cox it was originally published in the terrific UK bastion, *Black Static*, and then noticed by Paula Guran and collected in the *Year's Best Dark Fantasy and Horror 2010*. Andy also published my story "The Hanging Tree", which is almost not supernatural at all.

I'll note that Christopher Fowler and I ran a competition for *Black Static* called 'The Campaign for Real Fear', for which we selected twenty flash stories from the submissions and they were published in the magazine. Subsequently, I felt that I should also rise to the challenge of writing a horror short story in under 500 words, and "Water" was born – it was an Athena story: out in a jiffy, fully formed, and downright weird. It was also published in *Black Static*.

Two of the stories in the collection were written for themed anthologies. "A Rebellious House" was part of a beautiful volume called *The Madness of Dr. Caligari*, edited by Joe S. Pulver, and inspired by the black and white film *The Cabinet of Dr. Caligari* (1920). "Family" was included in another Pulver anthology, *Cassilda's Song*, whose stories were influenced by the King in Yellow mythos by Robert W. Chambers.

I spent a long time writing and rewriting "The Tamga", which demonstrates my abiding interest in animistic/shamanic worldviews. "Y" arrived in my mind after seeing a strange pattern in an underground car park, rather like the protagonist experienced, and then proceeded along its strange route.

New to this collection, the story "The Gift of the Sea" came partly from my admiration for the amazing Eileen Gray, an Irish designer/artist before her time who was a European sensation in the inter-war period of the twentieth century.

"Wake the Dead" is also original to this collection and is an Irish folk horror story featuring our eerie Straw Boy tradition. Set at Samhain, the Irish New Year, this story bucked under my fingers and attempted to become something different, which required that I retire from it until we could settle our differences. That détente resulted in the story missing a submission date for an anthology and gaining a sterling spot in this collection. What a sly gambit…

The collection gets its title from the new story, "The Boughs Withered When I Told Them My Dreams", which was inspired by a W. B. Yeats poem called "The Withering of the Boughs". I had been searching for a title for the collection when I read the two-line refrain:

'No boughs have withered because of the wintry wind,
The boughs have withered because I have told them my dreams.'

That last line gave me goosebumps, but while the metre worked for the poem it didn't work for a story title, so I cheekily amended it to suit my purposes. The story turned up in response to the title.

There is a Yeats connection to me as I live a short drive from Thoor Ballylee, the medieval fortified stone tower in which Years resided for years. It influenced much of his poetry, including his important volume *The Tower* (1928), and it's where he conducted magical work and seances with his wife George Hyde-Lees. Close by is the atmospheric wooded estate of Coole Park, former residence of playwright/writer Lady Augusta Gregory. Many of Ireland's literary luminaries of the late nineteenth and early twentieth centuries frequented this neighbourhood.

When I walk under the whispering branches of the knowing trees in Coole Park I am treading through the echoes of our creative past, and I am inspired, refreshed and uplifted.

Acknowledgements and Thanks

Writing is an act of magic, a conjuration from the self, but it is never completed in isolation.

I'll begin well by thanking Ian Whates: for his confidence in my writing, his astute editorial eye, and his labour in putting this book together. Plus a shout-out to the luminous Helen, who is always so kind and loves a snazzy piece of jewellery.

My dearest pal Kim Newman: I would name you a Prince, but you are a pragmatic socialist, so you are the Treasured President of True Friends. Thanks for the introduction and the many convoluted conversations about films, comics, and writing.

Kudos to Daniele Serra for the atmospheric cover for this volume. Good art always enhances a book, so I appreciate your contribution to this collection.

My husband Martin Feeney: you are my rock. I can never thank you enough for your love, faith in my work and fabulous meals.

To the editors who have bought and supported my writing, I thank you, especially Ian Whates (again, he deserves it), Andy Cox, Scott Gable, Paula Guran, Stephen Jones, Brian J. Showers, Joe S. Pulver, Kate Laity, Tim Deal, Sean Wallace, Paul Tremblay, Ger Burke, Chris Cevasco, Stephen Theaker, John Greenwood, and Jennifer Dawson.

My Clarion West mentors were hugely helpful and inspiring during an intense six weeks in Seattle: fist-bumps to Paul Park, Maureen F. McHugh, Ian R. MacLeod, Nalo Hopkinson, Ellen Datlow, and Vernor Vinge. Les Howle and Neile Graham have my eternal love. You were the stalwart guardians of the Clarion West eighteen and were vital to our experience. To my fellow classmates: ditto to you all, and I appreciated the critiques and the cheers.

There are many friends who have been important in my life and have helped steer my way.

The New York crew: Lorraine Artinger, Greg Artinger, Kevin Fay, Jack Gold, Kathryn Gold, Bruce Gilmour, and Samantha Janus. The 'Dubliners': Martina Murray, Claire Fitch, Karlin Lillington, and Eileen Mageean. Lit mates Tracy Fahey, Lynda E. Rucker, Sean Hogan, Kate

Laity, Michael Carroll (and Leonia Carroll), Robert Holdstock, and Paul McAuley. Love always to my heart sister, Sinead Fine.

James Bacon requires his own paragraph because of his unstinting friendship and support over so many decades, despite him constantly egging me into volunteering to run events. I know James, *finish up and get back to writing!*

This book is dedicated to my parents, Margaret & Padraic McHugh. My horror/fantasy obsession in my teens perplexed you, but I made a career of it in the end! Thanks for the love and support!

And big love to my sister Anne (forever missed) and my brothers Patrick and Brendan.

Maura McHugh
June 2019

More New Titles from NewCon Press

Simon Morden – Bright Morning Star
A ground-breaking take on first contact from scientist and novelist Simon Morden. Sent to Earth to explore, survey, collect samples and report back to its makers, an alien probe arrives in the middle of a warzone. Witnessing both the best and worst of humanity, the AI probe faces situations that go far beyond the parameters of its programming, and is forced to improvise, making decisions that may well reshape the future of a world.

Once Upon a Parsec – Edited by David Gullen
Ever wondered what the fairy tales of alien cultures are like? For hundreds of years scholars and writers have collected and retold folk and fairy stories from around our world. They are not alone. On distant planets alien chroniclers have done the same. For just as our world is steeped in legends and half-remembered truths of the mystic and the magical, so are theirs. Now, for the first time, we can share some of these tales with you…

Best of British Fantasy 2018 – edited by Jared Shurin
Jared spread his net wide to catch the very best work published by British authors in 2018, whittling down nearly 200 stories under consideration to just 21 (22 in the hardback edition) and two poems. They range from traditional sword and sorcery to contemporary fantasy, by a mix of established authors, new voices, and writers not usually associated with genre fiction. The result is a wonderfully diverse anthology of high quality tales.

Maura McHugh – The Boughs Withered
Kim Newman provides the introduction for this, the debut collection from one of the most exciting writers around. Twenty tales, including several original to this book, which represent the best short stories from an award-winning writer of fiction, non-fiction, comic books, and plays. A series of contemporary visions and murky pasts that draw upon the author's Irish heritage and so much more.

www.newconpress.co.uk